Fetch Out No Shroud

by the same author

THE NOOSE OF TIME
SALTY WATERS
A COOL KILLING

STEPHEN MURRAY

Fetch Out No Shroud

St. Martin's Press
New York

Library of Congress Cataloging-in-Publication Data

Murray, Stephen.
    Fetch out no shroud / Stephen Murray.
        p.   cm.
    ISBN 0-312-05086-0
    I. Title.
    PR9619.3.M85F4   1990
    823—dc20

                                                            90-37119
                                                            CIP

First published in Great Britain by William Collins Sons & Co. Ltd.

First U.S. Edition: December 1990
10 9 8 7 6 5 4 3 2 1

FOR JOHNNY

Do not despair
For Johnny-head-in-air;
He sleeps as sound
As Johnny underground.

Fetch out no shroud
For Johnny-in-the-cloud;
And keep your tears
For him in after years.

Better by far
For Johnny-the-bright-star,
To keep your head,
And see his children fed.

John Pudney

CHAPTER 1

The grey concrete river flowed arrow-straight until the eye could no longer discern it as a separate entity; but far in the distance a swathe through the plain of barley showed where still it ran, sluggish, broad, impassive, towards the skeletal trees on the far horizon. Tiny parallel ripples coarsened its surface; here and there the play of the September sun threw changes of texture into unnatural relief, revealed the smooth skin pitted and stained, roughened here and there, as if by age.

No birds sang. Distant machinery whirred or whined, out of sight. Nothing, no one, moved.

A shadow rippling across the distant grain heralded wind, a gentle gust which rolled onwards until the nearer barley soughed and swayed. Somewhere a tap, tap, tap began, metallic and arhythmic, and died again as the breeze passed.

Andrew Hunter gazed out across the airfield with a sensation of familiarity. Though he had never been here before, this was his world; his work. The runway flowing away to the horizon; the forlorn huts; the hard-standings tangled with briar; the crumbling brickwork mottled with blackberries. It was like revisiting the street where one was born, finding a building more or less, a gap opened here or closed there; but always recognizably the same.

He looked at his watch, and turned so that he could see the way he had come. Still no sign that there was—ever had been—any presence but his own. The props—dusty, makeshift, tawdry enough—were still set out but the run had obviously been unsuccessful for the stage had been abandoned, the actors long since packed up and gone home. What did that make him? he wondered whimsically. The critic? The prompter? Both of these. Far from home, he yet knew himself to belong here.

Some tiny disturbance of the stillness caught his attention. He turned; and what he saw made him turn back and force his protesting legs into movement, into a run, clumsy and painful, blundering away from the concrete into the waist-high barley, on to the ankle-jerking soil.

'Stop! Andrew!'

He stopped, and turned, his arms spread in supplication, his eyes fixing in the very instant in disbelief on the tightening finger: the finger which plucked him from the stage forever.

Somewhere in the wide sky a quiet hum was born, and swelled; and the man who was left lifted his gaze at last, thrusting the shell cases deep into his pocket. His eyes—which seemed accustomed to the task—scanned the unremitting blue of the sky, assessing.

His gaze dropped to the distant horizon and suddenly he turned, as if something had been settled, and disappeared in the direction of the square grey building which stood forlorn amid the barley.

The sound of the aeroplane grew.

The bright stained glass suddenly dulled as Alec started to read the Lesson and before the long passage from *I Corinthians* was half-way through heavy rain drops were being flung like handfuls of gravel against the panes. There was a general reaching for umbrellas as the minister followed the coffin up the aisle. They emerged into the little churchyard to be buffeted and teased by the sodden wind, and women clutched hats and steeled themselves to what the ragged, wet grass would do to high heels and stockings.

As suddenly as it had come the squall passed, leaving them slithering in weak sunshine up the slight slope towards the freshly-dug grave by the churchyard wall. Alec put a hand to his sister's elbow, as much as token of the shared moment as for any real help, and they followed Jeremy's overcoated back towards the place where the coffin rested on the wooden boards and the bearers stood thankfully back, grateful to have negotiated the slope without mishap.

The little gathering stabilized around the grave. The wind still soughed among the tops of the elms; beyond the churchyard wall sheep grazed placidly, equally unconcerned by weather or by human mortality. The undertaker's men lowered the body, and the minister said the words: *In the midst of life we are in death. Thou knowest, Lord, the secrets of our hearts. Suffer us not, at our last hour, for any pains of death, to fall from thee.* Jeremy stooped, knowing as always what was expected, and a handful of clods thumped on the boards. Tessa clutched her handkerchief to her face; and Alec looked down at the coffin and thought of his father's body lying invisible behind the elm boards, and of the eternal, commonplace enigmas of death and life.

The house seemed already changed: no longer informed by the personality of his father. Jeremy attended to people, thanked them for coming, accepted their condolences and their tributes with proper sensibility.

'He looks as if he's always been here,' Tessa murmured at Alec's elbow.

Alec turned. Her face had the washed-out look of someone who has recently cried and has now put the past behind them.

'Do you mind?' she said.

'Jeremy in Father's place?' He shook his head. 'He'll fill it better than I could.'

They watched their brother together for a moment. 'It wouldn't have done,' Tessa said eventually. 'Jeremy's cut out for it. Look at him. It would have been death to you.'

'I don't mind,' Alec said again. 'I'd rather he had it.'

'You've too much to do,' Tessa said, 'to allow you to be content. What is it now? Chief Inspector?' She smiled a wan smile of pride in his achievements and was suddenly perilously close to more tears. Quickly, she looked away, made a vague gesture which embraced the elegant room, the books, the guests. 'All this,' she said. 'It's a pleasure to him; it would be a burden to you.'

Alec glanced at her and met her gaze, and returned the rueful smile he found there. 'Come on,' he said ironically. 'I'll get you nice cup of tea, then we must do our duty.'

'I'll miss him, you know,' Tessa said. 'It was just knowing he was here. Now we're on our own.'

'Yes,' said Alec flatly. 'I'll miss him too.'

On Monday morning James Parker decided the weather looked more promising. For the last three weeks it had been too unsettled to risk starting the harvest. There had been breaks when the sun had shone warmly and the ground had steamed, but always by the time it had dried out enough to begin, the clouds had gathered again and heavy premonitory drops were spotting the concrete. And all the time the year was ebbing away, and the day drew nearer when the grain must be cut, or rot in the fields.

Now Parker glanced up with cautious optimism as he tugged the heavy tarpaulin clear and folded it into a rectangular bundle, finally dragging it into the shadow of the big square control tower. The sky was blue again, not the blue of high summer, but cornflour blue, with high, clear clouds drifting from the Forest towards the North Downs, and a sun once more brazen and warm to the skin.

A sudden stutter from the direction of the farm told of the tractor being started up, and a brief puff of black smoke appeared above the roofs. James swung himself up into the cab of the combine harvester; he should be cutting the first swathes, so that by the time Marty appeared with the tractor and trailer there was room for it to follow him on the stubble receiving the grain. James stabbed the starter button and kept his finger on it while the engine ground over and eventually fired. As it settled down, he briefly allowed his eye to roam over the whole wide expanse of pale barley; then he glanced over his shoulder; the tractor, a blue dot, was already nosing out from between the distant buildings.

He engaged power, lifted the cutting table clear of the concrete, released the brake and swung the ponderous yellow monster from under the lee of the control tower towards the waiting sea of grain.

Forty minutes later the combine crawled across the landscape spewing grain into the trailer drawn by its acolyte. For once the weather looked as if it might hold. James snatched a glance from the rotating blades and saw the clouds higher, whiter, scudding before the mild breeze. Yes; with luck, it was going to hold.

He looked back at his work; caught sight of something; looked again and stamped on the brake. The engine raced briefly before he cut the throttle and Mart on the tractor, taken by surprise, overshot so that yellow grain poured into a cone behind the trailer before there was a chance to shut off the flow. James pushed open the cab door and half-rose from his seat; then, seeming to have second thoughts, he reached back and killed the engine.

Down on the naked stubble he hesitated. Mart, puzzled, switched off the tractor and jumped down beside him. In the sudden silence after the all-enfolding racket of the harvest the crunch of the stubble beneath their boots was unnaturally loud.

'What's . . .?' Mart looked at James questioningly, and then followed his eyes, bewildered, to the uncut barley in front of the silent blades, where something lay in a shadow of dull colour.

James grimaced, and started forward to get a better look, and Mart hesitated, then took a step or two after him.

James Parker stared down at the ungainly huddle of clothes and the outflung arms. Then he looked slowly up and across the expanse of uncut grain, and around the blue horizon. 'That's torn it,' he said quietly.

But Mart had seen for himself and turned quickly away

and, one hand on the ribs of the tractor's front tyre for support, was doubled over being comprehensively, noisily, sick.

'I'd like an initial cordon round from here to . . . here, and then running back to where the concrete starts. Got the tape?'

'Don't tread it down . . . we'll want to go over this area with a toothcomb. Fletcher here yet?'

'That's his car turning in, I think.'

''Scuse me, let's just get a shot of . . .'

'Nelson . . .'

'Yes, sir. Hey! Simms! Keep the cars well away. Far side of the runway. No, those that are already here had better stay where they are. But make a parking area and make sure everyone uses it. No exceptions!'

'Right, Sarge.'

'We'll want to cut this stuff down piece by piece. Well?'

The police doctor rose from where he had been squatting by the body and shook his head. 'I'll leave him for Ransome.' He followed Alec's gaze to the object that had once been a man. 'He's waited long enough. A little longer won't bother him now.'

'Right. Mr . . . Parker, is it?' Alec looked round and addressed the farmer who was standing nervously by the big front wheel of the combine. 'We're going to have to cut this barley bit by bit, so that we can search the area without trampling it down. Have you anything we can use? Scythes?'

Parker regarded him distrustfully. As if you'd expect to find scythes on a farm these days! On the other hand, this man, who seemed to be the boss, knew barley from wheat . . . and as it happened, there were three or four of the things in a cobwebby bundle in the old loft. Though what the blades would be like after these years . . .

'What about my combine?' he asked. 'Can't I get on? I'd like to crack on while the weather's holding.'

The policeman, lean and experienced, cast his eyes round the horizon and the sky in a curious, circular movement, like a sailor assessing the chance of a squall, and then glanced up at the yellow machine squatting mantis-like beside him. 'Wait till our Scene of Crime people have had a chance to see it—that's one of them getting out of his car now, so we shan't keep you long. Then we'll want you to take the combine out backwards, so as not to make any new tracks. Can you do that? We can't move the body.'

'All right. I'll need that, too.' Parker nodded towards the trailer, abandoned on the stubble. Tracks led from it in a wide circle back towards the farm, where Marty had gone to get help. A little heap of vomit showed where the front wheels of the tractor had stood; it was parked now the other side of the control tower, Mart sitting beside it leaning against one of the back wheels. 'Mart can bring it back over the same tracks,' Parker volunteered. He was badly afraid that this policeman was going to refuse; he only had the one decent grain trailer, and there was no chance of borrowing another with every farmer in the district combining while the weather was good.

Alec looked from the trailer to the blue tractor and back again. 'I don't see why not. But you'll have to leave all this area uncut, I'm afraid, until we've done. And we'll want to speak to you again—this evening will do. OK?'

Parker nodded, relieved. He had waited while the police gathered in his field like gulls behind the plough; had stood patiently while someone junior had taken down his account of finding the body; had watched the morning slip past and realized that he would be lucky indeed to be able to get any more work done that day. Now, keen to get on, he grunted, 'I'll see about those scythes,' and started towards the tractor to explain to Mart what they were going to do. Alec watched his retreating back a moment, then turned briskly and gave his attention to the matter in hand.

*

By early afternoon the scene looked very different. The trailer and the combine had both gone, and a distant whirr and clatter told of the harvesting carrying on on the far side of the old airfield. Nearer at hand two uniformed policemen, jackets off, sleeves rolled up, stood red-faced and ruefully considered their blistered hands. Most of the cordoned-off square was cut now, but it would have been hard to discern any pattern to the scattering of policemen and civilians delving, noting or simply standing chatting on the stubble. In the centre of the square a small island of barley stood uncut. Among it, completely disregarded, the bundle of clothes with its out-flung arms lay where it had first been found.

'Here he is!'

'Not before time.' Alec waited for the tall, rumpled civilian to get his case from the boot of the car, then walked across to meet him.

''Afternoon, Doctor.'

'Sorry to keep you. Been an accident on the Caterham Bypass. Queued back to Purley. What have you got for me?'

The two men walked together towards the bundle which now, with the pathologist's arrival, was the focus of every eye.

'Shotgun, you say? Good. There's usually quite a bit we can tell from those. Here we are. I see . . . big chap, isn't he? . . . yes . . .'

While Ransome arranged with the photographer for some preliminary shots, Alec let his eyes roam again over the body. You could shut yourself off from the blood, and the smell, and what the shotgun pellets had done to the face, because it was only so much data. Like the clothes: blue trousers, good brown shoes with a thick sole, oatmeal jacket—flung wide with the open arms, and much stained.

It was difficult to see what colour the shirt might have been. No tie. Problems with the face, but the hairline had barely started to recede. He was as the doctor had said a big chap, and heavily-built. The body had that natural— that is to say, unnatural—look which suggested it lay where it had first fallen: the rag-doll look, as Alec thought of it in his own mind.

The pathologist was muttering into his dictaphone, and broke off to question Alec. 'How carefully have you searched this bit?'

'Pretty carefully. We left the barley uncut round the body until you'd seen it.' Now the two perspiring constables were clearing the grain stalk by stalk under the eagle eye of Fletcher from Scene of Crime and the civilian forensic expert. 'So far, nothing.' He paused. 'He's been shot pretty close to, hasn't he?'

'Pretty close.'

Then both men must have come from the direction of the control tower. There were no tracks in the standing barley where anyone had trodden it down: ergo, they must have come from the direction of the tower, where Parker had already combined before he saw the body.

The pathologist, who had been bending over the body, sat back on his heels and scrutinized the thermometer. 'OK. If you want to get him bagged up. Where's he going?'

'East Grinstead. That suit you?'

'I'd do it back at King's if it was up to me—' he glanced at Alec, and stood up, easing his muscles—'but that'd involve moving the body out of the district and a lot of fuss with the coroner. The Queen Vic will do me fine.'

Alec nodded. The Queen Victoria Hospital at East Grinstead was, moreover, only a few hundred yards from the police station where already the murder centre was being set up. 'I can have the body there for you within the hour, if you like.'

Ransome shook his head. 'No good, I'm afraid. I've another to do. First thing tomorrow, though. You know,' he continued as they walked across to the cars, 'it's lucky the weather's changed.'

'He thinks so,' Alec agreed, nodding towards the far side of the airfield where the combine was droning away.

'Lucky for us, too. That chap's been there the best part of a week. Much longer in this warm muggy weather we've been having . . .'

He drove off across the wide expanse of concrete with a parting wave. Alec turned and looked back at the figures dotted across the stubble and frowned. Now the questions really begin, he told himself.

By nightfall an area one hundred yards square had been examined with painstaking thoroughness. So had the concrete of the nearer part of the old runway and closest of the hardstandings. Another thirty or forty acres, comprising mostly the runway and access roads back to the gate into the lane, had been combed more generally by a team of four men walking slowly to and fro in line. The gateway, and the adjacent verge, had received especial scrutiny, and Scene of Crime had photographed two sets of tracks made in the soft verge, and taken a cast of one set where they had left deep indentations across a patch of bare mud.

At eight Alec called a halt. It was not quite too dark to see, but dark enough for the risk of overlooking some clue to outweigh the advantages of going on. He arranged for two of the men to return in the morning to poke among the farm rubbish and dilapidated buildings along the perimeter hedge.

'What about these, sir?' The constable indicated the scythes with distaste.

'Lean them up against the wall here,' Alec said, nodding towards the control tower. He looked across the luminous, sighing barley: away in the darkness, a mile away maybe, the drone of machinery still sounded, and yellow light wavered across the darkened landscape. Parker and Mart would stop only for sleep and meals now, until all the vast sea of grain was reduced to stubble.

Cars started to leave the scene. Headlights came on and

swept round. A rabbit, caught standing foolishly on its hind legs in a clear patch of stubble, suddenly began to run to and fro in senseless diagonals. The lights swept over it; it vanished in the darkness.

Fletcher was waiting for him. Alec cocked his head interrogatively, and they fell into step together.

'The proverbial needle in a haystack,' Fletcher commented.

'Mm. And a killer who kept his head.' He ticked the points off on his fingers. 'No cartridge cases; no trampling of the corn round the body . . .' He broke off. 'You know, one thing's puzzling me.'

'Only one?'

'But doesn't it strike you?' Alec turned to look at the older man, who nodded.

'I know. The shot should have been in his back, shouldn't it.'

'If he was running away . . . saw the gun, and ran away, like that rabbit, senselessly, just to put as much space as he could between himself and it . . . Ideal from the murderer's point of view, of course. No pools of blood on the tarmac; one path into the corn, and the body lying at the end of it. So the shot should have been in his back, surely?' He shook his head doubtfully. 'Maybe Ransome'll be able to shed some light on it after he's done the PM.'

'Maybe.' They had reached the cars. Nelson stood waiting by the blue Escort which had brought them from police headquarters. Fletcher turned away to his own car, fishing for his keys.

'By the way,' Alec said, looking back the way they had come. The afterglow of the sun gleamed on the windows of the old control tower. 'That padlock. Didn't it look rather new?'

'On the control tower?' Fletcher stopped and turned to glance in his turn to the dark, angular tower where it bulked against the sky. He hesitated. 'I'll have another look at that. Neither new nor old, I'd say. It'd open, with a key.'

'It was just a thought. 'Night, David.'

''Night.'

'OK, Nelson, let's get home.'

CHAPTER 2

'It's probably one Andrew Hunter. Lives in Nottingham. He's a freelance journalist, author, that sort of thing. His wife reported him missing last week when he didn't ring home from a business trip. The local CID made what inquiries they could, reckoned he'd maybe been keeping another woman on the side—he made quite a lot of these business trips, it seems—and had chosen last week to make it permanent. They sent us a picture, but that wasn't much help of course. But the clothes are right, if it is Hunter.'

'Is the wife coming down?'

'She's already on her way, sir. Her local station sent someone round last night to break the news, as soon as we'd made the identification.'

Alec grimaced. 'OK,' he agreed. 'We'd have had to see her, anyway.'

'Want me to go to the post-mortem, sir, or will you go yourself?'

'I'll go. We'll do the formal identification afterwards, when they've had a chance to make him a bit more presentable.' He fiddled with the paperknife, frowning. 'I wonder why he never had all that concrete taken up?' he mused.

'Sir?'

'The farmer. Why did he never have the runways taken up, do you think? How many acres must there be under concrete there?'

'No idea, sir. Quite a lot, I suppose. There's all those huts, and the hard-standings too. He'd had some of those up, though. There were piles of bits of concrete, weren't there?'

'Only right by the gate. Money troubles, do you think?'
He shook his head to clear it. 'Something else you can ask
him. No, what I really want to know is whether he saw
anyone on the airfield in the last week. Any cars on the
verge. Heard anything. Does anyone use it—kids learning
to drive, parachute club—you could still land a light plane
on those runways, despite the cracks. Anyone have a lease
on any of the buildings? Ask him for keys of any that are
padlocked, and we'll have a little nose round this afternoon,
perhaps. We're probably talking about Thursday or Friday
for the date of the killing, but I'll let you know for sure when
Ransome's done his stuff.'

Sergeant Nelson looked thoughtful. 'Parker won't take
kindly to stopping work for a lot of questions.' But as he
spoke the lines of light and shadow on the carpet blurred
and vanished and a sudden spatter of rain hit the windows
like grapeshot.

'There's your answer. Better get out there right away.
See you back here at lunch.'

The Queen Victoria Hospital at East Grinstead wasn't
equipped to the standard Ransome was used to at King's,
but it had all that was necessary; and after all, he mused as,
green-gowned and wellingtoned, he followed the mortuary
attendant through from the changing-room, his requirements were simple enough. The dead were a lot easier to
treat than the living. You couldn't ask them questions, of
course; but nor could they mislead you with answers which
were coy, or devious, or simply bloody-minded. You had a
body—here it was: a collection of data; and you disas-
sembled the data piece by piece, and reassembled it into
the truth. Simple! Huh.

Alec, as he walked back from the hospital to the police
station at East Court two and a half hours later, reflected
on how much easier it must be to diagnose the living than
the dead. What a vast deal of time he would save if it were

only possible to address questions to the corpse with any expectation of a reply. And whereas illness and disease followed well-charted and logical progressions, a murder could be affected in a thousand ways by that most imponderable of phenomena, human nature.

This particular body had yielded up a good deal of information, but nothing that was immediately helpful in understanding why it had been lying amid the barley on a disused airfield in Sussex. The forensic expert had watched with eagle eye as Ransome picked out each piece of lead shot from the mess of flesh and clothing, and had carried off his prize for weighing and analysis. With normal luck, they would soon have the weapon identified, and be able to say how far the murderer had been standing from the victim when he pulled the trigger.

Clothing had proved to be unremarkable, but Alec had made a note of the contents of pockets and wallet before they too were carried off to the laboratory for examination. Nothing, unfortunately, saying 'Meet me at the old airfield at midnight, signed X'; but there was no doubt the dead man was Hunter, and the rail tickets and the hotel key and the other bits and pieces would go a long way towards reconstructing his last days.

He wondered whether Nelson had had better luck at the farm. It was vexing that the airfield was so accessible: the old main gateway, it was true, was blocked by a tangle of barbed wire, backed by a barrier of dumped soil; but there were any number of gates from surrounding lanes into fields adjoining the perimeter track. It would be worth having a word with the local bobby in Hartfield to see what problems they had with joy-riders or vandalism; but the fact remained that anyone could have got in—and out—much as they pleased. And there were worse places to carry out a killing than in the middle of a deserted airfield.

And then Parker himself, who had behaved as if finding bloody bodies in the path of his combine was an everyday occurrence; not like his tractor-driver, whose colour had varied only between white and green the whole time they were there. Still, farmers were like that: all that mattered was the harvest—or the ploughing, or the milking, or the spraying—and to Parker anyone who couldn't appreciate that would no doubt be a mere townsman and an idiot. There might be a body; but there again, it might be too wet to harvest tomorrow, and that was a more immediate concern.

Janice Hunter could never be glamorous, but her sharp, small features would have been attractive enough before her misery rendered them drawn and ugly and plain. A short, dark-haired woman in her early forties, she was sufficiently in command of herself to mutter a reply when Alec greeted her as she was shown in.

As he watched the uniformed WPC settle her into a chair and put the cup of tea within reach, his compassion was moderated by a more pressing anxiety that this woman should tell him what he needed to know without a great fuss. If she was the sort by whom even tragedy is grimly relished as a rare moment of limelight, the going would be tedious.

'All right now?' the WPC was saying comfortingly. 'Chief Inspector Stainton is just going to ask you a few questions and then I'll be able to take you to your friend's.'

Janice Hunter clutched her balled handkerchief and looked up. Her eyes as they met Alec's, though puffy and dark-ringed, were resolute enough.

'I'm sorry I have to ask you anything while you're still so upset,' he began; 'and I want to thank you for being so brave about the identification. Now, let's see if we can clear up one or two matters to start with . . .' And he commenced, matter of fact and unemotional, to draw her story from her, and as she talked Mrs Hunter too seemed to treat the matter as questions of fact, and that seemed to help her.

What had hurt most, she explained in a tart Midlands accent, was the assumption of the Nottingham police that

Andrew had run off with another woman; that she, Janice, was merely shutting her eyes to a common enough fact of modern life. As if she had never faced that possibility for herself! But they didn't listen when she told them that while it was theoretically possible, in practical terms it was the last thing that could have happened.

'I know Andrew spends a great deal of time from home,' she said with pathetic dignity. 'When he's researching for a book, or an article, it can take him all over the country; abroad, even.' She looked up at Alec. 'Do you think I haven't wondered sometimes, when I'm lying in bed alone, whether *he*'s really alone too?'

'What I couldn't get across to them is that if he'd . . .' She swallowed, and went on firmly, 'If he'd left me, he wouldn't have gone without his work. He was two-thirds of the way through a book, and he left all his notes, everything, at home.'

'Everything?'

She thought, then looked up. 'I don't know,' she admitted. 'He'd have had some papers in his briefcase; he took that. But all the rest, it's still at home. That was what worried me. Oh, of course, that Sergeant Gurney thought I was shutting my eyes to something I didn't want to see. Dear God, I'd put up with more than that if I got Andrew back! But his work—he'd never leave that. That's why I knew it wasn't a woman. That something had happened to him.' She pulled the balled handkerchief apart, and pressed it into a different ball, and wiped at the corner of her eyes as if removing a streak of mascara. Alec thought of television grief, and stage grief, and the grief that relatives who ought to be sorrowing but weren't sometimes presented for his consumption, and was obscurely grateful for the genuine article.

'What was it he went away for? Research for his book?'

She nodded. 'Partly. And he'd been asked to speak. A reunion: men who had fought together in the war. You know.'

Alec raised his eyebrows. Mrs Hunter smiled emptily, a brief mechanical gesture that left the grief in her eyes untouched. 'Oh no, he wasn't old enough for that. Andrew was a war baby: born on VE day, he always said. Perhaps that's what made him so interested in it. Most of his books, you see, they were about the war. His history of the Yeomanry regiments—' Alec shook his head fractionally—'well, it was a sort of authority.' Another half-smile, with something of pride and nostalgia in it, passed across her face.

'And so he was asked to speak at this reunion in his professional capacity, so to speak; as a historian?'

Mrs Hunter shrugged. 'It's what his present book is all about, you see: South Africans in the RAF. They were all South Africans: there was to be a dinner, and speakers, and outings, over the weekend. I don't know what Andrew was going to speak to them about. I suppose they forget . . .'

Alec frowned. 'When was this?'

Apparently, Hunter had left home on Thursday of the previous week—the day, according to Ransome, he had almost certainly died. The dinner was to be the next night, Friday, and his talk was set for Saturday morning. He'd been invited to stay over for the whole weekend. He'd gone a day early because, he said, he wanted to do some research at the Imperial War Museum first.

'Yet you rang the police on Saturday to report him missing? Even though he wasn't expected home until the next day?'

'He always rings home,' she said, shamefaced. 'To say he's arrived safely. Sounds daft, doesn't it, in a grown man.'

'And when he didn't?'

'I rang the hotel.' That was on the Friday, and they had told Janice that her husband had checked in, but couldn't be found. She had sat and thought about that for a bit, still hoping that he would ring, and went to bed definitely worried. She woke to remember that if her husband had

been to the Imperial War Museum he would have seen
Trevor Letts there; so she rang Trevor Letts.

Andrew Hunter had never been in the Imperial War
Museum that week. A quick search in the library confirmed
that he was not there now. She checked the hotel again, and
spoke to one of the organizers of the reunion. Andrew had
been absent from the reunion dinner, had failed to appear
to address the assembly as scheduled, and generally was
not in very good odour in consequence. Janice had sat
staring at the telephone thinking nervously of the trouble
she would be stirring up; then picked up the receiver and
dialled the local police.

Alec mentally collated Janice Hunter's account with what
could be deduced from the evidence on the body. It all made
sense, of a sort. Whether Hunter had ever intended to go to
the Imperial War Museum was academic. What was certain
was that he had had a more pressing appointment.

'I'd like to send someone up to Nottingham,' he said, 'to
look through your husband's notes; also his diary, if we
may. I suppose he didn't mention anyone he was expecting
to meet in London? Was he nervous; tense; anxious about
the trip?'

'No,' Mrs Hunter answered definitely. 'He was just as he
always is.' For the first time her voice wavered, as if the
recollection of normality was suddenly poignant. 'He always
was a bit vague when he was in the middle of a book; you
know, as if he had something on his mind. But that was
normal. There was nothing else as I noticed.'

Then, Alec reflected, the notes and the diary were the
best bet; and with luck they would illuminate the link
between Andrew Hunter, military historian, from Nottingham and a bleak expanse of barley and concrete which
once, more than forty years ago, had been RAF Hartfield
Park in Sussex.

CHAPTER 3

'I'm going to send Johnson up there first thing tomorrow,' Alec said, 'to make a thorough examination of Hunter's papers. There's a diary, too, Mrs Hunter says. It may show us who he arranged to meet at Hartfield, and why.'

The Superintendent grunted. 'He'd more likely have had it with him. Have you checked his belongings at the hotel?'

'Nelson's doing that this afternoon; should be on the way back by now.'

'And what do you reckon to this trip out to Hartfield? Research for his book?'

'I don't know,' Alec admitted frankly. 'It looks a possibility, doesn't it, given the sort of field he was working in. But then why not tell his wife about it?'

'And you believe the wife?'

'I think she's telling the truth as she knows it,' Alec answered cautiously. 'And I think her grief is genuine. I also think her reasoning is probably correct about there not being another woman, although I haven't completely ruled out the possibility that his little story about going to the Imperial War Museum may have been a cover for that, rather than for his visit to Hartfield. Don't forget,' he added, 'that though Hunter didn't go to the IWM he definitely did go to the hotel. And we checked the reunion. That's certainly genuine. So he didn't leave Nottingham for black silk sheets in a docklands penthouse.'

Blackett frowned. 'You're not leaving us much if you rule out the wife and you rule out another woman. Money worries?'

'She says not. I've told her we'll want to see bank statements. She says he has an account in his own name, and she doesn't know about that one, but the joint account's healthy enough.'

'And Hunter got to Hartfield when? And how?'

Alec hesitated. 'At the moment we're working on Thursday afternoon for Hunter's arrival at Hartfield Park. Ransome says it's likely on the medical evidence, but they're doing some checks on the larvæ and so forth to make sure. There was no car at the airfield, of course. The murderer could have taken that away with him; or for that matter, murderer and victim could have arrived together. Hunter had the return half of a ticket from Nottingham to London on him, but nothing further than that.'

'Meaning that he didn't travel on from London by train?'

'Not necessarily,' Alec replied. 'It only means he hadn't initially bought a through ticket, which suggests the visit to Hartfield Park may not have been part of his original plan. Suppose he went to his hotel first, checked in, and then decided to make the Hartfield trip. You can only get day returns provided you're travelling both ways off-peak, so if he went by train he'd have had to buy a single—and he'd have given up his ticket at the barrier in East Grinstead. In that case, I'd have expected to find a bus ticket in his pocket; but he could have thrown it away, or got a taxi.'

'You're checking, naturally.'

'Taxi-drivers? Yes. And train and bus times to see when he could have got to Hartfield. And if he did get to Hartfield by public transport, there's a good chance that someone saw him walking on the road out to the airfield: it's a mile or more out of the village.'

'Hm. No other wounds?'

'No. We're still waiting to hear whether it was one shot or two; the forensic chap thinks only one, but he's not convinced we've found all the pellets, and he's having Fletcher's boys go over the ground again in case we missed any.'

The Superintendent leant back in the chair, which creaked its protest. 'Good. And the farmer says he saw nothing?'

'Yes. I'm a little doubtful about that. When Nelson

asked him generally about his movements last week he said Thursday he was muck-spreading on the far side of the valley. But his tractor driver backs it up.'

Blackett heaved himself to his feet. 'You seem to have it all under control.'

Alec rose and followed the other man to the door. 'I suppose so. But while we know who the dead man was, we haven't the slightest clue to who killed him; or why.'

'It usually becomes apparent.' Blackett nodded and left. Alec, shutting the door behind him, wandered over to the window and gazed thoughtfully down until he saw the Superintendent's foreshortened figure emerge into the car park, fish for his keys and drive away; then he returned to his desk and lifted the phone.

The hotel, just off Hyde Park, was a plush one; not so much displaying as thrusting its four stars at the visitor: button-leather on the reception desk, uniformed staff, braided (but teenage) doorman. Nelson waited for two white-mackintoshed Americans to check out, then approached the desk and proffered his warrant card.

The assistant manager, duly summoned, was condescending. Perhaps Nelson and Liz Pink in their inconspicuous plain clothes were insufficiently impressive; perhaps they did not properly smell of money; perhaps he regarded the four stars as a personal accolade. At any rate, he inclined towards the amused and dismissive.

'I couldn't tell you,' he replied in response to Nelson's initial inquiries about Andrew Hunter's arrival the previous Thursday.

'But you did have a party here, a group of South Africans over for a reunion?'

'The conference facilities had been booked, yes. Naturally several of the delegates arrived a day or two early. And some stayed on, one or two are still in residence. Whether your Mr . . . Hunter was among them, I really couldn't . . .'

'Find out,' Nelson ordered shortly.

There was a pause. The assistant manager's features flushed slowly pink, then paled with anger or pride.

'Find out, and stop giving me the run-around. And while you're at it, I want to know what time Mr Hunter checked in and what happened to his luggage.'

'Don't you talk to me like that. I'll have you know that—'

'Oh, put a sock in it,' Nelson cut him off. 'I haven't time to waste on your high opinion of yourself. Just do it, will you? Please?'

He turned to Liz as the man sulkily walked out, and winked at her.

Five minutes later the assistant manager was back, a register in his hand.

'Mr Andrew Hunter arrived at eleven twenty-five on Thursday morning. He had Room 433; a single. He was due to check out on Sunday, but did not do so.'

Nelson raised his eyebrows. 'That concern you?'

'Guests often stay on a day or two.'

'Did you think to check whether his bed had been slept in?'

'The chambermaid would have noticed, of course. I would hardly have been likely to concern myself with that.'

'You mean, you don't care whether your guests are here or not, so long as they pay for their rooms.'

'How they spend their time is their own business.'

'And if he didn't check out, it meant you could charge him for an extra day!'

'Do you have to be so . . . so offensive?'

'For crying out loud!' Nelson exclaimed. 'Right. So his luggage is still in Room 433?'

'I imagine so.'

'Good. We'll take it with us.'

'If you pay Mr Hunter's bill, naturally.'

Nelson shook his head wonderingly. 'You do try it on, don't you. And don't get any ideas about sending the bill to Mrs Hunter. It'll do your four-star image no good at all to have it known that you sent a bill to a widow for a room her dead husband never occupied.'

'A widow?' the assistant manager faltered.

'And,' Nelson went on, 'our forensic people will want to have a good look at that room. So will you please have it locked, until they say otherwise.'

'You ask me to take a room out of commission . . .'

'Tough.'

Alec sat back in his chair in the borrowed room in East Grinstead and considered what Liz had told him. 'One suitcase?'

'Yes, sir. He hadn't even unpacked. They were still going over the room when I left. Sergeant Nelson's going to bring the case back with him when he comes.'

'Nothing else?'

'It was only going to be a long weekend.'

'Of course. All the same . . . By the way, did you see anyone from the conference?'

'There was one South African couple there, sir. They were the only ones left. I got a list from them of other delegates. They thought they'd mostly be staying on in this country for a week or two, sightseeing or visiting relatives, but one or two might have taken the opportunity to see a bit of Europe. They said there was some annoyance when Hunter failed to show up,' Liz went on. 'They knew no more than that. I presume the conference organizers established that Hunter had checked in to the hotel, but this couple knew nothing of that.'

'The organizer being?'

'A man called Patrick, Jack Patrick, sir.' She added apologetically, 'Who could be anywhere.'

Alec got up and took his jacket from the peg, fishing for the car keys in the pocket. 'It's a start, though. We have a body; and we're beginning to have some idea of times and movements. Now we need a murderer.'

CHAPTER 4

James Parker had had plenty of time to consider the macabre discovery he had made. Sitting in his air-conditioned cab high above the whirling blades of the combine he had to keep the routine half of his mind very much on his work: on the dials and lights before him; on the rate at which the machine spewed out grain and chaff; on Marty's tractor keeping station with him, and the rate at which the trailer filled; and on the uncut barley into which his machine sailed as a steamer cleaves the waves: attentive for wire, for dumped mattresses, for cans or old rope or any of the hundred things which shouldn't be there, but if they were would turn his expensive and delicate combine into so much stationary junk.

All this occupied the subconscious part of his mind. But the other half, the speculative half, was free. Often he listened to a cassette on the headphones. Sometimes he mentally planned out a new building, or the alteration to the kitchen Diana had been nagging him to do after the ploughing and sowing was over—both highly speculative projects, money being as tight as it was. Today, he pondered the presence in his barley field of a dead man.

He'd been more shaken then he'd shown; at least as unnerved as Marty, though he'd controlled it by his concern to get on with the harvest. Like most farmers, Parker was used to treating shotguns as tools of his business. They were no more dangerous, after all, than the deep slurry pool, or the fumes when they cleaned out the grain tower, or the whirling PTO behind one of the tractors. Each season such dangers claimed lives or limbs somewhere in the neighbourhood.

But it was the first time Parker had seen what a shotgun could do to a human being, and shotguns weren't going to be quite so neutral for him again. The blackened, decaying blood; the obliterated features, the gaping chest; and of course the smell. Farm smells were one thing—innocuous because familiar, a by-product of the day's work, each element recognizable. The smell which had assailed him as soon as he opened the cab door yesterday afternoon had been a different matter altogether.

That the police suspected him of having a closer connection with the death than merely discovering it, he was fully aware. He had stood around apparently ignored most of the time, but what attention he had been paid had that guarded politeness which meant they were reserving judgement—or were already inclining against him. Even waiting on the stubble with Billy Standish, the Hartfield constable, had been unnerving; he had drunk in the Anchor or the Huntsman or the Gallipot time without number with Billy—after hours, too, on more than one occasion—but having him there in his barley, uniformed and official, had been horribly different. Billy had been changed, frighteningly changed, into PC Standish, the custodian of the law; and Parker had been very conscious that, by being the one to discover the body, he had placed himself in suspicious proximity to the gravest crime in the book.

When the plain-clothes men had arrived, the ones who ferreted, and the ones who seemed only to stand and ponder, it had been impossible to separate who was who, civilian or police. The youngster who took his statement must have been a detective, since he wore plain clothes. So, too, must the other man, the spare man in his mid-thirties with the cool energy, whose glance had been direct and remorseless, and to whom Billy Standish spoke with such punctilious deference.

The thing was, Parker would have suspected himself, in their position. Almost the first thing they had asked him was whether the barley had been trampled down around the body, and he had denied it. So how had the body come there? And where had the killer been? Parker glanced across

the airfield to the old control tower and tried to estimate
how far the body had been from the edge of the concrete.
With no indication of the presence of anyone else they *had*
to suspect him.

They hadn't returned last night, which was a mercy; he
and Marty had been able to get on with the combining. It
had been ten o'clock before they ceased. This morning
there had been the detective-sergeant, asking about where
he had been and what he had been doing this last week.
And there would be more visits, more questions, he knew.
And they would ask about his shotguns, and take them
away maybe, to work out when they had last been fired.
And it wouldn't be Billy Standish who came to do the
questioning, he knew. It would be a younger man, faster-
witted, sceptical; with no preconceived prejudice in Parker's
favour. Harder to convince. And harder to lie to.

Eddie Zablonski was a small, gnarled man with a shrewd
eye. Owner of a small chain of radio shops in Capetown, he
was clearly prosperous in an understated way. His wife was
more flamboyant, noticeably well-dressed rather after the
manner of an American matron. Nelson placed her in her
late fifties, and her husband eight or nine years older.

They were in England, Mr Zablonski told Nelson, for the
reunion to mark forty-five years since the end of the war,
and they were the only ones to have stayed on after the
weekend using the hotel as the base for their sightseeing.
Did Nelson know Little Rissington? Yes, Nelson did, dimly.
Eddie Zablonski had served at Little Rissington.

Nelson asked about the reunion weekend and learned
that it had been a great success, marred only by the non-
appearance of Andrew Hunter. The little South African was
not much worried by that, though inefficiency galled him,
and anyway, Brian Schumaaker had taken the opportunity
to fill the time with his reminiscences of first coming to
England and that, striking a chord with all of them as he
recalled mud and fog and girls who said yes when they

meant no, and no when they meant yes, had kept them all
better amused than any historian could have done.

'Don't get me wrong,' Eddie assured Nelson earnestly. 'I
respect history as much as the next man. If you think about
it that way, we *were* history. Know what I mean?'

Nelson mentally added the capital H's and knew exactly
what he meant.

Eddie and June Zablonski had arrived at the hotel on the
Thursday, a day before the reunion proper. Nelson perked
up at that; could they have seen Andrew Hunter? But if
they had, they had no way of knowing, and the description
of a heavily-built middle-aged man in jacket and trousers
was pretty vague. Maybe later they'd have a photo to try
them on.

The formal part of the weekend finished on Sunday
lunch-time. About half of those who had attended stayed
on for Sunday night at the hotel; the rest, shrewdly weighing
the difference between the price of a hotel in London and
one in Bath or York or Inverness, or conveniently provided
with friends or relations to offer hospitality, checked out on
Sunday afternoon. By Monday lunch-time, at any rate, the
Zablonskis were the only ones left.

Nelson thanked them, looked in on the two youngsters
from the police laboratory who were going over Room 433,
found he was in the way and headed for Victoria.

CHAPTER 5

Johnson, whose images of Nottingham had been moulded
by teenage readings of Lawrence and Sillitoe, was vaguely
annoyed to find himself caught up in the morning rush hour
in a modern city thronged with cars. What had he expected,
he asked himself derisively, Victorian grimy brick and trams
to Trent Bridge and men leaning against street corners in
mufflers and cloth caps?

It took him three circuits of the one-way system before he was able to find the exit which led to the police station, but once there the natives were, as Mr Stainton had predicted, both friendly and cooperative.

But not helpful. The problem was, of course, that there was nothing much to be helpful about. Andrew Hunter was not a notorious criminal; he was not constantly being bound over for beating his wife, or taking a knife to the neighbours; even his motoring was law-abiding and without offence. Historians do not tend to fill police notebooks and there was nothing, literally, which the local CID could tell Johnson about him, beyond the bare fact of his address and a vague generalization about the area he had lived in.

Johnson grimaced ruefully. 'Thanks, anyway. It's information of a sort, I suppose, even if negative.'

'You want to go and have a word with his local station,' the bearded detective-sergeant suggested. 'They might have a bit more.'

'You'd better show me where it is on the map, if you don't mind. Don't want to lose my way among the slag-heaps.'

'Ha-bloody-ha. You won't find many of those where you're going, son.' They walked together across to a big wall-map and found the village where Janice Hunter lived. 'That's your best way: take you about twenty minutes, I should think.'

'It'll take me twenty minutes to find my way off the ring-road,' Johnson retorted sourly.

'It won't be so bad now,' the other man remarked blankfaced. 'They'll all be at home exercising their whippets.'

Johnson grinned. 'Thanks, anyway. Do the same for you some day. Come and see how the other half lives.'

'I already know,' the bearded sergeant said, turning away. 'That's why I'm here. Best of luck!'

'Thanks!' I'll need it, Johnson thought wryly. Nobody likes to feel they have embarked on a wild-goose chase, and that, Johnson decided as he skirted the city centre again and headed westwards, was exactly what he was on.

*

'Perhaps it would help if you could give me an idea of your husband's movements over the last few months,' Johnson said patiently. It had not been a comfortable half-hour, and he wished Liz Pink had been given this job instead of him. 'Just in general terms. He's been working on a book, hasn't he? That must have involved him in a lot of research.'

'All his work involves a lot of research,' Janice Hunter retorted sharply. 'That's what his work is. He doesn't make it up, you know!'

'No; I didn't imagine he did,' Johnson replied evenly. 'I suppose what I'm trying to get at is where your husband's visit to Hartfield Park fits in to the picture. So where else did his work take him; who might he have gone to see?'

Mrs Hunter got up and walked around the room, putting an ornament straight, fingering a pulled thread in one of the curtains. She had not offered him tea or coffee. The tearful ones were easier to deal with, he thought; the dry-eyed sort hurt more inside where there was no way of reaching them.

She turned and faced him. 'Are you still trying to prove he was seeing another woman?' she asked directly.

'No; no, I'm not trying to prove that. We don't really think he was, you know.' Or if he had been, it was merely peripheral to his death.

'Because I've faced that now. I've faced the fact that the wife is always the last to know. It's what the neighbours think, of course. What they've always thought, I wouldn't be surprised.' Her voice with its stark Midland vowels was flat and accusatory.

Johnson made a little bustle of turning to his notebook and readying his pen. 'Just give me a few things to work on. What you remember. That's all. Where did he go last? Let's start with that.'

Piece by piece he extracted the sparse and unpromising details. Two trips to the Imperial War Museum, in February and May. Three days in July, referencing gravestones in

the churchyards of Kent and Sussex – on consideration,
Johnson underlined that one; a day trip to Ashbourne to
talk to a South African who had stayed on in this country
after the war, and another to Hereford for the same purpose.
Half a dozen absences from home, maybe, in the last twelve
months.

'But he didn't give you any indication that he was planning to call at Hartfield Park on this last trip? You knew he
was addressing the reunion, of course.'

'Yes; he's done that sort of thing before. I didn't know he
was going anywhere else. Apart from the Imperial War
Museum, that is; and apparently he didn't go there, did
he?'

'No. All right. What about letters he might have had
recently. Had anyone written suggesting he meet them?
Was he involved in any disputes? Might one of his books
have upset someone, who harboured a grudge, perhaps?'

Mrs Hunter looked at him queerly, then walked out of
the room. Johnson followed dubiously. A door, which had
been shut when he arrived, was open on the other side of
the hall, and he saw it led into a room where the garage
must once have been; probably converted from the garage,
in fact.

It was crammed from floor to ceiling. Three green filing
cabinets filled the only wall-space not occupied by shelving
and cupboards. Above them, a wall-map of Britain and
Northern Europe, fully six feet square, marked with pins
and flags. Mrs Hunter stood by the big desk that covered
much of the floorspace, a funny quizzical smile on her
face.

'This is his life, here. This is all I have of him now, this
and a few clothes in the wardrobe upstairs. Letters?' She
pulled open a filing cabinet and he saw folders crammed
with correspondence. She banged the drawer shut and
pulled open another: the same. 'And you ask if he had any
letters,' she said with a queer little laugh.

Suddenly Johnson realized—and he didn't take himself

for the world's brightest psychologist, but he saw this—how much Janice Hunter had resented her husband's work. During his lifetime it had been a rival more real than any physical mistress. That was why she could take the idea of his infidelity so calmly: because she had been forced for so long to endure the presence in her very house of his true mistress. Andrew Hunter had had an affair, right enough; and he had pursued it blatantly, callously, negligently, right here.

It must have been, Johnson pondered, much like himself being forced to look on while his girlfriend embraced some other bloke. Not a pleasant thought, and he thrust it from him as he turned to consider the daunting treasure-house of Andrew Hunter's study.

This was going to take some time.

Alec left his car on the verge a hundred yards short of the gateway. A couple of men in plain clothes were swatting the vegetation in the ditch half-heartedly; they straightened up as he approached.

'Got anything?'

'Not a dickeybird, sir.'

'Mr Fletcher around?'

'No, sir. He was looking at the buildings earlier, then he said to have another go by the entrance here. He'll be back at Headquarters, sir, if you want him.'

Alec glanced across towards the huddle of dilapidated buildings and shook his head. 'Later,' he said. The airfield stretched nakedly into the distance. The air was empty of the sound of machinery: it seemed almost unbelievable that all that prairie of barley had been reduced to stubble already.

Simms and a uniformed constable had got on well with their house to house visits. There were maybe twenty houses between the airfield and Hartfield itself, and of these fifteen had had someone in—and another two, they learnt, were occupied only at weekends. On the other hand, nobody

recalled anyone walking along the roadside the previous
Thursday.

'He came by bus, sir,' Simms confirmed, when Alec
tracked them down near the old station. 'We're pretty sure
about that. It dropped him at the corner at two-fifteen. But
after that . . . Part of the problem is that round here nobody
walks—if they have to go into the village they all go by car.
So no one would actually have met Hunter on the road.
We're down to hoping someone might have overtaken him
in a car, or looked out of their window just as he was going
by. And so far, no one did.'

'Never mind; if we know he used that bus, that answers
most of the questions for us. How positive was the identification?'

'Pretty positive, sir. The person we spoke to remembered
enough to describe his clothes reasonably accurately. Most
of the passengers are regulars, you see, so a stranger is
noticed. We had a bit of luck there.' He glanced at his
colleague, and Alec realized they were looking rather pleased
with themselves. 'We met today's bus that goes through at
the same time and spoke to the driver.'

'Well done.' A delivery van whizzed past. Somewhere
down the road the clop of hooves on tarmac could be
heard.

'Thank you, sir. Bit of luck, really, that it was the same
bloke. Apparently Hunter got on at the railway station,
wanted to make sure it was the right bus, didn't know the
fare . . . If he was trying to be noticed he couldn't have
done it better.'

The three men stepped back on to the verge as a couple
of horses appeared round the bend in the road, moving with
steady effortless gait. Two girls looked down with casual
interest and answered Alec's nod with non-committal
smiles. The animals were glossy and well-cared-for, sinews
rippling fluidly beneath chestnut coats.

Alec glanced at his watch: it was a thought! 'Excuse me!'
he called. One of the girls glanced over her shoulder and

saw him gesturing, and reined in. Alec went up to where the two animals stood steadily on the tarmac.

They listened cautiously while he asked what he wanted. 'About what time?' the older girl, dark-haired and handsome, asked. She turned in the saddle, to address her friend. 'What time did we come out last Thursday, Jill? It usually is much this sort of time; early afternoon,' she said in an aside to Alec.

'Didn't you stay behind?' the second girl queried. 'You had the blacksmith coming, don't you remember?'

'Was that Thursday? No, that was Wednesday. This gentleman wants to know if we passed anyone walking along the roadside.'

'Not that I recall. Is it important?'

'It is, rather.' Alec fished out his warrant card and the leathers creaked as the dark-haired girl leant to read it. She met his eye, as she sat up, with astute interest. A few yards up the road, the other horse snorted, and shifted its weight, its shoes clacking on the tarmac.

'This is to do with the body on the airfield, isn't it?' the girl said shrewdly. He nodded. She turned in the saddle. 'Wasn't there someone in Butcherfield Lane one day last week?'

'A man,' the other girl agreed. 'Not local. Not a walker, either. I mean, not a rambler, or anything. More as if his car had broken down.' Her horse, bored, lifted its tail and casually defecated steamingly on to the road. Simms backed away, nose wrinkling. The uniformed constable sniggered.

'Remember anything about him?' Alec asked. 'Big? Small? Old? Young?'

'Dunno. Biggish, maybe. Yes, he was. Age? I don't remember. You pass someone, you don't really notice. Especially from up here.'

'Not bald,' the first girl said humorously. 'That's something you do notice, from this vantage-point. Otherwise, as Jill says . . .'

Alec fished for a card, and scribbled a number on it. 'Ring

me on this number if you remember anything else. I'll
have someone come round and take a statement from you
anyway. And you are . . .?' He wrote it down.

'By the way,' he added, 'can you tell me what he was
carrying, this man?'

'Was he carrying anything? I don't recall. Yes, he was,
though! He was carrying a briefcase. Black, with combi-
nation locks. My husband has one just the same.'

Alec heard a piece of the jigsaw fall into place with a
sharp click in his mind, but only nodded. He smoothed
the chestnut's glossy neck and slapped it affectionately. It
turned its head and blew its sweet rich breath through its
nostrils to him.

'You're honoured,' the dark-haired girl said with the
slightest of emphasis.

Alec met her steady appraising gaze. 'Thank you for your
help,' he said.

'You're welcome.' The girl tossed her head and her horse,
as if in mimicry, tossed his, and the two riders resumed
their steady way.

Alec turned away, to find the two constables looking
aggrieved. He knew what they were thinking: we spend all
day slogging from house to house getting nothing; then
Chief Inspector bloody Stainton breezes along and witnesses
fall over themselves to speak to him. Even the bloody horses
talk to him. Alec grinned inwardly. That was life; in the
police force, at any rate.

In the two borrowed rooms in the East Grinstead police
station at East Court things began to settle into some sort
of routine. Lab reports; correspondence; copies of this, that
and the other to senior officers, to the pathologist, to the
coroner.

Johnson returned from Nottingham late on Wednesday
afternoon, goggle-eyed from the driving and the hours spent
poring over papers in Andrew Hunter's study, and bearing
as trophies several bulging envelopes of correspondence, a

desk-diary, an address book, and three blue ring-binders which represented the raw material of Hunter's proposed book on South Africans who had served in the RAF.

Andrew Hunter's desk-diary was more or less in plain English, but depressingly businesslike in its brevity. Several days would be blank, then a note would record some banality: books due back to the library; a TV programme on the Desert Rats to be watched; his wife Janice to be collected from the station.

For the previous week there were two entries only: the page for Tuesday said 'Collect suit cleaners pm'. Two pages on, Thursday's entry said simply 'London 8.50'. Alec looked at his list of trains and ran his finger down the times: the train which left Nottingham at ten to nine arrived in London at eleven-five. Allow for a taxi or tube ride to Victoria, and Hunter could have caught the eleven-forty to East Grinstead. That seemed a little early—he hadn't caught the bus to Hartfield until half past one. Ah, but Hunter hadn't gone straight to Victoria. He had stopped off at his hotel to check in and leave his suitcase; according to the hotel, he had arrived there at eleven twenty-five. That would just leave him time for a snack in the buffet at Victoria before catching the East Grinstead train. It could fit.

If Hunter's original plans involved going to Hartfield he would surely have got a through ticket: therefore, it had been an afterthought. Caused by what? Alec stared at his scribbled notes. There would have been time for Hunter to have met someone, certainly; or he could have collected a message at the hotel that made him set off for Sussex. In that case, he must originally have had a serious intention of working at the Imperial War Museum, or why travel down on the Thursday, when he didn't have to be in London until the Friday evening for the reunion?

Alec tapped his pen rhythmically against the desktop. Probably the reason for the visit was more trivial: Hunter's work concerned the war, and the RAF; presumably Hartfield Park came into the picture somewhere and he had gone down on the spur of the moment to check some detail on the spot.

The plain conundrum remained, though: if Andrew Hunter had gone to Hartfield Park on a whim, how had the murderer known he was to be found there?

'It's always the same with a borrowed nick,' Nelson grumbled. 'The coffee-machine's better than your own. Ours never produces stuff like this.' He set one of the steaming cups down by Alec's elbow.

Alec leant back, and indicated the diary in front of him. 'What do you make of that?'

Nelson picked up the top sheet and frowned at it. 'Not a lot, sir. So far as I can see there's nothing to suggest any appointment, anyone he planned to see in London, any reason for going to Hartfield Park.'

'Therefore?'

'Therefore maybe the answer isn't in Hartfield Park.'

'Reasonable enough; but where does that lead us? He wasn't killed in Nottingham, was he? Which would be the place you would expect if it was domestic, for example.'

'There's always the lady-friend,' said Nelson dubiously. 'We don't *know* there's nothing in that.'

'True. So the lady-friend, though hypothetical, remains in contention. What about this reunion? That isn't hypothetical, is it?'

'Old comrades. Pilots. I see that all right, sir . . .'

'There's a link: the question is, how much of it is natural coincidence? Hunter's researching in that area . . . and he was going to meet, the day he died, or at least that weekend, presumably some of the very men he was researching. But then his body's found, of all places, on a disused airfield. Now, is that too much of a coincidence?'

'It's a good point, sir.'

Alec sat back in disgust. It was a lousy point. For of course it wasn't coincidence at all that the pilots figured in the research and at the reunion. It was *because* he was an expert in that field that he was invited to address the reunion. Alec watched Nelson working that out for himself; their eyes met, and Nelson shook his head dubiously. 'It's a leap in the dark, sir.'

In the end, it was the blue files which Alec selected to take home with him. Apart from anything else, they ought to be intrinsically interesting, if he could penetrate the shorthand they were written in. Forty-five years . . . ten years before he himself was born. When Eddie Zablonski had been a skinny youth of twenty; when Alec's own father had been a twenty-five-year-old hero, and his mother cool and beautiful in the Wrens . . . and both of them alive. When lads in their teens were errand boys one day, and the next piloting a bomber to the Ruhr, or driving a tank in the dusty deserts. Or dead. And men of his own age were old, he told himself ruefully.

Half an hour poring over the thick files after his meal was enough to show him that while he could sit and dream over them on his own, if he wanted to know their secrets he needed help. He walked over to the telephone, thinking, then flicked through his address book.

'Tony? Alec. Fine. You? Good. Look, I'm ringing in case you can help me . . . yes . . . it's a sort of historical matter. Second war; not quite your period, I know, but I thought you might . . . no, air force. About 1944, I think. I've got some research data here I'm trying to puzzle out.'

He leant against the wall. 'Pity. No, I just thought you might . . .' Suddenly he straightened up and reached for a pen and the pad. 'Walker, you say? Francis Walker. Yes . . . yes . . . got that. Is that the home number, or is it daytime only? Thanks. Thanks, Tony. Yes, we must get together when it's cleared up and I'll tell you about it.'

He put the phone down, considered the number written on the pad, glanced at his watch. It was after ten o'clock, but not long after. Too late? Probably not.

'Hello.' Female voice. Neutral, cautious.

'Hello. I'm trying to contact a Francis Walker. Have I got the right number?'

'Who is that?' More than cautious; in fact, decidedly chilly.

'My name's Alec Stainton. Detective Chief Inspector Stainton. Is Mr Walker there, please?'

'There is no Mr Walker here.'

'Perhaps I could leave a . . .'

'This is Frances Walker speaking.' Oh, hell! Not Francis. Franc*es*. That was *not* a good start. No wonder she was cool.

'I'm sorry.' Angry with himself, his voice was clipped. No point making things worse with an apology. 'Tony Dexter gave me your number. He thought you might be able to help me with a little problem. I gather you're interested in history . . . the second war.'

'Look, Inspector whoever-you-are, it's a little late in the evening to start ringing people with your problems. Call me tomorrow, if you have to.' She gave him the number curtly. 'I'll speak to Tony Dexter,' she said ominously, and rang off.

Alex, furious, cursed her and went to run a bath.

So thoroughly did a hot bath and a good night's sleep erase the indignity of the rebuke that when the telephone rang in the office at nine-thirty the next morning and the switchboard told him it was a Dr Walker he had to ask them to repeat the name before he grasped who it was that was calling.

The morning Dr Walker was rather less abrasive than the evening version.

'Chief Inspector Stainton? I wanted to ring to apologize for my bad manners last night.' There was a certain warmth —or at least a diminution of coolness—in her voice, a nicely calculated measure of contrition. The fault, he gathered, was still to be his, but she regretted having overreacted to it.

'Please don't apologize. My fault entirely for ringing you

so late.' Deliberately, he un-gritted his teeth. He could eat humble pie with the best of them, when he wanted a woman's help. Besides, he admitted, it had been rather late last night.

'I'd had rather a bad evening with my little girl; only just got her off to sleep,' Dr Walker went on, 'so I'm afraid . . . but then I rang Tony Dexter this morning and he told me who you were . . . I'm afraid I thought you were wasting my time with some triviality. He said that from his experience that would be unlikely. Will you tell me how I can help you?'

Alec thought quickly. It was not a matter easy to explain over the phone; and besides, he needed her to see the files. 'Look, where are you ringing from?' he asked.

'My office in Redhill.' A moment's hesitation. 'You're welcome to call if you'd rather talk face to face.'

'I think I'd prefer that. Perhaps I could come in your lunch-hour. Is there somewhere we could talk? It shouldn't take too long; I don't want to get you into trouble.'

'Oh, you won't do that.' There was an undercurrent in her voice that he did not understand, as if he had suggested something vaguely improper. Alec suggested a time; she agreed, and told him where to come.

'And he saw nothing?'

'That's what he said, sir.'

'Didn't see a man walking along the roadside? Didn't see a car on the airfield? Nothing!'

Liz Pink shook her head apologetically. 'Nothing at all,' she replied sadly.

She had known as soon as James Parker opened the door to her that she was going to come away empty-handed; known it as soon as she saw the flicker of triumph, the infinitesimal relaxation of tension when he saw that this time they had sent a woman. And though Liz had been severe, and brusque, and sly, she had never really regained the initiative.

All Parker would confirm was what was in the statement
he had given Nelson: if the barley had been trampled down
he hadn't noticed. Yes, he would have expected to notice,
given that it was his barley. Yes, he had been on the airfield
the day before he found the body, and seen nothing. No, he
had seen nothing in the previous few days either. No, he
had seen nothing the previous Thursday.

Liz herself had looked from the farmhouse's kitchen window, to find that only the merest sliver of the airfield was
visible between the big elder bush and the corner of an old
outbuilding; she had sallied into the yard to see whether
more could be observed from the door of the machinery
shed, or the bullock pen, but in vain. It was perfectly
possible that whole bus-loads of intruders had been on the
airfield and James Parker, unable because of the weather to
cut his barley, had seen nothing of them.

Parker's own movements that important Thursday he
accounted for quite plausibly; a trip into East Grinstead
after an oil filter for one of the tractors and a farm sale in
the morning; muck-spreading in a field the far side of the
Medway in the afternoon. It was a slightly more circumstan-
cial account then he'd given Nelson, but there were no
discrepancies.

There was one marginal gain from the visit, in that she
met the other members of the household. James Parker had
a wife, a dressy woman more suited to being a stockbroker's
than a farmer's wife; who scorned, if Liz was any judge, her
husband's work and the perpetual mud and labour and
sweat it entailed, and who fought a bitter battle of silence
with the third occupant of the house, Parker's mother, whose
presence was the one which filled and formed the farm.

Liz spoke to both women. Old Mrs Parker must have
been in her late sixties and was bound to her chair by
arthritis. She had better things to do than gawp out of the
window, she sneered; though what those things might be,
except endless watching of television soap operas, was un-
clear.

The younger Mrs Parker, disdainful and trying to be superior, was pointedly unhelpful. She might have gone shopping. She might have been up to town. Of course she had not gone with her husband to some bloody farm sale; what on earth would she want to do that for? Pressed, she grudgingly admitted to having been out riding in the afternoon. No, she had seen no little man with or without briefcase trudging along the road, and no, nothing on the airfield, which she stayed clear of anyway because there was only barley and bloody concrete, and James moaned if she rode in the one, while the other damaged the horse's feet.

'Wonder if she met the other two?' Alec mused. 'I encountered two riders myself. In fact, I meant to ask you to follow them up for me. It seems to be the primary activity for Hartfield womenfolk, doesn't it?'

'Nothing much else to do, I suppose,' Liz observed with unwonted tartness. 'They can't spend the whole day playing lady of the manor.'

'Pity Parker didn't take to you rather more.' It was Mr Stainton's way of saying she had messed it up, Liz thought bitterly. She hated the fact that her gender was something to be played with: would this man, or that, respond better to a WPC than to a man? Respond in what way, for God's sake? It should just be left out of court, she told herself angrily. Why must it always be made something of? Why must even Mr Stainton see it as a counter to be played with?

Perhaps it was that flash of anger that made her say, more definitely than she had intended to, 'He's lying, sir.'

Alec looked at her thoughtfully. 'You think so? In what respect?'

She hesitated. 'I don't know exactly. Only that he . . . I don't know, he seemed to think he'd got away with something,' she ended lamely. 'As if he'd duped me and I'd fallen for it.'

He didn't query it, she noticed; didn't ask if she was sure, or laugh it away. She watched his expression change as he pondered what she had said and what, maybe, Parker hadn't.

'I wonder . . .' He glanced up, changing tack. 'You brought his guns back?'

'Yes. Two: a twelve-bore and a four-ten.'

'Where did he have them?'

'Cupboard, sir; good stout one in his office, properly padlocked.' You still found farmers who had the damn things hanging over the door, Firearms Act or no; but then, farmers didn't often saw the barrels off and hold up banks . . . or kill trespassers on disused airfields. 'He didn't make any fuss about them,' she added.

'Humph. I'll bet they got a good clean on Monday night, all the same. Get them down to the lab, let Alan Hancock have a look at them.'

'Right, sir. Sergeant Nelson says what about the South Africans? From the reunion. Apparently they'll be flying home soon.'

'How many has he traced so far?'

'Not many; about fifteen, I think sir.'

'OK, he can have Johnson to help him. We'd better interview all we can before they leave.'

Liz grinned. 'If we miss any, sir, I'm volunteering to fly out and see them over there. I've always fancied spending Christmas on the beach.'

'If this case isn't tied up by Christmas you'll be spending it right here,' Alec retorted briefly. 'Along with the rest of us. You can tell Nelson that, too. It might just concentrate his mind on tracking down his missing heroes.'

CHAPTER 6

It was just on one o'clock and office-workers were emptying into the streets in search of sandwiches and hurried shopping when Alec turned into the car park of Delta Communi-

cations on the outskirts of central Redhill. He slipped the
dusty Bristol into the only vacant slot between a van em-
blazoned with the company logo and an overflowing dustbin
and climbed out. A garish Porsche couched nearest the
entrance, and he eyed it sceptically.

The lobby was bare of anything except, on the wall, a
phone unit and a brief note: All Visitors Lift Receiver and
Wait For Receptionist to Answer.

He lifted, and waited. They might know the last thing
about communications, he thought sourly, but they had
patently forgotten the first.

Nevertheless, in a surprisingly short time he was climbing
the stairway behind a girl in a surprisingly short skirt—a
gentleman would have ascended first, he mused; but then,
a lady would have let him—and being ushered into a bright
office which seemed to be some sort of creche, provided with
ten telephones, all of which were ringing.

In fact, he corrected himself as the door shut behind him,
there was only one child, a serious-faced little girl of—
so far as he could judge, and he knew himself to be none
too competent in this field—eight or nine years of age,
who raised her head from her copy of *Asterix the Gaul*
to stare politely at the visitor; and there were only three
telephones, although it was true that two of them were
ringing.

A woman was listening to the third telephone and watching Alex expressionlessly from grey-green eyes as she sat at
the desk, the receiver hunched to her shoulder. She might
be thirty-two or -three, he thought. Her face was the adult
counterpart of the child's, solemn and probably not quick
to laugh—though when she did, it might conceivably be an
occasion worth waiting for. Her expensively-cut biscuit-
coloured suit was plain but avoided severity by a soft blouse
open at the neck. Her shoulder-length hair was neutral in
colour, drawn back to one side to highlight high, delicately
sculpted cheekbones. She nodded briefly as their eyes met
before turning back to the business in hand, speaking a few

brisk words, putting one phone down, picking up another. Alec helped himself to a chair, and waited till she should be free.

When eventually the shrilling telephones were dealt with and Frances Walker turned to him, Alec found himself on the receiving end of a disconcertingly straight, appraising gaze.

'I see why it's easy for you to take your lunch-hour in your own time,' he remarked drily.

'There are some advantages to being the managing director,' she matched his dryness.

'And having your daughter with you is another?'

Dr Walker's expression softened as if a hidden key had been pressed. 'She should be in school. But we had a bad night last night, didn't we, sweetie, so Lucy's come with Mummy today.' She switched her gaze back to Alec. 'So far as lunch goes, does that give us problems?'

The woman's self-confidence was daunting. She was neither chary of showing her love for her child, nor was he to be in any doubt that witnessing it accorded him no privileges. Her manner was, faultlessly, neither warm nor cold. Her telephone call that morning had expressed contrition, but it was clear that she was not on that account prepared to look on Alec more favourably. Her poise was undisturbed, and as for her judgement, he would have to take his chance.

He shook his head. 'No problem so far as I'm concerned.' Provided, he mentally reserved, the child is as innocuous as she looks. If she turns out to be a miniature version of her mother, the next hour or two may be rather wearing. 'If there's somewhere you'd both enjoy?'

Frances Walker's mouth twisted down in a sharp flick of amusement. 'You don't have to take us on a Sunday School treat, you know. Look, how long is this likely to take? So I can warn my PA?'

He considered. 'No longer than you want at this stage. But if you decide to help us, and you find you're able to . . .'

'You mean, if *you* decide I'm able to,' she put in, with a look of cool shrewdness from the grey-green eyes.

'. . . then it'll be a case of arranging for you to study some documents we have. I don't know how long: an evening; maybe more. Depends how long they take you to decipher.'

She raised her eyebrows. 'Sounds intriguing.'

Speedily, Dr Walker (doctor of what, he wondered?) made arrangements for her assistant to cover for her. Lucy was fastened into coat and gloves; Dr Walker collected her own and led the way out of the room.

The Porsche in the car park must be hers, of course. Nevertheless she took it as a matter of course that they would travel in his car, and he noticed she ran an appreciative palm over the smooth coachwork as she waited for him to unlock the passenger door and lean the seat forward for Lucy to climb into the back.

On her directions, they followed the old A25 to Godstone. The White Hart had a family room and Lucy sat, silently as she had sat for the short journey, considering what she would like to eat while Alec helped her mother off with her coat and bought them both orange juice and, after a moment's consideration, the same for himself.

'OK,' Dr Walker said when they had ordered, 'fire away.' And she leant forward with her chin resting on her tented fingers and gave him her attention.

'So that's about the size of it. It's double Dutch to me. To someone in the same line it's probably very simple. It's someone in that line I'm looking for.'

'OK.' She considered a moment, and then said, 'I don't know how much Tony Dexter told you about me. One: yes, it is my subject. Don't ask me how I got into it, it's a long story. To do with my father, whom I never knew. And don't remark what a strange occupation it is for a woman.'

'I wasn't going to,' he said drily.

Just as drily, she said, 'If I thought you would, I shouldn't be here. Two: I'm good. It's a hobby, as you obviously

realize, fitted in round the edges of Delta, but I make it pay
its way: articles for magazines, two books, one on the Italian
campaign, one on the Balkans; and a half-share in the
standard work on the Desert Air Force. And that means—'
she gave him a direct look—'if you show me these notes
I'm going to know whose they are.'

'I imagine,' Alec remarked, 'you have a pretty good idea
already.'

She smiled, as if she had suddenly realized that she was
about to enjoy herself, and leant back. The waiter brought
their food and Lucy set solemnly to, the knife and fork large
in her pale small hands.

'Dr Walker . . .'

'You'd better call me Frances, Chief Inspector. If it
doesn't cause you too much confusion.'

'I'll do my best to cope. Right. On the basis of what
you've said, yes, I'd like your help. And I think you won't
take offence if I say now that I am dealing with rather a
serious matter. A murder. That . . . imposes responsibili-
ties.' He met her eyes. It wasn't a point he'd have to make
twice, if he was any judge. Frances Walker was a woman
who would keep her own counsel and trust her own judgements. A woman, in her field—in her two fields—as successful as himself; if you judged by material rewards, a sight
more successful.

'I . . . understand that,' she said, and her clever eyes were
watchful. 'You know no more of me than I do of you.' She
thought for a moment. 'All I can say is, I'll still be happy
to help. If you'd like me to. As to whether I have the right
qualifications—inside—I must abide by your judgement,
of course.'

They regarded each other a moment across the table,
each assessing and submitting to assessment. Alec nodded.
'All right! I've brought the files with me. When we've eaten
I'll fetch them from the car and you can tell me what you
think.'

Dr Walker nodded too, and turned back to her meal. The

girl Lucy, watching them both unnoticed beneath downcast lids, slowly resumed her chewing.

Alec drove away in a pensive frame of mind, having dropped Frances Walker and Lucy back at Delta Communications. The precious files he had left in Dr Walker's keeping. Not only the wisdom, but also the propriety of this caused him concern: quite apart from their value as evidence, the files belonged to Janice Hunter, and they represented her husband's next book; and here he had delivered them into the hands of an admitted rival in the same sphere of scholarship.

Nevertheless, there was a murder to be solved, and if those notes contained a clue they must be made to yield it up. Moreover, he had made his decision on the basis of his judgement of Dr Walker; and he did not think, in this instance, his judgement was likely to prove unsound.

If there was a threat to that soundness, he admitted, it was in that Dr Walker was a woman; but that came, in the order of things you noticed in her, quite low on the list, after her directness and perceptive intelligence and shrewd humour. In any event, he would have further opportunity to judge when she was ready to give her verdict on the contents of Andrew Hunter's notes. They had made a provisional arrangement to meet the next evening. Dr Walker, when she worked, worked fast.

He wondered whether the solemn-eyed Lucy would be present, a tiny chaperone, reserving her own judgements, on that occasion also.

'Mr Patrick, sir. Chief Inspector Stainton.'

Alec came forward to greet Patrick and gestured him to a chair. In the end Jack Patrick, the man who had organized the reunion weekend, had proved easy to trace: he had simply left a forwarding address with the manager of the hotel. He was a large, loose-framed man who put Alec in mind of a cow-hand in an old Hollywood western, moving slowly—though age might have something to do with that.

'I'm grateful to you for coming. I hope this won't spoil your stay in England too much.'

'Last time I was here I was the one being shot at,' Patrick said. He talked as lazily as he moved, so that each word seemed to have a weight of consideration behind it, but the vowels were the tight Teutonic diphthongs of the white African, not the drawling rusticities of the frontier American. 'It took the wind out of my sails when your man told me Andrew Hunter had been murdered, I can tell you.'

'Did you ever meet him?'

'No. Would of met him at the reunion for the first time. I made most of the arrangements by letter, and he replied the same way. I fixed up the whole reunion, they maybe told you that. Booked the hotel. Talked SAA into giving us discount flights. That sort of thing.'

'Were the reunions a regular affair?'

'Nobody I know makes a regular affair out of flying six thousand miles to meet a few blokes he could meet as well in Capetown or Jo'burg. Look: we had a get together in nineteen-sixty-five. That was twenty years after the war ended. I'd say about two hundred of us got together then, that was in Salisbury, Rhodesia. Well, we originally planned to hold a special reunion for the fiftieth anniversary of the end of the war, that'd be in five years' time. But then it began to look as if not so many of us might make it.' Patrick looked at Alec shrewdly from beneath bushy eyebrows. 'So forty-five would have to do.'

'And because it was going to be a big celebration, you wanted to have it here in England where it all happened.'

'Because it was going to be the *last* celebration,' Patrick corrected. 'Uh-huh. We reckoned we'd come to England. Nobody was belly-aching at an excuse for a holiday abroad.'

Alec leant back, his hands linked behind his head. 'So who came?'

'Fifty-one,' Mr Patrick said without hesitation. 'Plus some of them brought their wives, of course. Seven blokes from the UK—you know, stayed on here after the war. One bloke flew over from Switzerland. Couple from the States. All the rest from South Africa.'

'And these were . . .? I mean, what was it they had in common?'

'All aircrew. You know what I mean when I call them that? People who flew from here.' Alec nodded. 'Include ground staff,' Patrick went on, 'and it all gets too unwieldy. Besides, there were ground staff and aircrew that never exchanged more than a few words. There were pilots treated their fitters like so many servants. You could have friction there, if you weren't careful.'

'Tell me the format of the weekend.'

'I'll do better than that.' Patrick flicked open his briefcase and slipped out a thin document with a blue cover representing some sort of flag featuring an eagle. He passed it across the desk. Alec leant forward and flicked through it.

The programme was on the third page, and Alec ran his eye down the schedules carefully. 'So Mr Hunter's lecture, address, whatever, was to be on the Saturday morning?'

'Right. There was a man coming from Vickers, he was speaking first; then your Mr Hunter after the coffee-break. Then p.m. we had the coach trips. Oxfordshire, or Kent and Sussex. Saturday night was the dinner; and Sunday two blokes from the modern RAF and then one who used to be in the Luftwaffe. Finish Sunday lunch-time.'

'What were these coach trips you mentioned?' Alec queried.

'Just nostalgia,' Patrick explained. 'Where people went depended where they served, what they flew.'

'The men who had been in bombers went to Oxfordshire, and those who had been in single-seaters to Kent and Sussex?' Alec guessed.

'You got it.'

'What about those who weren't in either? Who had been in Coastal Command, for example?'

'Well, that's just too bad. But you can't get to Pembroke Dock or Wick in an afternoon jaunt from London. We had a third trip to Duxford, to the museum, for the odds and sods.'

'Tell me about the Kent and Sussex trip: where would that have gone to?'

'OK, well, I didn't make that one myself. I took myself off to Duxford with the odds and sods. The fighter types, they went to—' he ticked them off on his fingers—'Kenley; Tangmere; along to Hawkinge; West Malling; then back to Biggin Hill where your RAF laid on some tea.'

'Quite a trip.'

'Sure; but most of 'em had served on one of those stations at some time.'

'But you had to miss out, say, everything north of the river.'

'Uh-huh. Plus all the fields that have been built on, like Croydon and Gravesend—there's no point that I know of in going to look at a whole lot of houses—or were too far away to get to, like Manston and Exeter; you want to go somewhere where there is still something for them to see, keep everyone happy. The other trip, that went by Fairford and Abingdon and Banbury, and the American Tactical Fighter Wing put on a real good do at Upper Heyford to finish with. Lot of the guys flew from Lincolnshire or Yorkshire, but they're too far. The Duxford trip? That stopped off at North Weald on the way.'

Alex said, 'Nobody went to Hartfield Park.'

'None of the coaches did, for sure.'

'Was there anything to stop someone going off on their own, if they didn't fancy the coach trips?'

'Not a thing. If anyone wanted to shop, or see the Tower of London or stuff like that, that was their business. There was nothing they *had* to go to until the Reunion Dinner, and that wasn't till eight.'

'Would Andrew Hunter have had an invitation to that?'

'Uh-huh. Him and all the seminar speakers would.'

'Get a good guest speaker?'

'Carl Stocker,' Mr Patrick said with some pride.

Alec raised his eyebrows in polite surprise. 'Big stuff!'

Patrick grinned. 'We were just lucky he was going to be over here for the Amnesty talks. And one of our blokes, Bill Janssen, he and Stocker are pretty good pals: on the same boards of directors, that sort of thing, you know the score. So he twisted Stocker's arm some. 'Course, Stocker flew Sabrejets in Korea, so we pulled the old pals a bit. He couldn't join us for the rest of the reunion,' Patrick commented. 'Only the Reunion Dinner.'

'Just so.' Alec sat up. 'Good; I think that covers it for the time being. I'll just have someone photocopy the programme and list of delegates if I may.'

'Right. I'll be around for a week or two yet,' Mr Patrick commented aimiably. 'If there's anything else you think of, I'd be happy to help. This bloke Hunter, I never met him, but if he was as good as his books suggest it's too bad someone had to kill him.'

'It usually is,' Alec agreed drily, and rose to see Jack Patrick to the door.

CHAPTER 7

On Friday evening Alec called for Dr Walker at Delta Communications as most of the staff were leaving. The Hunter files were at home, she said, and if he'd like to follow her there she thought it would be worth his while: they were, she said tantalizingly, exceptionally interesting.

Alec thought of his skimped roll at lunch-time and the steak he had promised himself, and mentally tightened his belt.

'There will be,' Dr Walker said, reading his mind, 'a meal, too. We do eat, and I have to repay your hospitality.'

The red Porsche was certainly distinctive, but it was not so easy to keep it in sight on the commuter-crammed roads. Dr Walker drove it skilfully and, Alec thought, unnecessarily provocatively; no doubt for his benefit. The Bristol was no sluggard, but several times he wished for a car with the Porsche's agility as he glimpsed it flicking through the traffic, getting further and further ahead. Once on the M25, though, Alec slipped into the overtaking lane and made the Bristol stir itself. Dr Walker was not foolish enough to try and lose him, and they settled into safe convoy until the Porsche began indicating for the turn-off at Riverhead. Ten minutes of twisting, deep-sunk lanes brought them to their destination. Alec mentally added a couple of noughts to his estimate of Delta Communications' turnover as he followed the garish Porsche up a sweeping drive and parked beside it in front of a low, timbered house.

'Darling, I'm home!' Dr Walker dumped her bag in the large hallway and strode through into the living-room, pulling off her gloves. Alec followed more circumspectly.

Lucy sat solemnly on a sofa. A book was in her hand. There was a big, expensive television in front of her, but it stood dark-faced and silent.

Dr Walker crouched down to kiss her. 'Had a good day, darling?'

'Yes, thank you.'

'Lovely.' She gave her daughter a look almost of fear, Alec thought, then straightened up and turned to the girl who had come in. 'Oh, Bridget, thanks. You pop off now if you like; I'll make dinner.'

Alec nodded to the girl (Irish? Italian? Welsh? Dark and Celtic) who slipped past him through the doorway and waited until Dr Walker should have time for him. The girl Lucy was explaining patiently about the corn dollies they had been making in school for harvest.

Widow? he wondered. Single? Divorced? There was no ring on Dr Walker's finger that he could see. If it was Delta Communications which paid for the house, though, Delta Communications must be doing a good deal better than its unprepossessing exterior suggested: and *that* wasn't any of his business, either.

'Eat first,' Dr Walker pronounced, turning to him, 'and work afterwards.'

But it was quite a long time afterwards that they finally sat down in the beamed living-room with the three blue files on the coffee table in front of them. The meal had been good, and agreeably simple. Then there had been Lucy to be played with, and the bookshelf to browse through while Lucy was bathed and put to bed and read to. Clearly Dr Walker took her daughter seriously; but the recollection of the child's solemn patience prompted Alec to guess that maybe the burden of responsibility did not lie totally on one side.

'Right,' Dr Walker began, putting down her coffee and reaching for one of the files; then she seemed to change her mind, and left it lying on the table as she turned to consider Alec. 'Probably best to give you some background first. Hum! Most of Andrew's—I take it these are Andrew Hunter's work; it's fairly distinctive and I do,' she added drily, 'read the newspapers.' Alec nodded. 'Well, most of his notes here are what I would call raw material. I don't ·know if you've read any of his books. They tend to be meticulous, and very detailed. His research is thorough, the detail faultless. You would go to one of his books if you wanted to know exactly what the order of battle was at Alamein, for example, although not necessarily if you wanted to know what it felt like to be a private soldier taking part.' She glanced at him. 'Do you know what an order of battle is?'

Alec smiled inwardly. 'Yes.' Perhaps his smile wasn't only inward, for her glance lingered speculatively for a moment before she continued.

'In the present case he was collecting data for a book on South Africans serving with the air force here in the Second War. There was no secret about it; the book was commissioned by the publisher, and it was pre-sold abroad as well.

'The bulk of his notes refer either to crews or to squadrons;

their order of battle at any given time—how many planes available for operations, how many under maintenance, and so on; dates of operations and which planes took part; and the purpose and destination and success of those operations.'

'Hence the multitude of numbers.'

'That's it. The squadrons have numbers; individual aeroplanes have numbers; the dates are expressed numerically; and so forth. Look!' She pulled one of the files towards her and leafed through a couple of pages until she came to a good example. Alec leant closer to see. Her perfume was faint and expensive; her features hidden by her hair as she leant forward.

'Here: that's a squadron number. Always in arabic numerals. That's the serial of a particular machine: a Halifax, in this case, from 429 Squadron, at Leeming in Yorkshire. The date—that's in a mixture of arabic and roman numbers. And the destination, Magdeburg, which he's abbreviated to Mdb.'

The jigsaw fell into place. Alec looked at the page heading: Pegg, A. J. The man's career lay before them now as a coded message reveals itself when the words are written in clear beneath the code groups. Andrew Hunter's notes charted his path across wartime Britain to lonely Yorkshire and the bleak full stop a line or two later, relating to his last trip to Stuttgart: DNR. Did not return.

Dr Walker had followed his gaze. 'Yes; you forget that it's not just data for some academic book. Dead at twenty-one. It was a hell of a price to pay.'

They sipped their coffee. 'As I said, I read the papers, you know,' Dr Walker said after a moment or two. 'About Andrew Hunter's death. About where his body was found.'

'And?'

'And I guess I asked the same question you're trying to find the answer to now. Why there? Why Hartfield Park?'

He shook his head. 'I don't see it quite like that. To me, getting an answer to that question is a step on the way to something else. Not an end in itself. I want to know who killed him.'

She met his eyes. Hers were green and serious; little crowsfeet lurked at the corners.

Alec looked away deliberately. 'So is the answer here?' He gestured to the blue files.

Dr Walker bent to refill their cups from the percolator. 'No. That is, I don't think so. Not the answer to your question, anyway. To mine about why he was there . . . maybe. I'd better clarify that.' She clasped her hands in front of her lips like a child at prayer.

'I take it Hartfield Park is mentioned in there,' he said, thinking to help her.

'Oh, sure. In all its guises. OK, let's start with that. Hartfield Park began life as a bare grass field. A satellite to Redhill during the Battle of Britain. After that had ended they took it out of commission to make a proper airfield out of it: still grass, but with a perimeter track, a couple of hangars, administration buildings. That took until 1941, autumn. By that time requirements had changed rather. It wasn't needed for its original purpose, and no one quite knew what to do with it. For a while it was used as a sort of outstation to Tempsford—cloak and dagger stuff; dropping agents and so forth. Then a PRU unit went there for three months. By then it was the beginning of 1943 and it was taken out of commission again for the building of concrete runways.

'By that time, we were beginning to look forward to the prospect of getting back into Europe. But Hartfield Park was never going to be any good for bombers, or airborne forces, gliders and what-not: it was too small, and the situation between the North Downs and the high ground of Ashdown Forest made it tricky for heavy aircraft.' She glanced at him doubtfully, as if unsure how much he followed. 'So it became a base for Typhoons and Mosquitoes. The Typhoons came in April 1944 and the Mosquitoes a month later. In August the Typhoons left, to go over to

France to operate from captured German airfields. The Mosquitoes stayed until the end of the war. They were operated by a Royal Air Force squadron which was originally designated as a South African unit,' she concluded. 'Later it became more mixed, but there were South Africans serving in it until the end of the war.'

'Hence Andrew Hunter's interest,' Alec said thoughtfully. 'And hence his visit, maybe.'

Alec leafed absently through the file. The initials HP fairly leapt at him from the page. 'What are these abbreviations, do you say? Targets?'

Dr Walker nodded. 'Probably mostly airfields—the squadron was supposed to be flying intruder missions, much of the time to Denmark, eastern Germany and Poland, trying to catch German aircraft at their own fields with their pants down, so to speak. A fair amount of shooting up of trains went on too; general disruption of the Germans' rear areas to hamper their resistance to the advancing Allies.'

So: had Andrew Hunter gone to Hartfield Park to see for himself where his South Africans had lived and flown? Perhaps he had made a habit of such trips; Janice would be able to tell him. It was innocuous enough, a harmless piece of archæology, a painstaking recording of the not-now-so-recent past. It didn't really seem likely that anybody could have taken serious exception to it, any more than it was likely that Parker had been so plagued by trespassers that he started taking a shotgun to them.

Curious to find the pedantic Hunter's enthusiasm shared by this competent, forthright woman. Perhaps that sort of research was more fascinating than it appeared from the outside. After all, men did many things in wartime. And, he reminded himself, not all of them were honourable.

Alec realized that Dr Walker was watching him, and looked up. 'I'm very grateful for your help,' he said.

'Good. I . . . could do some more work on those last entries if you think it would help. I haven't worked out all the references in detail,' she went on. 'I might see if anything emerges that sheds light on just what Andrew was doing at Hartfield Park.'

She had already done plenty, but better by far her expert scrutiny than his amateur one.

'All right,' he said. 'I accept. Provided you can spare the time . . .'

'You mean, will I kindly not take too long about it!' she replied with a glint of amusement. 'I'll ring you the day after tomorrow. No: that's Sunday, isn't it? I imagine we both prefer to keep that to ourselves if we can. Monday, then. I'll either have worked it out, or be hopelessly stuck by then. Will that do?'

He smiled. 'That will do very well.' Out in the hall a clock began to tell the hour and he looked at his watch. Ten o'clock. The darkness had fallen long ago, turning the windows into black rectangles like polished mediæval mirrors.

'Stay and have a drink,' Dr Walker said, noting his glance. 'I go to bed about eleven; I'll throw you out then. What can I get you?'

'What have you got?' he asked cautiously, hoping for something innocuous.

She regarded him speculatively, then rose from the sofa with sudden energy. 'One glass of good red wine. How about that? It'll help me sleep, and it won't prevent you getting home safely.'

At five to eleven he rose and thanked her again for her help. It had been an unexpectedly pleasant evening, and he had no need to counterfeit gratitude. 'You cook a good meal, Dr Walker; I enjoyed it.'

She accepted the compliment with something of her sardonic flick as they walked to the door of his car. 'I'm glad you think so. And it's Frances. No more of this Dr Walker nonsense, please!'

'All right. And I'm Alec. Thanks anyway.'

'Good. I'll ring you on Monday.' Businesslike, she smiled,

framed in the doorway against the light of the hall. But when Alec looked back before turning out of the drive into the lane to raise a hand in farewell she was gone. Alec shrugged and let up the clutch, and the hedge cut the house off from his sight.

CHAPTER 8

'There are three ways we can approach this.' Alec leant forward and tented his fingers, frowning slightly and wondering why there was always this compulsion to start the new week with some statement of principles. 'Route one is to delve further into Hunter's life. By that I mean his life in Nottingham; his friends there and elsewhere; hobbies, activities; this hypothetical mistress that he could have been meeting when he went on his research trips. Though at first sight,' he added, 'it looks unlikely that anyone from the Nottingham end should choose to kill Hunter down in Sussex.'

Johnson, who had been about to make that very point, sat back again, glad he had kept his counsel. 'In fact, though,' Alec went on, 'a moment's thought will suggest that a competent murderer might very well want to stage the killing on foreign territory. So we can't assume that someone from Nottingham didn't know about Hunter's plan to visit Hartfield and take the opportunity of paying off some score there.

'Secondly, there's the place itself.' He looked around the little group as if searching for the precise words he wanted. 'I mean by that, Hunter had a link to Hartfield Park. Therefore, anyone else who has a link to it also had a link to Hunter. That's plain enough. That means, for example, everyone at the farm. Anyone who used the place for unofficial driving lessons. For poaching. For dumping their unwanted fridges and bedsteads. A link with Hartfield Park is a link with Hunter, and the closer in time the association is, the stronger the association.'

'Can't we limit it further,' Nelson offered, 'and just concern ourselves with people who were at the place last Thursday?'

Alec shook his head. 'We've no way, at present, of knowing who *was* there. We've got to come to that obliquely.' He paused. 'The last route is via Hunter's work: his research.'

Liz Pink looked doubtful. 'Isn't that the same as the second route, sir? I mean, surely his work *was* Hartfield Park.'

'No. His work was the South Africans who flew here in the war. And before that, it was—what was the name of his last book?'

'About the Normandy landings, sir,' Nelson supplied.

'Right. For both works he must have talked to a host of people, ferreted out hundreds of forgotten facts. Historians must make enemies, if only of other historians. It must be possible for us to chart his footsteps, see whom he talked to, where he might have stirred a controversy or rubbed the scab from an old wound.'

'Seems a bit dubious, sir,' Nelson said sceptically. 'You don't take a shotgun to someone just because you say the battle of Waterloo happened on a Thursday and they say it was a Friday.'

'Would you feel the same way if someone's scholarship destroyed your life's work? Or your reputation? If someone suggested that a battle was won in spite of, not because of, your leadership, for example? It's a mistake to think that ivory towers are peaceful places.'

Liz Pink was looking thoughtful. 'If we can look for the murderer among his work; and we can look for it among people linked to Hartfield; then surely anyone who fall into both categories is much the likeliest suspect.'

Alec hesitated. 'I know what you're thinking. The South Africans who flew from there. Some of whom are over here for the reunion. And I'd like to think so too, because it would make our job a lot simpler. But it doesn't work. Because both factors occur, it doesn't make them twice as likely to be the killer. In fact, the probability isn't increased just because the person falls into both categories.' He looked at her. 'You obviously don't agree!'

'If you say so, sir.'

'So how do you want us to divide up?' Nelson asked, before Liz could dig herself further into trouble.

Alec sat back. 'I'd like you to gnaw away at the Nottingham end for a bit. I've arranged for the local CID to be asked to give us what help they can. Whatever there is, isn't just lying on the surface waiting to be picked up, we know that already. We'll have to rely on Janice Hunter quite a lot for details of her husband's life. Neighbours, social clubs, finances, details of his journeys away from home—follow those up. Find the hotels he stayed in when he was away. OK?'

'Right. How long do you want me to keep at it?'

'We'll see what you turn up. If anything looks promising I'll send someone to give you a hand. But if nothing's surfaced after, say, two or three days then we can probably use you better down here.

'Liz, I want you to take the local end, but not Parker: you've had one go at him, now I think you'd better leave him to me. But there's nothing to stop you going through the general area pretty thoroughly. The clergy; the rambling clubs; the WI; the schoolkids; once you get enough data you can start to piece it together, perhaps; give us a picture of who might have been in or near the airfield at the important time. Find out who goes where, and when. See if you can sniff out any busybodies who know everyone's business and find out what they know about that Thursday.'

He turned to Andy Johnson. 'That leaves you and Simms to follow up on Hunter's work. I've got someone on to going through his notes; with luck they'll tell us whom he talked to, where he went for his research; then you can chase them up and see if you come up with anything. Meanwhile, take over from Sergeant Nelson on tracing the South Africans who were at that reunion. Where were they all that Thursday; and where are they now?' He glanced at Liz and smiled briefly. 'And Hunter's notes will also tell us which of them may have flown from Hartfield Park forty-five years ago. Because while I don't think that makes them instant candidates for the role of murderer, it might, it just might, have led one of them to go back there on a sentimental visit of their own. Just for old times' sake.'

Nelson stayed behind after the other two had filed out. Alec gestured him to pull a chair up. 'Nothing on the shotguns,' he informed him economically.

'No, sir? Doesn't surprise me.'

Alec pushed the lab report across the desk and Nelson glanced through it. One of the guns could be ruled out altogether: it was a four-ten, whereas examination of the pellets and the wad, which had been found near the body, showed that Hunter had been shot with a twelve-bore from approximately six yards' range. The other gun—which was indeed a twelve-bore—had been examined in some detail. It was, the report said, certainly lethal: to anyone who tried to fire it. Although it had been recently cleaned the barrel was excessively worn and the breech no longer gas-tight, and it had certainly not been recently fired. The presumption was, indeed, that it had been unused for several years: the bore was pitted with rust which the cleaning had failed to touch.

'He's trying it on,' Nelson remarked.

'I think so.'

'We asked him to turn in his guns and he's hunted around for a couple of old hacks to keep us happy.'

'Knowing that we would find that they couldn't have been the murder weapon?' Alec speculated.

'Possibly. Maybe he didn't expect us to look at them as closely as we have. I see the lab haven't done a test-firing on this twelve-bore.'

'I don't blame them,' Alec remarked drily. 'The thing is,

did Parker know that it was a twelve-bore that shot Hunter? I couldn't tell, just by looking at Hunter's body. I doubt if anyone could. And, if Parker has handed these two in—what has he kept back?'

'And why?' Nelson added, setting the report down.

'Just so. And if he's tried this little piece of deception: what else has he lied about?'

Alec was still speculating about that matter as he drove through Hartfield that afternoon and turned up towards the airfield. He slowed as he passed the gateway on to the perimeter track. The stubble had already vanished, to be replaced by the evenly turned furrows of the plough; but no tractor was to be seen crawling across the landscape, and he drove on to the track down to the farm.

James Parker was in the yard, attending to something on a big four-furrow plough cocked up behind the blue tractor. He looked up briefly as the car turned in, and bent to his work again.

'I've come at a bad time, it seems,' Alec said, standing behind him.

'You could say that.'

'Got trouble?'

'What does it bloody look like.' He straightened up, his hands slippery with hydraulic fluid, and looked Alec distastefully in the face. 'I thought I'd done with you people.'

'I rather doubt that,' Alec replied briefly. He nodded towards the house. 'Anyone else in?'

Parker's eyes flickered. 'Yes.'

Alec said, 'I'll go and have a chat until you're finished. Don't keep me waiting too long, will you?' He walked towards the house, wondering just how long Parker would give him; not long at all, if he had any sense.

His knock was answered by a woman of his own age. She was within millimetres of being beautiful; but suffering, or bad temper, or habitual resentment with life for denying her what she fancied she had a right to, had hardened her

features and sharpened the contours of a face which in a
woman on better terms with her lot must have been lovely.

She looked Alec up and down insolently, *de haut en bas*.
Every policeman knows that look, and Alec had long ago
come to terms with it. Probably this woman regarded everyone that way.

'Mrs Parker?'

'Yes.'

'I'm Detective Chief Inspector Stainton.'

'Oh God. I thought we'd seen the last of you after that
girl came.'

'May I come in?'

'I suppose you're going to, whatever I say,' she replied
gracelessly, and turned away. He stepped inside and closed
the door. It was a side hall—the front of the house faced
the other way, but was probably never used—empty except
for a fancy wrought-iron table, on which were piled letters
and bills and a Yellow Pages. The walls had muddy scuff-
marks where boots had been left against them. Ahead was
a closed door, and another door to one side, open, from
which echoed the cacophony of canned laugher. He grimaced, and went on through.

The woman who had let him in was slumped in a chair,
watching the TV. At first Alec thought she was the only
occupant, then a pair of bright, suspicious eyes drew him
to the figure of an old woman watching him from the far
side of the room. No; on second thoughts, not as old as all
that; sixty-five, maybe.

More laughter spilt importunately from the television.
The volume was turned right up. Maybe the old woman
was deaf, but he wondered how the younger one could stand
it, all the same. Alec walked across and turned off the set.

The older woman said nothing, but her gaze sharpened
still further in what could have been amusement. The
younger one gave a pout of boredom and continued to stare
at the dead screen, pointedly ignoring him.

'You're Diana Parker then; James's wife,' he began. 'And

you,' he asked, looking across at the other woman, 'must be Mrs Parker senior?'

'What if I am?' she answered tartly. Not deaf, then. How old was James, he wondered? Anywhere between his late thirties and mid-forties. The old woman must have been here since at least the war, then. Alec guessed her husband had been dead some time: the household was fossilized in a long-established mutual enmity, the enmity of women of different generations, with no natural affection for one another, forced into proximity through their link with the same man. A mother who despised the girl who had usurped her son; and a wife who saw and hated in the older woman, what she herself would become in course of time.

'You can see a portion of the airfield from this window,' Alec remarked. Out in the yard Parker was still tinkering with the tractor. Beyond, the bare chocolate soil stretched to the distant trees. 'You must have been curious about all the commotion last Monday. Must have wondered what a lot of policemen were doing swarming over your land.'

Diana Parker shrugged uninterestedly. Old Mrs Parker watched him with her sharp eyes. 'I'm tied to my chair,' she said at last. Her voice was like her eyes, sharp and wary, and she lifted her hands an inch or two from the chair arms so that he could see the twisted, arthritic fingers. 'Aren't I tied to my chair, Diana?'

'Yes, Mother,' Diana responded, bored.

'And you?' He turned to Diana, pressing her.

'I saw some men wandering around. Cars. If that was your lot. James was out there. Let James sort it out, I thought. Whatever it is.'

'You were busy?'

She shrugged again. 'Don't remember. What was I doing on Monday, Mother?' She turned to the older woman, raising her voice slightly as to a stupid child.

'How should I know?'

Alec tried a different tack. 'I believe my WPC asked you about the previous Thursday too. That's when we think the dead man was killed.' He turned to Diana. 'You went shopping, Mrs Parker. And out riding in the afternoon; I believe that's what you said.'

'If that's what I said, then that's what I did, I imagine.'

'And you, of course,' he turned to the older woman, 'would have been here as usual.'

'Do you see me wandering around the airfield shooting at trespassers?' the old woman jeered. 'Of course I was here.'

'Do you have many murders in this part of the world?' Alec asked.

'Don't be bloody stupid,' Diana Parker ejaculated inelegantly.

'Then,' Alec said quietly, 'perhaps I can suggest that you're taking the matter surprisingly calmly. A man killed on your farm and you were neither of you interested? Perhaps you were neither of you surprised, either!'

The two women looked at each other: a look, he thought, of mutual distrust, mutual need. Choosing to hang together rather than hang separately?

He waited for one of them to speak. In the end the old woman had more staying power and it was Diana who said, conciliatory, 'Perhaps it's because it's so . . . upsetting that we're not quite ourselves. It's not a very nice thing to have happen on your land.'

'No,' Alec agreed tonelessly. 'Not nice, at all.' He paused. 'You know who it was, who died?'

'Some . . . some author, James said. Historian. Military archæologist. Something like that.'

'His name was Hunter. Andrew Hunter.'

'Was it?' she asked. Hard as she tried, she couldn't keep the uninterest from her voice.

'You'd met him, I imagine.'

'I doubt it.' Suddenly her eyes narrowed, became like the old woman's, flinty and feral. 'When should I have done that?'

'No? I thought perhaps he'd have been here before. Since

he was interested in the place. To learn its history.' He turned to the old woman. 'You'd have been able to tell him that.'

'Eh? What could I tell him! All past, gone. What use is it to anyone to go back . . . No. He never came, Detective-Inspector Whatever-your-name-is. No.' Her voice trailed tiredly away. Her face was slack, as if pain from the arthritis was dulling her. 'No; he never came here. Not to me. I never told him . . .'

'Of course you didn't, Mother,' the younger woman said impatiently. She turned to Alec. 'OK, I'm sorry he's dead. But he means nothing to me. How could he?'

Alec regarded her speculatively. 'I suppose, though,' he said after a moment, 'your husband was pretty upset? To have found the body . . . not a pleasant one, either. Not after four days . . .'

Diana Parker's face was stony still, not yielding an inch. There was the sound of the outside door banging open and of boots being kicked off. A sour smile leaked over Diana Parker's face. 'Now you can ask him,' she said, and turned pointedly away.

Parker looked round suspiciously when he came in the room, as if trying to divine what had been said, what accusations hung in the air. Alec kept his face impassive, masking the dissatisfaction he felt with the women's resistance to his inquiries.

'I was asking,' he said bleakly, 'about Andrew Hunter. About when he came here before; asking questions for his book.'

Parker looked from one to the other of the women. 'He never came here,' he said abruptly.

'Shouldn't you have said, "Who's Andrew Hunter?"?'

'That's an old trick,' Parker sneered. 'Everybody knows that was the bloke's name; the dead bloke.'

'And you say you'd never met him before?'

'Never met him at all,' Parker retorted, 'unless you can call finding his corpse in my barley meeting him. That seems to me to be going a bit far.' His manner had gained something in assurance and his voice was stronger, as if some threshold had been crossed.

Alec said pleasantly, 'Show me where you keep your guns, if you don't mind.'

'Got a warrant?'

'For the purpose of making an inspection under the Firearms Acts,' Alec said easily, 'I don't need one. You know that. Besides, I generally only find myself obtaining a warrant when people have something they'd rather hide.'

'Get off my back,' Parker said roughly. 'I've nothing to hide; that doesn't give you the right to come here and treat me as if I was a criminal.'

'All right; show me where you keep the guns, then.'

Parker looked at him suspiciously, then led the way through to the next room; it was roughly furnished as an office, with a battered desk heaped with accounts and the discarded carton of a veterinary medicine. In the far corner was a grey steel cabinet, shoulder high. The key was in the lock. Parker opened the cabinet: it was empty except for a carton of cartridges.

'When am I going to get my guns back?'

'Soon.'

'I don't keep them for sport, you know,' he retorted sarcastically. 'I don't suppose you'd realize that rabbits eat young crops. My winter corn'll be coming through in not many weeks.'

'Use them a lot, do you?'

'I've a licence for them!'

'Which do you prefer?'

Parker hesitated. 'I . . . mostly use the four-ten.'

'That's a boy's gun. Why don't you use the twelve-bore?'

'I . . . haven't been using that so much recently. It's a bit old. You know how guns get.' He turned and swung the door of the gun cupboard shut, turning the key, then marched back across the room, leading the way back into the sitting-room.

'If you've seen all you want to, you can go.'

'Yes,' Alec said decidedly. 'I think I've seen enough. To be going on with.' And he nodded to the two women, and let himself out through the hallway. Parker watched stolidly as Alec climbed into his car, turned it, and drove out of the yard. Then he went back through to the office and reopened the door of the gun-cupboard and stared at the open half-used box of twelve-bore cartridges.

'Damn,' he said savagely, and then again, under his breath, 'damn it to hell.'

CHAPTER 9

'These are the ones you want. I've removed the sheets and tagged them together. The files are marked where they were taken out.'

'That's very efficient of you.'

Dr Walker smiled tolerantly and relaxed back in her chair. They were in her office in Redhill, surrounded by the curious stillness a place of work has when those who work there have departed. A clutter of papers and files was piled on to a table at one side, the VDU pushed back on its stand out of the way so that they could spread the files out on the desk.

Alec picked up the slim sheaf of A4 paper, each sheet dotted with Andrew Hunter's cryptic notes in his legible, painstaking hand, and weighed it thoughtfully.

'There are twelve of them,' Dr Walker clarified. 'Two flew from Hartfield Park in the Battle of Britain. That's Collis and Lynch. Smith was with the Typhoon squadron that was at Hartfield before the invasion and went over to France that autumn. The other nine all flew the Mosquitoes at various times: three two-man crews, two navigators who flew with pilots of other nationalities, and one pilot who wasn't there long enough to be allocated a navigator.'

Alec leafed through the papers. 'Binney, Fernyhough, Green, Janssen, McAllister, Murdoch, Phillips, Dixon and Taylor.'

'That's right.'

He fiddled with the tag, separating the sheets out one by one on to the desk in front of him. He looked at them in turn, turning over the page where the notes continued on to the other side. Then he gathered up five of the sheets and put them to one side.

'Murdoch, Collis, Fernyhough, McAllister, Binney,' Dr Walker said, her eyes not on the papers but on him.

'Yes. If they didn't survive the war they're not of much interest to me. Have you a photographic memory?'

She shook her head, but he wasn't looking at her. He fished a slim notebook from the inside pocket of his jacket and flicked through till he found what he wanted, then picked out two more of Andrew Hunter's sheets. There were now three piles before him.

'Lynch and Green,' he said. 'Those two, so far as we know, are at this moment in South Africa, and haven't left it.'

'Lynch must be pretty old,' Dr Walker remarked. 'He was one of the original Battle of Britain pilots. That makes him seventy, at least.'

'Yes.' It was a consideration not to be overlooked. Turning to the paper on Green, for example, he saw that his date of birth was given as nineteen-fifteen. Thirty at the end of the war; seventy-five now. No great wonder he too had stayed safely at home rather than jaunting to England with the mere striplings of sixty-five. Janssen, he saw, at barely sixty-three, was the youngest of those who had made the trip; Dixon at sixty-eight the eldest.

That left five sheets: Janssen, Phillips, Dixon, Smith and Taylor. Alec gathered them up and tagged them together. They were the first line of investigation: the men who had flown from Hartfield Park and had been in the country for the reunion at the time Andrew Hunter was killed.

There still remained the other forty or fifty men who had come over for the reunion but had flown from other airfields. There was no real reason why one of them, assuming there was a motive for killing Hunter (and looking at it now in colder blood, it did seem improbable that a motive could flourish across six thousand miles and forty-five years) should not have met him at Hartfield, knowing he was to be there, and done the deed . . . So they would all have to be checked.

Dr Walker helped him; as Alec read out the names she located them in Hunter's meticulously arranged blue files, withdrew the relevant sheets, inserted a slip saying what had been removed, and made a fourth pile on the table. It was slow work.

'There. That's the last.' Dr Walker snapped the ring-binder shut. 'Oh, one other oddity. A man called Paul Napier. There's a sheet with his name at the top, but no other entries. Whether that means Hunter hadn't come up with any information, I don't know. If Napier was aircrew, there should have been something that could be put down, even if it was only that he was killed in training.'

'He never made the reunion anyway,' Alec commented. 'His name's not on the list.'

Dr Walker nodded and sat back, weary. Alec remembered she must have been ten or twelve hours in this office already today, and mentally chided himself for forgetting it. Her goodwill had been invaluable; it would be foolish to squander it now; and ungrateful.

'OK.' He smiled; he was tired himself. 'I'm immensely grateful to you, Dr Walker—' he corrected himself— 'Frances, I mean. I'm only sorry to have kept you so late. You must be sick of the sight of these files.'

She shook her head. 'I said it was my hobby. I take my hobbies seriously. And it's not every day that one is asked as a favour to run through the private notes of one of one's biggest rivals.'

'Was he good?' Alec asked curiously. 'I mean, in your field: was Andrew Hunter respected?'

'Oh, very much.' Dr Walker was emphatic, urgent. 'Don't underestimate him. This is all first-class stuff. His book would have been *the* book on the subject; no question. I suppose,' she added hesitantly, 'you don't know what's going to happen about it? I mean, in the circumstances?'

He looked her straight in the eye. 'I don't.'

She met his look. 'I haven't photocopied those files, Inspector.'

He relaxed fractionally. 'If you had, it would mean I'd misjudged you. You'd better ask Janice Hunter about the book, hadn't you? The notes are hers; it's her decision.'

'Sure.' She looked thoughtful. 'I could always suggest . . . you see, I want this work to be published. Who does it . . . that doesn't matter so much. But once the research has been done it would be wrong to disperse it again, or bury it in an attic.'

'I don't know much about these things,' Alec said diffidently, 'but I imagine Mrs Hunter might be glad for someone to complete the book as a tribute to her husband. Properly acknowledged.'

Dr Walker's eyes lit up. 'If she would, I'd do more than that. I'd have it published under his name. And,' she added, 'she could keep the copyright and the royalties. I don't exactly need them.'

Alec began to gather his things together, and suggested a meal in the town; or was she keen to get back to Lucy? She was, but—with a businesswomanlike glance at her watch, and a sharp glance as if she suspected she was being teased—she had an hour and a quarter before the baby-sitter was due to depart. A meal would be fine; and over it she would run through the notes she had made clarifying Hunter's references on those important five sheets, so that he had it clear in his mind.

A competent, decisive businesswoman, Alec considered as he waited while she locked up. Not perhaps altogether relaxing as a social companion; but at a time like this, as a co-opted colleague, a godsend.

Dr Walker switched on the alarm and pulled the last door to, locked it and took his arm.

'I don't know what you had in mind,' she said, 'but there's a restaurant I favour just near the playhouse. This way, then.'

And Alec, not without an inward smile, allowed the decision to be taken out of his hands and submitted to being propelled firmly in the necessary direction.

CHAPTER 10

It was a cool, still September day. Out here on the perimeter track the ever-present heady odour of high-octane aviation fuel was muted, mingling seductively with the equally heady, more delicate scent of late-mown hay. Out of the hedge twenty yards away a pheasant erupted with its hoarse squawk and a rattle of russet plumage.

'Bang, bang!' Kenny Taylor—jaunty, athletic, flamboy-antly moustached—swung off his bicycle and fell into step with the stocky pilot plodding, heavily laden, along the edge of the concrete track. 'Coming down the Dorset Arms?'

Janssen kept on walking. 'All right. Gimme fifteen min-utes to get rid of this kit. Taking Bertha?'

'Carburettor's a bit dicey. Suppose we might risk it. Dicky coming?'

'I'll tell him. What about Babe and Doug?'

'Oh, Doug! Talking mumbo-jumbo with his ground crew when I passed them. He's a bloody old woman, that man, I tell you; a bloody old woman!'

'If it gets him home . . .'

'. . . Wants to air test this afternoon. I tell you, a bloody old woman! See you by Bertha, then.' He put his foot on the pedal and hopped along for a couple of paces, then swung the other leg precariously over the cross-bar. 'Ten minutes!'

'Hey, you said fifteen!' Janssen protested, as he was left behind.

'Get a move on, then,' the cyclist called over his shoulder, as he rode off in the direction of the distant huts. 'Come on, run! Hup, two, three.' The bicycle jerked as it met one of the joins in the concrete and the rider hurriedly transferred his attention to the question of balance and rode off, his cap tilted at the inevitable angle.

Janssen, plodding on with his burden, grinned. 'Silly bastard,' he muttered to himself; and then, glancing at his watch, hitched the parachute and dinghy pack higher on his shoulder and lengthened his stride.

A hundred yards short of the crew-room he heard the racket of the old Austin truck overtaking him. It rattled past, and two men tumbled out of the cab as it drew to a halt; a third clambered over the tailboard. The truck swung round past him, and the girl at the wheel gave him a cheerful wave as it headed in the direction of the watch office.

The atmosphere in the crew-room was as sweaty and smoky as ever. Dimly seen figures moved around the lockers or bent over the table.

'Beat you to it,' someone boasted. 'You should have waited for the truck.'

'Lazy bastards.' He moved over to the lockers and began stowing his burdens away. 'And what were you doing sitting in the cab? That's my seat.'

'First come, first served, chum. Besides,' came the inevitable taunt, 'we thought we'd do Alison a favour; let her have someone handsome to talk to for a change.'

He looked across at Doug, who caught his eye and grimaced sympathetically. Doug McAllister didn't speak much, and when he did he spoke quietly, as if he didn't have to shout to make his point. If there was line-shooting going on he didn't speak at all. Kenny was right, he was a bit of an old woman when it came to questions of detail, Janssen thought critically, but it was difficult not to be impressed by the air of maturity about him. Hardly surprising, perhaps: look at those wrinkles round his eyes. Lots of the chaps had lined faces these days, but not like those: those were the real thing. Old Doug must be at least thirty.

That made the contrast between Doug and his navigator, bending over the table ticking off something in his notebook, looking barely fourteen, all the more piquant. So they called the nav 'Babe', offered to buy him lemonade in the bar and made a great show of patiently explaining their ribald jokes to him. Sometimes he fancied Babe found it all rather hard to take. Still, he was a bloody good nav; and Babe and Doug made a good team, despite the disparity in age—or maybe because of it. One of the best.

'We're going down to the Dorset.' Already it had grown from a suggestion to an established party. Someone slammed a locker door and turned to the others. 'Who's coming?'

'You're on,' he said. 'Anyone seen my nav?'

'Doug?'

'Uh-uh. I've some letters to write, and we've got an NFT at three, if the boys can sort out that mag. I'll give it a miss.'

'What about you, Babe? C'mon, I'll buy you a fizzy. What about it?'

Babe glanced at Doug. 'Well, I've . . .' Outside, the rumble of an engine and the screech of worn brakes cut off Babe's reply. A door slammed, and Kenny Taylor burst into the hut, his battered cap pushed nonchalantly back and his oil-stained jacket hanging open over a rough roll-top jersey.

'All ready to go? I've got Bertha just ticking over. Daren't switch her off. Doug?'

'Doug's staying . . .'

Bill Janssen bundled the last of his things away; the others were already pushing out of the hut again; Babe followed, with an apologetic glance at Doug. He shut his locker door and hurried after them.

'I'll send your nav on if I see him,' Doug said as Janssen made for the door. He met his eye, more seriously. 'Get Babe back in one piece for me, Bill. And this time it really had better be lemonade. If the air test's OK . . .'

He didn't need to finish the sentence. The weather was good; it was fair odds they'd all be flying that night. Janssen nodded soberly. 'I'll get him back.' Then he let a crafty grin spread across his face. 'Give Joan my love. Letters, my foot. You don't fool *me* with that bullshit!'

Doug's eyes crinkled, and he clapped him on the back as he hurried out to join the others. 'Too sharp for your own good,' he laughed. 'Alison's a lucky girl.'

And he grinned back, not sure whether the glow he felt was because of Alison's love or Doug's approbation. He gained the back seat of Bertha just as the old car began to move and, the door still flapping, squealed away from the hut towards the main gate.

'Don't bother, Kenny.'

Dicky Dixon shouldered through the door into the snug as Kenny was leaning on the bar, teasing his moustache lovingly and waiting for the landlord to emerge from the other bar. He put a cautionary hand on the sleeve of Kenny's jacket. Bill and Babe and Stu Phillips, semi-circled round the corner table, looked up questioningly.

'We've to get back,' Dicky said, grimacing. Bill let his breath out with a deep sigh.

Kenny looked down at the hand on his sleeve. Dicky withdrew it. 'Sod that,' he said forcefully.

'I came to tell you! Got the word just as I was on my way down to join you.'

'I'd better get back,' Babe began, clambering to his feet; 'Doug . . .'

'Bugger Doug,' Kenny said. 'I came here for a drink, and so did you. You didn't get here just yet. You can arrive after Fred's fetched us this refill, all right?'

'Not for me, Kenny,' Bill said, getting to his feet also.

Babe was already standing by the door, his expression fearful and anxious. 'Let's be going.'

'Nobody's going,' Kenny said reasonably, 'until we've had this second pint. Got it? Fred: four pints. One for you, Dicky? No? All right, sod off, then. You've done your good deed, you've come and told us. We'll be back in fifteen minutes. Hitler can wait a quarter of an hour, I take it.'

Bill sighed, and turned to Dixon. 'How did you get here?'

'Got the bike. I can take one of you, but . . .'

'Go on: you can take us both. Babe's only a lad.'

'That's what you said last week,' Dixon said drily. 'Before we had that monumental prang.'

'That was because you were tight,' Bill said, grinning. 'This time you're sober. Come on, then, Babe, old son.'

The three of them pushed out of the snug, and a moment later the two who were left heard the motorbike splutter into life and rumble into the distance.

Stu sat alone at the corner table, the empty glasses before him. Kenny stood stiffly at the bar, fighting down his rage, his fresh beer untasted beside him.

Their eyes met, and locked, and each recognized in the other the same terror.

CHAPTER 11

SAA had made out all the tickets in the same way. Jack Patrick had tried half-heartedly to get them to issue open-ended tickets, but really he'd been pretty satisfied with the deal he'd got, and he didn't think the guys would want to pay the earth for the chance to get to Europe a month earlier or stay on later.

DC Johnson ran a pen down the details, and glanced at the calendar on the wall: the tickets fixed the outward journey for the fifteenth, a week before Hunter's body had been found but only a matter of days before his death. Return had to be either on the thirtieth, or on the eleventh of the next month. Individuals could choose which of the two dates they wanted to return on, but they had to let the airline know within forty-eight hours of their arrival in Britain. With very few exceptions they had opted for the later date.

The five names on Mr Stainton's list were not among those exceptions. It was now the twenty-eighth. They had just over a week. It seemed curious that the killer, if it was one of the South Africans, had not waited until the last moment before they were due to leave for home before doing the deed; that way, by the time the inquiry got under way, it would be immeasurably complicated by the vicissitudes of international cooperation.

Johnson turned to the telephone directory, then with his finger still keeping the place picked up the receiver in the other hand and stabbed out the number.

Alec Stainton sat at the table in his flat and considered the limited time at his disposal. The unadorned simplicities of the *Temps Pascal* oozed from the speakers of the stereo as he set about collecting his ideas into some sort of order; that apart, the flat was quiet, insulated by stout Victorian construction from the other of the two flats into which the big house had been divided, and by the remnants of the Victorian kitchen garden and 'wilderness' from the rest of the world, the flesh and—in so far as he was to be found in this part of Sussex—the devil.

The situation was not altogether unpromising. Previous murder cases with which Alec had been involved had been unhelpfully foggy: few facts, and a great deal of human irrationality, so that the solution lay more within the competence of the psychologist than the logician.

Here there were at least facts. Not, as yet, decisive ones like retrieving the shotgun or finding bloodstained clothing or an incriminating note; but good enough to start with, and to suggest that a sensible mind ought to be able to arrange them into some sort of satisfactory order.

Andrew Hunter was linked to Hartfield Park, and perforce to James Parker, who had moreover discovered the body. He was also linked by the nature of his work with fifty-odd South African war veterans, now scattered throughout the United Kingdom (and possibly Europe generally; he must not forget that) and due to return to their lawyers' offices and farms and supermarkets in a week or so's time.

But five of those South African airmen had their own link with Hartfield Park as the scene of their youthful triumphs and fears. Of their youthful passions, too, perhaps: was there any significance in that? He made a note to remind Liz Pink to listen with particular care to anyone in the area old enough to remember wartime scandals of that sort.

Nelson, with the aid of a detective-constable helpfully loaned by the Nottingham CID, was sifting thoroughly through the daily details of Andrew Hunter's life. First priority must then be to check up, if possible, on those whom Hunter had visited on his recent trips gathering material for the current book. It was always possible that his digging had uncovered something which someone was determined should not see the light of day.

Locally, they had not had conspicuous success. Liz Pink's patient and polite inquiries had uncovered nothing beyond a complaint about unlicensed riding of motorcycles along bridleways and a lengthy diatribe directed at James Parker.

Parker had apparently been so unreasonable as to lose his temper with one of his neighbours when he caught her dumping rubble, the product of refitting the kitchen, over one of his hedges. Fair enough, Alec thought, given the cost of repairing damaged machinery; but it had perhaps been rather excessive of Parker to swear that he would take a shotgun to the neighbour if he caught her at the same trick again. The diatribe had sidetracked into a condemnation of the police for allowing farmers to keep shotguns and thereby increasing the risk of armed hold-ups and psychopathic killings. Liz had tactfully refrained from pointing out that shotguns have legitimate uses too, and that it wasn't the licensed guns that caused the trouble, and moved on.

In Parker's case, though, Alec mused, it looked decidedly likely that his gun *had* caused the trouble. That there had been lies told him at the farmhouse he was in no doubt, in addition to the silent testimony of the cartridges in the gun-cupboard. Where was Parker's twelve-bore? We have left unsaid, he misquoted to himself, those things which we ought to have said, and we have said those things which we ought not to have said, and there is no health in us.

In so far as Liz Pink's inquiries had been aimed at obtaining corroboration of Hunter's movements once he got off the bus in Hartfield that Thursday afternoon, they had been conspicuously unsuccessful. Alec's chance encounter with the two horsewomen by the roadside remained the only help in that respect; but they too, revisited, far from adding to what they had already volunteered, seemed to have doubts about whether it really had been Thursday they had seen a figure at all.

The plainsong came to an end and the machine switched itself off. Alec stirred in his chair. Nelson was busy enough in Nottingham for another day; but then he, like Liz and Andy Johnson, would be back, looking to Alec for the lead and the direction; looking to him to give some evidence of a logical approach to the case, rather than a mere staggering from one point to another. Police work, he told himself for the umpteenth time, was like command in battle: to lose the initiative was fatal. Once you began merely to react to events rather than controlling them you were lost.

He drew a sheet of paper to him and began to sketch the priorities: trace the five South African airmen who had flown from Hartfield, and establish their alibis for that Thursday. Visit all those whom Hunter had visited in recent months, if only to confirm that they existed, and dispose finally of the ghost of his hypothetical mistress.

He hesitated. The next item should be, track through Hunter's work to make sure he had not stumbled on any scandals or skeletons. How to do that, without Hunter's own specialized knowledge, was problematic, and he knew he would have to prevail once more on Dr Walker to help him. Much as he shrank instinctively from involving outsiders in the inquiry, needs must, he told himself, when the devil drives; and Dr Walker was at least competent and (so far as he could tell) discreet. Perhaps he could set Liz to work with her in place of himself; but that was tricky. Dr Walker might not be so ready to help Liz; might, perhaps, resent being asked to aid a WPC where she had been quite willing to be consulted by a Chief Inspector.

Then there was the lab to ginger up. The post-mortem on Andrew Hunter's body had shown neither more nor less than would have been expected of the killing of a man with a shotgun. It had not taken the forensic lab long to establish that the murder weapon was of twelve-bore, and they were sure now that only one shot had been fired, from a distance of some ten yards, from a gun with a slightly worn choke.

That meant that the killer must have followed Hunter into the barley, for the body had been a good seventy or eighty yards from the edge of the nearest hard-standing; and it had been sheer bad luck—or had it?—that Parker had cut those swathes first, thereby obliterating the evidence.

There was still the puzzle of why the shot should have been in the chest, not in the back. Conceivably Hunter and his killer had been standing talking, and the dead man had no time to turn and run; or perhaps he had been mesmerized by the appearance of the gun . . .

Alec put the papers down and walked round the room, frowning. Something was nagging at him. Something someone had said, or . . . yes, he had stood in the cleared barley discussing that with David Fletcher, the Scene of Crime Officer, and Fletcher had added something about looking for oil-stains on the concrete where a car might have stood;

and he had looked across . . . He halted by the window and stared out into the blackness, unseeing.

Out on the drive below a pair of headlights turned in from the road, curved up towards the house, flashing briefly on a blank window, and extinguished themselves towards the garages at the back. A moment later there was the rumble of the door being lifted, following by the quicker rumble and clatter as it was slid down and the padlock thrust home. Alec turned away, content.

The task of locating the South Africans was a tedious one, and unglamorous to boot. Andy Johnson, beavering away at it as the hours passed, found himself resenting the way Liz Pink and Sergeant Nelson seemed to get all the interesting jobs, all the trips out and the chances to be taken into Mr Stainton's confidence.

From the practical point of view, the problem was knowing where to start. After the reunion the veterans had been free to go where they pleased, with only the deadline of the plane home to meet. How do you find someone who has the whole of Europe at their disposal and no one to answer to? The answer, Johnson told himself ruefully, is: with difficulty. In the event, he began with the car-hire firms and with snatches of conversation recalled by Jablonski and Jack Patrick and in less than two days he began to reel the first of them in.

'I'm investigating a murder, I'm afraid, Mr Dixon. Andrew Hunter. A military historian. Who was to have been a speaker at your reunion weekend.'

'I was looking forward to hearing him. From what I'd picked up, he was going to be pretty interesting. 'Course, I've seen his death in the papers.'

Cedric Dixon was big and burly. Alec, who knew him to be sixty-eight—he confirmed it briefly, glancing down at the extract from Hunter's file notes—would without that knowledge have placed him at no more than fifty or fifty-five.

His was the taut bulk of a young man, not the loose volume of the elderly. His square face was seamed, it was true, but the narrowed eye openings belonged to a man who spends much of his time out of doors under a wide sky, and in the sun at that. Muscle still stretched the shoulders of his jacket, preventing it from meeting across the plain blue shirt, which was open at the collar—and the collar, Alec thought, if it was ever to do up round that massive pillar of a neck, must be about the largest size obtainable.

'First,' Alec began, 'I'd better ask you formally for an account of your movements since you arrived in this country last week. I'm going to be asking everyone this, I may say.' Over in the corner, Johnson wrote 'Dixon' on his pad, and underlined it twice and then, on second thoughts, to avoid future confusion, put 'Mr' in front.

Cedric Dixon had, he confessed, been looking forward to this trip for months. Until retirement last year he had run a hardware store in Pietermaritzburg, on the eastern coast of South Africa.

The chance to come to England was fortuitous. In one go Dixon could visit the few friends he still had from wartime days—it would be his last chance, he said realistically; enjoy the reunion itself and a touch of forgivable nostalgia; and grasp the opportunity to fill his mind with new ideas, new sights, which were rather hard to come by these days back in his native country.

Dixon sketched out the programme he had planned to fill the days until his return home, and it was a demanding one. The man seemed, Alec considered, anxious to pack the time as full as could be, as if he knew it was a chance that would not, in the natural order of things, come again.

Alec put that consideration aside. The question was, where had this scheme taken Dixon on that vital Thursday? And the answer, though plainly given, was not itself plain. Like the rest of the veterans, Dixon had arrived at Heathrow on Monday night. That gave him three clear days before the reunion proper got under way, and he didn't intend to sit in some London hotel wasting them.

Tuesday, he had done little; allowing himself to recover from the journey. On the Wednesday he had been in Cambridge, dragooning an executive from a local machinery firm, who had once had the misfortune to attend a conference in Durban at which Dixon had been present, into showing him the sights. Alec made a note on his pad; that should be easily verifiable. Dixon had stayed Wednesday night at the University Arms.

Thursday was more nebulous. It had been allocated for more sightseeing: East Anglian wool churches, Norwich, Aldeburgh because of the musical associations. Little Gidding to round off this complete tour of East Anglia, before Dixon returned to London that evening.

'How did you get about?' Alec asked.

'Hired a car for the whole three weeks of my stay. I intend to get my money's worth out of it, I can tell you.'

Alec thought hard. A day's sightseeing would be difficult to corroborate; and Hartfield Park would be only—what? —two or three hours from Cambridge by motorway. Would Dixon have spoken to anyone? What about Little Gidding, for example? There was a book there, Alec recalled, where you could write your requests for prayers to be said by the community members: he and Jayne Simmonds had done so one wet February day, and he still recalled the tingle of sudden dim insight into what it was her faith meant to Jayne. Though his own prayers that day, he thought coldly, didn't appear to have been conspicuously answered.

If Dixon had written anything in that book . . . he glanced at him from beneath lowered eyebrows. He didn't look the type to go in for sentimental touches of that sort . . . But it was definitely worth checking; and worth speaking to anyone at the community who might remember Dixon—surely a memorable enough figure.

'Does your sightseeing and visiting of friends take you to Hartfield Park?' he asked directly.

'Going down there this afternoon,' Dixon rumbled with
zest. 'Don't suppose there's much to see now.'

'Still quite a bit,' Alec said, smiling.

'You go to college?' Dixon asked. 'You're probably nostalgic about your college, I guess,' he went on, not waiting for
the reply, 'go to all the reunions and stuff. Well, us old
fogeys get nostalgic for when we were fighting in the war.
Get two of us together and hear how we natter on. I tell
you, a couple of South African war veterans can talk the
pants off of the United Nations any day! It's because we
were young, I guess, that's all.'

'Are you seeing anyone in the area, Mr Dixon?'

'Oh, I'll see one or two. D'you know a place called
Tunbridge Wells?' Alec nodded. England was rather less
far-flung than the South African veld. 'And I guess I'll call
at the farm after all these years. The one on the field, you
know it?'

'To see . . . Mrs Parker?' It had to be; James would be
too young.

Dixon's eyes flickered a momentary blankness. 'Mrs
Pa . . .? Oh, sure. I beg your pardon; after all these years
. . . you think of people as they were then, you know? Forget
their lives have moved on too. Yeah, sure I'll see her after
all these years. I wrote and said I would.'

Alec said, 'Did Mr Hunter ever write to you? I was
thinking, for his research, he might have tried to contact
those of you who are still . . . whom he could still locate.'

Dixon burst out with a spurt of large laughter. 'We aren't
so easy to kill off, boy. Those of us the war didn't do for are
still mostly around. Did Andrew Hunter write? Not to me,
anyway. He could have buttonholed most of us at the
reunion, mind. Maybe he planned to do that.'

'Maybe he did.' It was a disappointment. Alec had felt
confident that Nelson's search in Hunter's study would
sooner or later show up a file of useful correspondence with
these South Africans.

'You think one of us could have done it?' Dixon asked

shrewdly. 'It'd have to be a good reason, to kill a guy you never met, who lives on the other side of the world.'

'Who says the killer never met him? And there could be reasons. He was a writer; he planned to publish . . .'

'Dirty doings in the war, huh?' The scepticism was barely veiled.

'Could be. Would that look like a good reason, to you?'

'It depends,' Dixon replied slowly, 'what you mean by dirty doings.'

'You tell me.'

But Cedric Dixon shook his head, smiling, keeping his memories to himself.

'Get anywhere, sir?'

Alec was standing at the window, looking down at the top of Cedric Dixon's head as the man marched purposefully to his car below.

He turned. 'Hello. You back? No I don't think he knows anything. Whether he feels anything, or suspects anything . . . but he's not the sort who's going to start raising hares for us to chase. What news from Nottingham?'

'Nothing substantial, sir. Hunter was a meticulous sort of chap, fortunately; kept copies of all his letters, that sort of thing. That's quite a help.'

Alec pulled a pad towards him and wrote down some names. 'Any of these figure in the correspondence?' He swivelled the pad round so that it was right way up for Nelson.

Nelson scrutinized it, brows puckered. 'Don't ring a bell . . . I'll check, of course. There is something Johnson missed, not that I altogether blame him, in that lot: a general sort of letter which Hunter wrote, which I guess he sent to those of the South Africans who were still alive: I took a copy of that, sir.'

'Do we know just who it was sent to?'

'No. The addresses are left off; that's what made me think it might be a sort of circular letter. Maybe he marked the

files somehow to show which of the survivors he'd sent it
to.'

'You could be right.'

'Anyway,' Nelson said gloomily, 'no record of any appointment to meet someone at Hartfield Park, and that's
what we were really hoping for.'

Alec took back the paper with the list of names and stared
at it thoughtfully. After a moment he reached for his pen
again and added one more name at the bottom: Paul Napier.
Silently, he turned the paper again so that Nelson could
read it.

'Yes,' Nelson said. 'Yes, I was going to mention him.
Paul Napier. Hunter certainly wrote to him all right; went
to see him, too. Lived in Hereford.'

'Lived?' Alec repeated, thinking he must have misheard
the tense.

Nelson glanced up and met his eyes grimly. 'That's right.
Paul Napier died a fortnight ago. The death was in the
Independent. Cutting out the obituary,' he said, 'must have
been about the last piece of research Hunter ever did.'

'What had Napier done to earn an obituary?'

'He was one of the country's leading experts on the
growing of bonsai trees,' said Nelson with a deadpan face.
'Oh, and he served in the war. You'll like this bit. As an
Intelligence Officer in the Royal Air Force. At RAF Hartfield Park.'

CHAPTER 12

Cedric Dixon did not go straight to the farm from East
Court. Instead he drove out to Ashdown Forest and found
a picnic area where he could pull the car off the road. He
added it to the row of cars ranged to take advantage of
the view and sat gazing out across the countryside
towards Lewes and thought of the last time he had seen this

countryside; and how different it had looked. From the air.

'Six minutes to coast, skipper.'
   'Six minutes it is. How long to the next change of course?'
   'Eight minutes; 085 degrees.'
   '085 in eight minutes. Roger, Dicky.'
   Cramped in his seat behind and just below the pilot's elbow Dixon struggled with his maps in the tiny pencil beam of his flashlight, then screwed round to peer down at the darkened landscape. A patch of water—pond or reservoir, it was too small to identify off the map—glinted in the moonlight. A dull red glow showed down and to starboard: some weary fireman building up his fire; then a little scatter of sparks and the light was extinguished as the train disappeared into a tunnel. Two minutes later they crossed the unmistakable margin between land and sea, and Dixon turned back to his map to check their position against the indentation of the coast.
   This was his sixteenth trip. Bill Janssen had been his pilot for all except the first two. You didn't have much say about whose hands you put your life into; all that mattered to Dixon was that Bill should get them safely back each time —and so far, so good. It was the only definition of a good pilot. Janssen was not as dashing as Kenny Taylor, nor as steady and painstaking as Doug McAllister, maybe; but still better than most; and then Doug was an exception.
   Doug must be coming up to the end of his tour; though Babe, who had joined him half way through after his previous navigator developed appendicitis, would have to stay on and fly with someone else until his own tour was over.
   Dixon smiled grimly in the darkness and thought that maybe Babe would be lucky to get to the end of a tour if the other guys didn't stop pulling his leg so much. Sometimes there was a look in Babe's eye, when someone was laying it on thick, which was disturbingly like panic. If he had a girl, now, and if she was the right sort of girl, that

would put him right, give him back his confidence; but kids like Babe didn't go for the right sort of girl; they went for the worst sort, to prove they were up to it, and got laughed at for their pains and ended up worse than before.

Dixon checked his watch. '085 in thirty seconds, skipper.'

'OK.' Pause. 'Turning on 085 now.'

The plane tilted with a little jolt, then settled back on to an even keel.

'What's our time to the Dutch coast, Dicky?'

'ETA the coast seventeen minutes, skip.'

'OK.'

Doug, on the other hand, would make the end of his tour. Then he'd get a chance of a break: a break from flying, and from watching over Babe the way he did. There was Joanie, of course . . .

Perhaps they'd marry, if she could square her parents— or even if she couldn't, perhaps. Piece of luck for her if Doug married her and took her home with him. Her parents were kind enough to outsiders—to him and Bill, for example— but he had seen how they worked the girl; seen the shame in her eyes when some of the guys turned up at the farm and she was skivvying in the kitchen or mucking out the byre. She'd live a different life on Doug's place back home, my word yes! And it couldn't be easy, in backwoods Sussex, to be known as the girl that's walking out with a South African.

He glanced up at Bill. After so many trips together he knew the signs now: the tighter grip of the knuckles as they left the English coast further behind and neared the continent. The restless search of the blank black sky. The needless checking and questioning and irritation of which he, Dixon, would be the recipient. Never mind. His own stomach told the same story every time; but he had no one to gripe at. And he'd put up with a lot from Bill so long as he kept on getting them home.

He wondered what other crews were like as they reached this moment. Difficult to conceive of Doug betraying anxiety by tics or nagging. And Babe, so helpless on the ground, was by all accounts completely impassive in the air, and the sharpest nav in the squadron, a natural.

'Enemy coast coming up, skip. Five minutes.' Their flight plan took them dog-legging up the North Sea, keeping just in contact with the coast, to cross over the Danish peninsula at Heide, near its narrowest point.

Kenny. Was he ever like this? Did he ever feel this weakening of the sphincter, dryness of the mouth? Not if you listened to his talk; but behind the line-shooting . . .?

He felt the momentary pressing down in his seat as Bill took the Mosquito up ready for the quick dive that would cheat the radar and take them safely through the point of most danger. Already the coast was faintly visible below the luminous circle of the propeller and the engine noise was changing as Bill banked and tipped the nose down and they were thrust against the harness.

'OK,' said Bill to himself. 'Here we go again.'

It was late in the afternoon and the autumn sun was sinking redly when Cedric Dixon turned the hired Fiesta down the track leading to the farm. The yard was empty; he parked tidily in a corner and levered himself out, and stood a moment as if trying to recall some elusive reminiscence.

With a glance up at the blank windows of the farmhouse he began to walk across the yard past the corner of the old dairy, past the feed hopper where the hens used to scratch, until he emerged on to the flat plain of the airfield. Overhead a jet bound for Gatwick cruised slowly over, its throttled-back engines keening mockingly. Dixon let his gaze scan from one side to the other as if he sought something more than the dozing brick shacks and the weatherbeaten control tower and the long concrete swathe and the chocolate ripples of the plough.

The jet was a dot over the distant horizon, its wailing engines dimmed to a muted rumble. Another, tinnier, sound caught the ear of the watcher and he glanced up and round in an unconscious habit, his eyes crinkling and narrowing, until he located the glint of the sun on a little single-engined aeroplane making its steady way south towards the coast.

Dixon turned and walked back through the yard and up the steps to the house.

'Hello,' he said quietly to the woman who at last opened the door and who moved, painfully, to one side to let him in. 'Hello, Joanie. Long time no see.'

Alec had taken for himself the journey to Hereford. It was partly for the very good reason that the lead looked promising: the letter from Hunter to this mysterious Napier, followed up with a visit; the tantalizing blank page in Hunter's notes. There was a direct link between this Napier and Hartfield Park, and all in all Alec had definite hopes. As that old war-horse Superintendent Blackett would have said, it smelled right—and then he would have snorted in self-derision; but chances were his hunch would prove shrewd. Alec hoped something of the same mysterious skill might have descended like Elijah's mantle upon his own shoulders.

There was also Alec's need to get away; to give himself the chance, by putting physical distance between himself and Hartfield Park, of distancing it mentally also. A different vantage-point, a different perspective, a different light. And, he reminded himself as he passed Oxford and turned the nose of the Bristol westward, Hereford was a pleasant destination on a still-warm September day.

As soon as he turned the corner and saw the cars Alec knew which house he was looking for; and knew that he was too late.

The young-middle-aged face which opened the door to him before he could ring was grim and unsmiling.

Alec asked for Mr Napier.

'Mr Napier's not in. What do you want?'

'First, to know who I am talking to.'

The man paused, as if the information might be somehow classified, not to be dispensed to strangers. 'Police,' he said at length, as if determined to limit the disclosures. 'What do you want?' he said again.

Alec felt in his pocket for his warrant card. 'I called to see Mr Napier,' he said. 'If I could have a word with the senior officer here I'd be grateful.'

With a doubtful look from the warrant card to Alec, as if checking whether the photograph might have been forged, the taciturn policeman opened the door a little wider. 'You'd better come in.' Alec entered. 'You'd better wait there. Sir.' The man was evidently not the garrulous type. Alec looked about him and wondered what had happened to the bonsai trees.

The little rubicund man who bustled out of the front room a moment later evened the score so far as garrulity was concerned. He must barely, Alec told himself, satisfy the regulations as to height; but the eyes that gleamed in the folds of pink flesh were younger and shrewder than first impressions might suggest.

'I appear to be interrupting,' Alec apologized. 'My name's Stainton.' He proffered his card again; the other man waved it away.

'Yes, yes. Not to worry, not to worry. I'm Robertson. What brings you here, then?' The last remark was shot at him with a keen glint from the alert eyes.

'I've a murder inquiry in hand. One of my leads brings me to Mr Paul Napier. I know he died recently. I arranged to call on the son, Colin, this morning.'

'Murder, hmm? Well, well, well.' All said very quickly, but as if murder was at least an extenuating reason for Alec's presence.

Alec said, 'Perhaps you'd better tell me what's going on.'

Robertson's eyes darted round the hallway, as if the answer might be concealed there somewhere; evidently it wasn't, for in the end he supplied it himself. 'You know about Paul Napier, you say? Hm. Well Colin Napier's in

the General Hospital, unconscious. He was attacked last
night by an intruder. Half an hour ago he was alive,'
Robertson added, glancing at his watch. 'He may yet croak.
Is that what you expected me to say? The old boy died ten
days ago. He was eighty, after all. To be expected, to be
expected.'

Robertson's small pink mouth clammed suddenly shut,
as if it had been issued with the day's ration of words and
had carelessly used them all up at one go.

Alec looked at him. 'I think, if you don't mind, you'd
better start at the beginning.'

Robertson hesitated, as his sergeant had done. The beady
eyes slipped this way and that, and then momentarily met
Alec's own. A small sigh escaped him. 'You'd better come
in here,' he said.

CHAPTER 13

The attack had happened at half past ten the night before.
Colin Napier had been out at his weekly meeting of the local
chess club and when he returned there were no strange cars
at the kerb, no lights on, or off, that shouldn't be, to warn
him. Consequently, when he opened the front door he failed
to notice that the door to the living-room, which he had left
closed, was ajar. He had turned to put the chain up for the
night, and been felled by a blow to the base of the neck.

The front room was barely touched, except that the
drawers of the desk had been torn out and the contents lay
spread on the settee, spilling on to the floor. In the back room
and the kitchen there were signs of a rudimentary search; it
was upstairs that the intruder had really got to work. In the
small front bedroom, which had been used as a study, it was
impossible to get in the doorway without treading on books
and papers, discarded box files and folders.

'He'd been up in the roof, too,' Robertson offered, gesturing into the bathroom, where the rooftrap sagged open and a pair of steps still lay canted on one leg where they had been pushed aside in a hasty exit.

Alec looked about him, then back at Robertson. He wanted to ask about the bonsai plants: where were they? Instead, he said, 'What was the weapon?'

'The famous blunt instrument used with a considerable amount of force. The intruder either intended to kill, or didn't care if he did. Or perhaps has not had much practice,' Robertson added with a humourless giggle.

And how far do you stretch coincidence, Alec asked himself. It was plain this hadn't been a normal robbery; valuable, portable items had not been taken, and the destruction, though superficially bad enough, had none of the nauseating malignance with which the burglar so often ruins what he cannot be bothered to take.

No, this intruder hadn't been looking for jewellery; not stereos and televisions: he'd left the valuables alone but he'd searched every folder, every pile of books and papers, every file of income tax returns, every letter and photograph album.

Alec looked up to find Robertson was still watching him shrewdly out of those absurd clown's features.

'I think,' Alec said slowly, 'your case and mine are one and the same. I think I can tell you what your man was looking for. What I can't tell you is whether he found it.'

Colin Napier was beyond giving any information: conscious, now, but in a poor way, unable to string words together, unable to recall more than setting out for his meeting the night before. Thus it was in an unsatisfactory frame of mind that Alec climbed into his car and drove from the hospital back to the house that afternoon to take his leave of Robertson.

He had done his best before he went to the hospital to follow the intruder's footsteps, meticulously hunting through every file, every bundle of papers, but the papers all related to the house, to Colin Napier's job as a teacher, to his work for the local constituency party, the accounts of the chess club, his pension, his car insurance. There was nothing to link Andrew Hunter to old Paul Napier who had died aged eighty, and who had once been Intelligence Officer at RAF Hartfield Park in the distant days of war. Yet the two men had met, that very spring. Hunter's diary was witness.

Come to think of it, he pondered, as he sat in the car outside the house, there had been nothing of old Mr Napier's in the house at all. For a man who had been dead barely three weeks, he seemed to have left remarkably little of the usual personal litter behind him. It wasn't just those damned bonsai trees which were missing. No pension book, no bank statements, no . . .

He climbed out of the car again and walked up the path. The front door was still ajar and Grimes, the taciturn sergeant, was standing suspiciously over a civilian from the forensic lab who was trying to collect fingerprints.

The sergeant looked up uninterestedly as Alec reappeared.

'When is the rubbish collected?'

Blank stare.

'Come on, man! When are the bins emptied? When is the rubbish collected?'

The forensic expert glanced up from his work. 'Wednesday, isn't it?'

It didn't take much finding: down by the side of the garage, a big black plastic dustbin on wheels. The top was not quite down, cocked up at an angle.

Alec lifted it up, and saw the reason.

The bin was full to overflowing with papers.

Today was a Wednesday. Another hour; another five minutes, even, would have been too late, for already there was a man walking purposefully up the drive towards him, and the rumble of bins being rolled out to the dustcart from the houses next door.

Alec met the man's eye and shook his head. 'Not this one,' he said. 'Police.' He showed his warrant card again; the man shrugged and walked away. Alec turned back to the black bin. 'I'll empty this one myself,' he said quietly.

'Of course, the thief may have found what he was looking for.'

'That possibility had not entirely escaped me,' Alec replied tartly. 'Just add these papers to that pile over there. Now: what have we?'

The contents of the black dustbin lay strewn over Nelson's desk, which had been cleared for the purpose. There may have been a superficial similarity to the contents of Andrew Hunter's study; but while Hunter's mountain of paper had been the meticulous result of a painstaking collection of data, this, Alec told himself resignedly, was the product of forty years of hoarding.

Or perhaps not, he corrected himself as he fingered a bundle of manuscript loosely tied together. Perhaps the old man had an idea that one day he would make of his memorabilia a book. Presumably he had overlooked the fact that his own chapter was drawing to its close. Paul Napier had left it too late, and death had overtaken him before he could add to the library of servicemen's reminiscences.

'There's nothing here that looks recent enough to matter,' Nelson observed despondently.

'Never mind! Look: who else is in? We'd do best to go through this lot fairly thoroughly.'

'Johnson's in; I sent Liz down to Hereford as you said, to catch Colin Napier as soon as he's able to talk.'

Johnson was fetched, and Alex explained how he wanted them to proceed. If the break-in at the Napiers' house was at all linked to the death of Andrew Hunter then there had to have been some matter that was significant to both events: a shared secret, a common purpose, something that might be revealed in a letter, correspondence, a notebook.

On the other hand, thought Alec wryly, if the connection

was the simple fact that both men had an interest in Hartfield Park, then they were in for a few more deaths: five more, to be precise. But it wouldn't come to that. It couldn't.

Maybe, he thought, whatever the intruder had sought was something Napier had without realizing it; but the presumption had to be that either Hunter had shared some vital knowledge with Napier or—more likely—it was Napier who was, knowingly or otherwise, the source; and Hunter and Napier being dead, the killer had set out to destroy the final remaining evidence.

Alec brought up short. If any of this made sense, the murderer must known that he still had one other item of unfinished business. Anything Hunter had learned from Napier must presumably be embodied somewhere in his research notes. Maybe Alec had already read it, passing casually over some brief cryptic reference without picking up its significance. The killer, then, would only be safe once those notes too were destroyed, surely.

The notes were safely back in the filing cabinet by the wall, and Alec's glance rested on it thoughtfully. But did the killer know that? Or did he think they had been left with Dr Walker?

He became aware that Nelson was addressing him; had been trying to gain his attention.

'Right,' he said forcefully, 'there doesn't seem to be much order about these, so we'll divide them into three. You—' he pushed a third of the papers roughly towards Nelson— 'take those. Andy, you take this lot over to the chair there. That leaves me with these.' He pulled a third heap towards him. The manuscript he put separately, earmarking it as his reading matter for the evening.

'A lot of this is sheets of rough notes,' he continued. 'Probably notes for a book. Read them all. The letters too. Anything promising put to one side and I'll look at it too. By promising I mean . . .' But what he did mean was not immediately apparent, even to himself, while Nelson, weary from wading through a study full of notes in Nottingham, presumably needed no telling.

They got down to work. Paper crackled, fingernails scrabbled at string. At first Nelson and Johnson erred on the cautious side, discarding almost nothing, asking frequently for a second opinion. As the morning passed they all three became more ruthless, keeping little, discarding the rest into plastic bin-liners.

Much of this stuff, Alec realized, had nothing to do with the war at all; Paul Napier had simply been a hoarder. Yellowing newsprint recorded the Queen's coronation and the Suez crisis equally with VE day and the dropping of the atom bomb. Colin Napier's school reports were indiscriminately bundled alongside a collection of stiff-back log-books filled with terse abbreviations. These latter, after a moment's consideration, Alec set to one side. He would take Dr Walker's advice there, he fancied.

But most dishearteningly there was no record of any correspondence with Andrew Hunter; and no hint in what Alec read of any scandal or crime or decent motive for murder.

He sat back and considered, while Nelson and Johnson sifted through the dwindling piles of papers beside them. If he were wrong in his assumption that the burglary and the murder of Andrew Hunter were connected—well, that merely put them back at square one with the investigation. But was he wrong? Surely there was, had to be, a connection; if it was not to be found in these papers, why, they must look further, deeper.

But in the meantime he must be sure not to neglect the other possibilities. And that meant, first and foremost, James Parker and his missing shotgun.

The Superintendent listened in silence.

'These are old men,' was all he said at length when Alec had summed up the state of play.

'I know, sir. But by the same token, men of that age are

often prominent in their way; in business, or in their local communities. Because they are merely visitors here, it's easy to forget that they might be important people where they come from. People who would not take kindly to having past scandals raked up. How do we know what else might be at stake?'

'You are suggesting, I take it, that one of them took—or created—the opportunity of the reunion trip to England in order to deal on the spot with Hunter and something Hunter had ferreted out.'

'I'm not going as far as that, sir,' Alec replied cautiously. 'I only wanted to give you a reasonable idea of the possibilities as they seem to me at the moment. I've two of these veterans to see tomorrow, Janssen and Phillips. Maybe I'll be a little clearer after that.'

'Your case would be a good deal stronger if we established for sure that Napier and Hunter had been in contact before their respective deaths.'

'We know Hunter at least planned to call on Napier, sir. I'm hoping to get more details from Colin Napier when he's in a condition to give them.'

'And also,' Blackett went on, 'if we could establish how the killer is supposed to have got wind of all this. Is Hunter supposed to have written to tip him off? To ask his permission to include this hypothetical material in his book?'

'I don't know the answer to that one. The supposition is that he received one of Andrew Hunter's letters asking for information, and panicked at what he thought Hunter was going to uncover.'

The Superintendent rumbled his dissatisfaction with the vagueness of it all. 'This hypothetical secret,' he suggested at length. 'D'you think Hunter would have made an attempt to turn it to account of another sort? Into hard cash, to be blunt?'

Alec chewed his lip doubtfully. The possibility had occurred to him; but it was piling speculation on speculation when they simply had not the information to help them one way or another.

Blackett shrugged. 'OK. I'm prepared to leave it to you. I'm glad you're not thinking of neglecting Parker, though. He seems to me much your best bet; far likelier than our South African friends.'

Alec headed for home in thoughtful frame of mind.

CHAPTER 14

That evening the telephone went or the doorbell rang every time Alec managed to get himself settled with Paul Napier's manuscript in his lap. Routine calls. An invitation; a friend passing on a new address; an insistent seller of fitted kitchens; the new edition of the church magazine at the door and yes, it was the month for renewing subscriptions; comes round quicker every year, doesn't it?

By eleven-fifteen the evening seemed to have evaporated, leaving not a trace behind, and the manuscript still stared reproachfully up from the table by the sofa. Alec sipped the last of his drink and stared back at it.

Other men's wars are like other men's loves, he mused. The fascination is in the intimacy, the glimpses of self-revelation. The mere chronicling of events, on the other hand, doesn't really hold much interest unless the chronicler —lover or soldier— is one who holds principalities and powers in his hand.

If the origin of Hunter's murder lay at Hartfield Park those nearly fifty years ago it must have the domesticity of private tragedy. The serious business of war was too impersonal to provide a reason for murder. Murder happened because people were cheated of their money or their girl spurned them or they couldn't abide the habits of those they lived with. But for none of those reasons, surely, would one wait forty-five years to pull the trigger. Yet whenever

Alec determined to quit Hartfield Park and seek the solution
to the mystery elsewhere something compelling pulled him
back. It wasn't just the place where Andrew Hunter's body
had been found; not just the place where he had been killed,
or the focus of his research. It wasn't merely the backcloth
to his murder: it was the very reason for it. The killing had
had its genesis there, in that windswept field where so much
killing had been initiated, and from which so many men set
out to their deaths.

That, Alec reproved himself severely, was a hunch; and
hunches must not through laziness be substituted for hard
work. He glanced at his watch. Half past eleven. There was
still time to begin. He poured himself another drink and, in
the silent flat, sat down to read back into the past.

Fifteen miles away old Mrs Parker sat, too, in a silent house,
alone with her memories. The television was mute. James
and Diana had gone up to bed. Time was, she thought,
when there would have been muffled giggles and faint
scuffles from the floor above, and the regular, faint rhythm
of a bed creaking. Now, a few footsteps, a lavatory flushing
once, and again, and then the old house was silent. We are
barren, she thought. Sterile. We have lost the facility of
love.

Sitting alone in the dimly lit room, Mrs Parker sighed,
and remembered. It hadn't always been so.

Standing at the sink in the farm kitchen you could look out
across the stack-yard, past the milking parlour and the
hen-run, to the ribbon of the perimeter track and half a mile
or so of the runway.

You imagined it had always been there. You imagined
there had never been ill-drained fields divided by hedges,
and coppices, and the pair of half-timbered farm cottages
that once, they said, had been the farmhouse, before this
one was even thought of. There had been nine months of
unbelievable rape, three or four years ago, when every day

saw a new landmark removed, a valley filled, a rise scraped
flat. The cottages had gone without her even realizing; she
left one morning to pick up a package from the station and
when she returned they had never been.

Now the airfield was there as if from time immemorial.
And one thing was for sure, she thought realistically,
whether the war was coming to an end or not, the airfield
would be there for a good while yet; perhaps for ever.

You could see a little; but you could not see the adminis-
trative blocks, or the hangars. So you couldn't see whether
Doug was on his way. But with Doug, she thought happily,
if he said he'd come, then he'd come, unless the war got in
the way; and you couldn't argue with that, could you? All
the same, it would be nice to have a bit of warning; she
hated him to find her slaving at the sink, or coming from
the hens in her pinafore and boots. A cloddish country girl,
that's what he must think her, when he found her like that;
but what could you do, with men to be fed and eggs to be
gathered?

She glanced at the clock, and reaching a decision, untied
the apron and lifted it over her head, instinctively patting
her hair into shape in the mirror. Doug told her she was
beautiful; men did, of course, especially in wartime when
so much living had to be crammed into so short a time; but
she knew herself to be too squarely built to be fashionable,
and trousers, which were more practical around the farm,
only made things worse. The cheap mirror threw back
tauntingly her familiar, too-pink face and the fair hair which
curled naturally, and straggled naturally too, and she knew
if she looked down she would see her hands rough and
swollen from the suds . . .

Only sometimes, when there was a dance in the village
hall, or when someone had taken her up to town for dinner
and they danced on some tiny, jammed dance-floor before
hurrying back through the blackout to catch the last train,
did she feel that in her evening frock and with her hair
back like Rita Hayworth's men were noticing her with

appreciation. The rest of the time, just another farmer's daughter with wind-roughened cheeks, she told herself ruefully.

She was still standing thoughtfully at the mirror when she heard Doug's step in the yard and turned to meet him and exchange that first greedy, wonderful kiss.

The orchard was a little way from the house, and sheltered by the big barn from the yard and the house windows. She and Doug had come here increasingly frequently as the summer months passed to sit with their backs against one of the old damson trees and snatch an hour from the rush of the farm or the station. Now their feet almost found their own way there, brushing the grassheads, spraying tiny showers of pollen which clung golden to her bare legs and Doug's uniform.

'I won't be coming tonight,' he said.

She nodded, and took the cigarette he passed her. He never told her in so many words that he was flying; it was shared superstition, that if he didn't tell her, fate would not be tempted, and he would return. She knew, because of what the others said and what her parents had picked up, that the Mosquitoes ventured deep into Germany, and even to Poland and Czechoslovakia, on intruder missions to shoot up trains and convoys, and to catch unwary enemy planes as they landed home at their bases. Something of the confidence the crews felt in the fast and agile Mosquitoes had conveyed itself to her; and also some of the relentless tension of those great flights so far into enemy territory.

She knew her parents resented Doug; resented him as part of the war which had stolen their land and robbed them of their son who, embarrassed and frustrated by the reserved status of a farmer, had manœuvred himself into the forces, and was now in France with the Guards Armoured Brigade.

They resented Doug too as a foreigner. True, he was not a black man or a lachrymose Pole or a drunken Australian; but an alien none the less, one of those with whom the war had flooded their country and their pubs and their newspaper. Doug's people farmed too, it seemed; but that was no affinity: their many-thousand-acre cattle lot was as remote in spirit from this business of paddling for a living in the Medway clay as it was distant in miles.

Guilt at betraying her parents was inseparable from her love for Doug; it grieved her bitterly that she could not please her parents in the placing of her affections; but there was a realistic, determined streak in her which she had inherited from them, and there was never any question of sending Doug away for their sakes. She had only one life; might not even have that if a doodlebug fell on the farm; and Doug might only have today . . .

He never, as so many men in uniform did, regarded the uncertainty of his life as a passport to her body. Almost, she regretted his delicacy in that respect. More than one khakied youth, in the long years between Dunkirk and Normandy, had tried to persuade her to make a personal contribution to the war effort and to the morale of the fighting men; she had sent them back to their training camps derisorily, and not felt guilty, for there were plenty of girls, she knew, positively eager to hear the same words and act on them. And how, anyway, was looking up at the starlight past an army haircut going to speed the defeat of Nazidom?

No, Doug was a man . . . there was no doubt about that; but a man could be virile, and gentle too; and that was the wonder of it.

She stubbed her cigarette out. 'Listen for us about three,' Doug remarked. 'We'll be going up for a couple of circuits. Assuming Babe comes back in one piece from the Dorset Arms.'

'You worry about him too much.'

'He's so young.' He smiled briefly, wryly. 'They all are.'

'Babe's problem is just that he looks it, and the others don't,' she retorted tartly. 'And the others lead him on. Especially Kenny.'

He put an arm round Joan's shoulders and leant back

comfortably in the silky grass. 'You're not very fond of Kenny.'

'Not much.' It was more than that. His heartiness and self-centredness repelled her beside Doug's quiet competence, or the more modest good spirits of the others, Bill and Dicky, say. But it wasn't just that; in some way she couldn't fathom, she was afraid of him. Afraid that sometimes beneath that high-spirited arrogance she could glimpse a real cruelty; an evil. 'He smiles too much,' she said at last; 'and boasts too much.'

'Takes all sorts,' Doug murmured, and his eyes closed and he relaxed, his head in her lap.

Later, he roused himself and sat up, brushing the hair back from his forehead and turning to look down at her.

'Time I was getting back.' He reached over to fasten the buttons of her blouse and she saw that the laziness was gone from his eyes, replaced by the preoccupation which she always saw there before an operation, and never let him know she had seen.

'It's only a quarter past two,' she protested.

'Yep. Time I was over at dispersal seeing how Bert's getting on with that mag.'

'Do you know all your ground crew by name?' she asked idly.

He flicked a smile. 'Uh-huh.' Then he stood up, dismissing further questions. 'Come on.' He reached down and helped her to her feet, and they clung briefly.

'Think of me, sewing a patch on Dad's corduroys,' she said lightly, as they crossed the orchard towards the gate into the lane. And I'll be thinking of you, she thought; listening to the planes take off at dusk; travelling with you the long evening, listening even in my sleep for your return.

'I'll think of you sewing a patch on mine in twenty years' time when I'm your father's age. You'll see how crabby a farmer can get then, I'll tell you!'

'You're on,' she said cheerfully, and they turned into the

lane, and began chatting lightly about the success of the squadron's cricket team.

At the yard gate they parted.

But all that, old Mrs Parker mused, contemplating almost in disbelief the arthritic fingers which lay painfully in her lap, was a long time ago. In another country. And besides, the wench is dead.

CHAPTER 15

A hundred and fifty miles away Colin Napier, more than half insensible from the combined effects of the attack and of the drugs which had been given to him since, had a dim sense of figures looming over him. Faces came into his vague vision and grew monstrously, stared into his eyes, then receded into the fog at the foot of the bed. Girls talked cheerfully, meaninglessly, as they pulled bedclothes briskly off him or tugged them briskly back again. Once or twice shadowy, sober parties took place around his bed, one voice holding forth and others supplying muffled counterpoint.

All the time he had a sense that there was one figure that stayed; just out of vision, but always there. At first it had been a threatening figure in its silent immobility, but with time it grew to be a comfortable presence, a steady reassurance of continuity: that there had been a past, and was a present, and would be a future.

Liz Pink watched the immobile figure from time to time, meanwhile leafing through endless copies of magazines from the day lounge: *Cosmopolitan* and *Woman's Weekly,* and then *Motor* and *Which?,* and eventually *Practical Householder* and *Model Railways,* till she thought she would yell if she saw another article on fitted kitchens or zippy family hatchbacks.

When Colin Napier began to stir, and his eyes to open

and try to focus, Liz put her magazine down thankfully. Perhaps now it would not be long. Nurses bustled about, or gathered in their cubicle at the end of the ward for a cup of tea. Soon one came over and gave Colin Napier a quick, appraising scrutiny.

Shortly a doctor came through and eyed Napier shrewdly.

He turned to Liz. 'He'll be a lot brighter in an hour or two. When the stuff we gave him this morning's worn off he'll be able to talk pretty rationally. Whether he'll remember much I couldn't say. How much time do you need with him?'

She thought quickly: better not to demand too much too soon. 'Half an hour should do it,' she guessed. 'But I may have to come back later.'

'Right. I suggest you go off now and get yourself something to eat. If you come back about three you can have half an hour. I'll look in about three-fifteen to see how he's taking it.' He smiled briefly, a human character infusing for a moment the rather tired mask of competence.

'OK,' she replied. 'And thanks.'

Bill Janssen was not much changed from the man he had been forty-five years earlier. Outwardly, true, time had played its usual tricks; though even here, with a light touch: Janssen was one of those men in whom, in certain expressions or by certain lights, the schoolboy they once were is visible.

So far as temperament went, the man probably hadn't changed much either, Alec judged. An average person. Averagely intelligent, averagely reliable. In short, Alec concluded, middle-of-the-road. *L'homme moyen sensuel*, perhaps, and *moyen* everything else, too. And yet this, with the possible exception of Kenneth Taylor, who had had some political success, was out of all of them the one who had achieved most: successful businessman, company director, with the ear of a man like Carl Stocker who really was a power in the land. A tycoon, he supposed, one would have to call him; yet here, out of his own country, just another tourist, an old man who had once fought in a war.

The woman with him, whom Janssen was quick to introduce as his wife, was more obviously interesting. Alison Janssen was much of her husband's age, mellowed from an unremarkable beauty to a remarkable grace, and there was something of English harmony beneath the South African melodies of her voice. Had Alec been in a position to compare the Alison he saw now with the young WAAF who had once driven the aircrew truck at Hartfield Park he would have thought the years had only added to her attractiveness.

'If you'd rather I waited outside while you spoke with Bill, I don't mind,' she volunteered.

'Well . . .' It was scarcely polite, but then police work often wasn't. 'Perhaps if you would. I shan't keep your husband long.' She nodded and left them and Alec, holding the door open, called to the WPC to ensure Mrs Janssen was offered tea.

'D'you want to know where we were when this guy Hunter was killed, is that it?' Janssen asked directly.

'Yes,' Alec said simply. 'And a few other things, too. I don't want to tell you just when we think Mr Hunter died, but I'd be grateful if you would tell me something of your itinerary before and after the reunion weekend. Will you do that?'

'No problem.'

As Bill Janssen talked, Alec began to cross him off the list of suspects. It wasn't just that the agenda of his stay in England was so logical and easy to verify: it was the man himself, speaking without anxiety or evasiveness. There was only one matter which required more going into, and even that no doubt would be easily resolved. The Janssens had stayed the first couple of days after their arrival, the days before the reunion gathering, with Alison's sister and brother-in-law in Edenbridge; not ten miles from Hartfield Park.

'How did you pass the time?'

'Mostly days out with Mollie and Jim. It was good weather —for England. Alison had a list of places she wanted to see. She likes South Africa. Just as well. But she's English; I guess you could tell that by the way she talks, even after all these years; and there's nothing like the place you grew up in, is there?'

'And did you go to Hartfield Park?'

Janssen shifted in his chair, looking shamefaced, as if nostalgia were a secret vice. 'Well, we did. Ali was stationed there too, you know. She wanted to . . . and it was so close, after all. Anyway, we had a quick look one day on our way in to Tunbridge Wells shopping.'

'What day would that be?'

'Oh, well . . . Wednesday, maybe. Ali would remember.'

'Can you at least recall what time of day it was?'

Janssen shrugged. 'Half ten? Eleven? I seem to recall we were in Tunbridge Wells for lunch.'

'Tell me, did Andrew Hunter ever get in contact; about the book he was researching?'

Janssen shook his head. 'Not with me. Of course, he would have been speaking at our reunion. Anything he wanted to know he could have asked then.'

'Yes,' Alec agreed. 'Yes, I suppose he could. And when you and your wife visited Hartfield again the other day, you didn't see anyone?'

'Not a thing. Ask Alison. Silent as the grave.'

'Yes,' said Alec heavily. 'Just so.'

'Good of you to spare the time, Mr Phillips.'

'Happy to help if I can. Sad business.' Phillip's accent was harder, more alien, than Dixon's had been, and less assured than Janssen's. He was on the small side, his hair thinnish but dark still—though perhaps that owed more to the medicine cabinet than to nature. He was, Alec already knew, retired; had held some post in the coils of the civil service. And forty-five years ago had flown from Hartfield

Park as navigator to Kenneth Taylor. Now he was waiting warily for Alec's next step.

'The reason I've asked you to call,' Alec said, 'and I shall be asking the rest of your party too, is in case the man whose death we're investigating, Andrew Hunter, gave any indication in correspondence with any of you that he was in any bother, or personal difficulties, or felt threatened in any way.' No need to tell Phillips they were each of them suspects for the killing; if he couldn't work that out for himself he must be very innocent—or very stupid.

'He didn't let on anything of that sort to me,' Phillips replied easily. 'Of course, I never met him; only got that one letter from him, and wrote one back.'

'You did get a letter, then? That would be asking for any reminiscences you had of your time in England during the war, I imagine.' Alec slipped the copy of the letter Nelson had found in Hunter's study from the file and swivelled it round so that Phillips could read it.

'Aye; that's the one.'

'When would you have received it?'

'Maybe . . . April; about then. I gave him one or two bits and pieces.'

'What was his angle?' Alec asked. 'He was hoping to publish a book, I believe. Was he after particular items of information? Or just what one might call general detail?'

'He wanted photos,' Phillips replied briefly. 'That's really what he was after. Plus copies of my log-book, if I still had it.'

'Have you?'

'No.'

'Go on, if you would.'

'That's it. I thought the guy had some nerve, as a matter of fact, writing to ask me to supply gratis the means for him to publish a book. I didn't waste much paper writing back.'

'I wonder how you look on those years?' Alec made his voice sympathetic, unemphatic. 'Probably as ancient history.'

'So I do. There's a lot of cods talked about the war being the best years of our lives. Just thank whoever you do thank that you were too young to be in it.' Phillips's voice was hard.

'Yet,' Alec reminded him gently, 'you are here. Taking part in a reunion; men who fought for—' what did South Africans fight for? He had been going to say, for King and Country. It might even have been true. 'For their country's freedom.'

'I'm here taking advantage of the best damned deal anyone's screwed out of SAA for many a year,' Phillips retorted. 'For that I can put up with the company of a lot of tedious old fogeys reliving their days of glory.'

Alec smiled faintly. 'And how have you been spending the time? Since the reunion weekend, I mean?'

'Sightseeing. Oxford, Bath, Stratford-on-Avon, the Cotswolds,' he reeled off.

'Hire a car?'

'Yep. I intend to get my money's worth out of it, too, I can tell you.' Alec made a mental note that South Africans seemed to be hot on value for money.

'And before the reunion? But you didn't have long, of course; only a day or two.'

'Yeah. I stuck around London the first couple of days. That was Tuesday and Wednesday. Tower of London, Westminster Abbey, all that crap.'

Alex winced. Never mind that it must be twenty years since he had last visited any of 'that crap' himself; there were times when tourists, of any nationality, were hateful. 'You did all that by bus and tube, I expect. A car's not much use in central London, as you'll have seen.'

Phillips shook his head. 'I had the car from the start. Fixed it up before I left South Africa. The other guys mostly did the same, then it was there at the airport and there was no being rooked by cab-drivers.'

'And,' Alec said, 'the Thursday. The day before the reunion proper.'

Phillips met his eye defiantly. He knew, as well as Alec
did, what was behind the question, though the date of
Hunter's death had not been given to the press, only the
date of the discovery of the body. 'Spent the day in Canter-
bury,' he said.

Alec looked at him impassively. 'The whole day,' he said,
in a tone that suggested he thought it a lie.

Phillips looked down at his lap, picking at a fingernail.
Alec said, 'I think you went to Hartfield Park too.'

There was a lengthy silence. 'Yes,' Phillips admitted
finally.

'When?'

'On the way back. Maybe half past four, five o'clock.'

'Thursday afternoon.'

Another pause. 'Yes.'

'For how long?'

'I reckon I was there an hour or so, poking about. It was
sort of different, though, so I didn't want to stay that long
when it came to it. The same—but different. Rather eerie,
to tell the truth.'

'Did you see anyone there? Most of it's farmland, of
course,' Alec said casually.

'Not a soul. Wherever the owner was, he wasn't visible
to me. Is it still the same people over at the farm? Well, I
reckon you wouldn't know. In our day it was some people
called Parker.' Phillips sighed, a long, sad exhalation.
'Young Joanie Parker, she was a nice girl. There was a bloke
called—' his face clouded, as if he found the memory elusive
—'McAllister. That's it. Doug McAllister. He and Joan . . .
but he was killed, of course, and she took up with someone
else for a bit, and then it sort of fizzled out. Losing McAllister
hit her pretty hard, poor kid.'

The reminiscences came haltingly, like long-pent grief,
and Alec was content to take all that was offered and make
his own analysis in due course. Besides, something Phillips
had said had sparked off a train of thought. Phillips was
staring at him still, sightlessly, his gaze fixed on the events

of that long-dead summer when he and Bill Janssen and Kenny and Dicky Dixon and Joan Parker had all been barely out of their adolescence, and when Doug McAllister had been alive.

Alec asked, 'Who was it Joan took up with? After the death of her boy?'

Phillips's eyes refocused as he considered the question. 'Oh ... Kenny Taylor. My pilot. Have you spoken to Kenny? He was Jack the Lad in those days. We all thought we were, I suppose.' He rubbed his chin thoughtfully. 'Except Doug. You know, it must be thirty years since I've thought of Doug. I had to stop and think, back then, to even remember his name. He was the opposite of Kenny in every way. Doug was good for Joanie; they were right for each other. Kenny couldn't have been more wrong.'

'McAllister never survived his tour?' Alec commented.

Phillips shook his head. The little room seemed stuffy with the memory of those dead years. 'No. They never came back from a trip to Rügen. Him and Babe. Babe Binney, his navigator. The best navigator in the squadron.'

That left the four of them, out of Andrew Hunter's list: Taylor and Phillips, Janssen and Dicky Dixon; and the fifth man, Smith, who had flown with the Typhoon squadron and gone with them to France that fateful summer.

Alec thought a moment. 'Does the name Napier mean anything to you? Paul Napier?'

'There was a guy called Napier who was our IO at Hartfield Park. He must be dead years ago. He was pretty old.'

'He was not quite thirty-five then,' Alec said drily.

Phillips looked shamefaced. 'I guess so. Makes you think, doesn't it?'

It certainly did.

Alec stood up. 'Thanks for your time, Mr Phillips. One last question.' He hesitated, and then committed himself. 'Did anything happen at Hartfield Park all those years ago, anything at all, which someone could possibly be so afraid of having made public that they would kill to prevent it?'

Phillips looked at him evenly. Forty-five years ago. What good could it possibly do now to recall old bitternesses?

'No,' he said steadily. 'Not a thing.'

CHAPTER 16

'So that's it, sir.' Liz Pink, weary and dark-eyed after her vigil and the long drive back, was clearly depressed at having no more useful news to report. 'Colin Napier was only interested in getting shot of everything: papers, bonsai trees, the lot. He was sick of it all. I'd say Mr Napier senior had not been easy to live with, what with his plants and his physical infirmities and his old man's ramblings about what he did in the war, Daddy.'

'Do you think he knew of Hunter's interest in the papers?'

'Probably. He says Hunter came to see his father back in May. But from Colin's point of view the only result of that was to revive his father's fantasies about writing a book. I don't think he thought of old Mr Napier's stuff as having real interest for a serious historian—didn't even realize that that's what Hunter was. Nor did he think it could be turned into cash. Otherwise he'd never have thrown it out. No, so far as he was concerned it was just so much waste paper. I did ask whether it was likely his father would have let Hunter take anything away, or make copies. He says not.'

'Paul Napier'd want to keep it for himself, of course. Especially if there really was anything controversial or new in it. I wonder,' Alec mused, 'whether Hunter had somehow sniffed it out despite the old man's secretiveness? Although it's difficult to see what could be new in the diaries of a mere Intelligence Officer forty years ago. Colin Napier didn't think of getting in touch with Hunter after his father's death, to pass the papers on to him?'

Liz smiled sourly. 'He says that the news in the paper of

Hunter's death scotched the idea, but reading between the lines I don't think he'd have bothered anyway. You mentioned the bonsai trees, sir. I found what was left of them among a heap of ashes at the bottom of the garden. Colin's reaction to his father's death was to get rid of every trace of him. Clothes to Oxfam, odds and ends to the jumble, papers to the dustbin. And the precious bonsai trees on the bonfire.'

Alec smiled rueful agreement. 'You've done well. It doesn't seem to get us terribly further forward, but don't get dejected about that. Even negative information's useful.'

Liz smiled dutifully.

'Tell me, if you had to pick from the bunch we're dealing with so far someone who would be vulnerable to scandal, who would it be?'

'It's tricky, sir,' Nelson, who had been listening silently so far, temporized. 'We don't know much about any of the South Africans. Parker, on the other hand, patently has *something* to hide.'

'Mm,' Alec agreed reluctantly. The trouble was, you never did know what anyone feared most. One person might laugh off a hint of sexual scandal which to another would be deadly; another might be felled by a suspicion of fraud. There were, he told himself, three sources of information about this assumed piece of past scandal. There was Hunter's research. There were Napier's notes. And there were half a dozen men and—he remembered Alison Janssen, and the two Parkers—women who no doubt for the sake of personal interest or consideration for their friends would lie like troopers if it suited them.

'All right, Liz. And thank you. I think it's time we had another word with James Parker.'

'If,' Nelson remarked as they drove out towards Hartfield, 'Phillips is telling the truth about his visit to the airfield on the Thursday, then it gives us a help on timing, doesn't it? I mean, we know Hunter was on the road from the village to Hartfield Park sometime after two. By four-thirty Phillips arrives at the airfield and there is no one to be seen. So Hunter was, by inference, already dead and lying hidden by the barley.'

'Mm. Would you put Parker down as a clever man? No, that's not quite the right question. This business with the shotgun, though. It's childish! Did he think we were to be deceived by him handing over some rusty old relic?'

'People frequently do think we are to be deceived, sir,' Nelson observed with unaccustomed dryness.

The interview with Parker was unsatisfactory. He was evasive when they asked him about the shotgun, at first clinging to the fiction that the two guns he had handed in were the only ones he possessed.

Alec gazed at him, disappointed. 'Perhaps we could look in your gun-cupboard again; or have you taken the precaution of removing the box of twelve-bore cartridges, mm?'

Parker looked crestfallen. 'They were old ones,' he muttered. 'I threw them out. It's dangerous, keeping old cartridges lying around.'

'Give it up,' Alec exclaimed wearily. 'You're fooling no one, Mr Parker. Do you think we aren't going to get to the bottom of this? Do you think we're tamely going to give up and go away and stop bothering you? You handed in two guns. One was a four-ten: irrelevant. The other was a rusty old twelve-bore that was probably last used in the Home Guard. Did you really think we would be satisfied with that? So where is your own twelve-bore; the one you keep the cartridges for? We'll know eventually. If I were you, I would make sure it was you that told us!'

Parker ran his fingers through his hair. His hands were the large, weatherbeaten implements of a farmer. Alec wondered whether Diana Parker shrank to receive the caress of such hands.

'I did have a twelve-bore,' he muttered. 'But I sold it. To a chap in Groombridge.'

Even now, Alec thought, Parker was an uninventive liar.

If he had said Crawley, now, with its large and anony-
mous population, or even East Grinstead! 'We'll check
the licences, then,' Nelson said. 'Should be an easy job
to track him down. He showed you his shotgun licence, of
course?'

'I . . . I don't recall.'

Nelson raised his eyebrows. 'Rather careless of you, sir.
That's the sort of thing that doesn't do your chances of
getting your own licence renewed any good. I suppose,' he
added with heavy irony, 'you didn't get a receipt, either?'

'No; no, I didn't. He paid me cash; it . . . it was the sort
of transaction where the paperwork rather gets forgotten.'

'Obviously.' Nelson glanced at Alec for instructions.
Alec's problem lay in deciding not whether Parker was
lying, but why. The fairy story about selling the gun would
stall them only for as long as it took to check it and prove
it false; to achieve that short respite Parker had confessed
to a misdemeanour, giving them an excuse—not a wonderful one, but it would do—to take him in for formal questioning. Was Parker subtle enough even to see what he had
done? Possibly.

He looked at Parker speculatively, pondering the nature
of his game. Were they really on the right track; or had they
stumbled on some other, private shame of Parker's which
led him to these transparent lies?

One thing was still unshaken, after all: Parker had the
best opportunity of anyone to kill Andrew Hunter; and if
they were right, he had had the means, too, in his vanished
shotgun.

But it was more than Alec could manage to fathom any
conceivable motive.

'Do you really think Parker killed Hunter?' Nelson asked
dubiously as they drove back to East Grinstead.

Do I? Alec asked himself dejectedly. But, he told himself,
I'd still like to know where that shotgun is.

When no answer was forthcoming to his question, Nelson
asked, 'So what's the next step, sir?'

'The next step, which is long overdue, is for us to have a little chat with Kenneth Taylor, Esquire.'

In the case of Kenneth Taylor, Alec mused, watching him as he settled in his chair, it was not so much a matter of glimpsing in the man the child he had once been, as having the sense of seeing now what the child, the young man, the middle-aged man, had foreshadowed.

He must have been handsome in his youth; still was, in a sleek-greying-hair, RAF-tie-and-moustache sort of way; but the effect of the years had been to crack the veneer of self-assurance and reveal the insecurity beneath. The aggressive stare had something of fear in it, and the lines in his face were not those of laughter, nor of character, nor even of meanness, but of anxiety. Not, Alec concluded, a man to trust overmuch; anything where his own interests were involved would certainly bear checking. He was a politician, of course, of a very minor sort, in his own country, and minor politicians, Alec thought cynically, were much the same wherever one met them.

'Good of you to come,' Alec began: an opening ranging shot, which might or might not provoke the opposition to react in such a way as to reveal their defences.

'One wants to do what one can.' Taylor's manner tried for that of the man of business who can just—glancing at his Rolex—spare you five minutes if you don't mind coming straight to the point, but there was unease in his eyes amounting almost to agony, which belied the pompous words.

'I'm sorry to break into your sightseeing. I hope you're enjoying your stay. I suppose you've seen from the newspapers that Andrew Hunter, who was supposed to have addressed your reunion in London, was found murdered a couple of days later. It's my job to find his murderer, and,' Alec added quietly, 'I intend to do so.'

'What has that to do with me?' Taylor asked tautly. 'I mean,' he corrected himself, 'of course, if I can be of any help—only too happy. But I don't quite see . . .'

'I'll be speaking to all those who attended your reunion before they go back to South Africa,' Alec said. 'At the moment, though, I'm especially interested in those who served at an airfield called Hartfield Park in 1944.' He caught Taylor's eye and held it. 'That's where we found Andrew Hunter's body.' He paused, then added, 'You flew from there, Mr Taylor, I understand.'

'It's a long time ago,' Taylor replied steadily. 'Not something to rake over. There was no great virtue in what we did. But we're old men now. Occasionally we get together to relive our days as heroes.'

'Were you a hero, Mr Taylor? I see you won the DFC.'

'They handed them out with the rations. Had to give the right proportion to the colonials to keep them happy; I was just next in line,' he explained. The throwaway modesty was a little pat for Alec's liking.

'So you have one memento, at least, of those days. What decided you to come over for the reunion?'

'I reckon there won't be another one! Chance to see the old country for one last time, too, I suppose.'

'How do you fill your time in South Africa? Retired?'

'Good Lord, no! At least, I suppose in a manner of speaking . . . I ran a modest little business; heavy machinery, earthmoving, that sort of thing. I gave it up five years since, when I got elected to the Assembly.' A certain complacency radiating from Taylor as he referred to the matter suggested that five years had not dulled the keenness of his self-satisfaction; and yet Alec had the queer sensation that all Taylor's cockiness was merely the thinnest, most delicate of shells over some nameless terror.

'Right.' Alec leant forward. This fencing was getting nowhere. 'Look, Mr Taylor, I'm investigating a murder. I'm looking for a man—or woman—who could have killed Andrew Hunter. And not only could have, but would have.'

Taylor was still; his eyes met Alec's, but wouldn't quite stay.

Alec contemplated the elderly South African pensively.

'Andrew Hunter,' he said deliberately, 'was doing his best to find out everything he could about the South Africans who served at Hartfield Park, of whom you are one. I think he may have found out something that someone—I don't know who—couldn't risk getting out. What sort of something could that be, do you think?'

He leant forward, his arms flat on the desk. 'What did he find out about you, Mr Taylor?' he asked softly.

Taylor looked back at him. 'He didn't find anything about me,' he replied. 'My conscience is clear.'

But his eyes told a different story.

CHAPTER 17

Alec Stainton's grey Bristol skimmed insect-like across the expanse of concrete and parked by the control tower. Fifteen minutes later, another car arrived.

Alec waited for the Scene of Crime officer to switch off and climb out. 'Thanks for coming.'

Fletcher grunted. 'OK.' He glanced up at the tower, grey and weather-stained. The low sun struck blood-red on the westward glass. 'Let's be about it, then.'

Fletcher selected one from a bunch of keys and fiddled with the shiny new padlock. 'What put you on to it?' he asked.

'The sunlight,' Alec replied apologetically. 'It was a bright day when Hunter's body was found; remember? I looked up at the tower when Ransome's car arrived and the sun was glinting on the glass. It was only afterwards I remembered there was a black circle which didn't glint.'

Fletcher grunted, and nodded. 'We gave it a more careful going-over this time,' he said, pushing the door open and looking round the big room. The air struck musty and dry, still. Forty years' emptiness and neglect was not to be so soon dissipated by a handful of policemen. 'I came over myself. The results were moderately interesting.'

Alec followed him in. The room was light, from the windows that surrounded it, though they were dusty with the years with the exception of the giveaway rough circle where someone had cleared a patch with their sleeve. A broad shelf ran along beneath the windows. In a corner a broken chair, one leg missing. There were light fittings, but they were cracked and cobwebbed and bulbless.

Alec moved over to the big front window and looked out. The effect of the extra height was dramatic, giving an overview of the airfield in which logic and design came to the fore; dispelling the sense of muddle which the ground-level perspective suggested, and simultaneously dispelling the years.

The mounds that had been visible in the distance formed themselves into evidence of Parker's half-hearted attempts to tear up the cross-runways; the length of the main runway was visible right to the far boundary. There was less view behind, to where the hangars and operational buildings had been grouped, but over beyond the perimeter track the huddle of the farm buildings was plainly in sight, though the angle prevented any glimpse of activity in the yard.

Alec turned back to the Scene of Crime officer. 'What did you find, then?'

'Some disturbance of dust on the floor. No identifiable shoe-prints—the dust's too powdery, it's dry in here.' He drew in his breath. 'Marks here . . . and here . . . where someone's leant on the shelf-thing.'

'With their palms?'

'With their knuckles, like this. In gloves. So no thumbprints.' He looked round the bare room assessingly. 'And something's been leant against the wall in the corner here. You can see where the bottom of it's stood.' He caught Alec's eye. 'I can't say for sure that it was a gun,' he warned, 'and there's no trace of oil.'

Alec moved back from the big windows until he was standing against the opposite wall. The main runway was visible still, and the more distant parts of the field; the farm was out of sight, and so too was the gateway from the perimeter track into the lane. He moved forward again to bring them into vision, and leant his weight on his knuckles on the shelf beneath the windows. 'Why lock it?' he asked himself quietly.

He turned to Fletcher. 'Why lock it? There's nothing in here to steal. Just to protect it from vandals, I suppose.' The padlock which had originally been on the door lay in its plastic bag on the corner of the shelf where Fletcher had placed it when they came in. Scratches of bright metal showed livid against the russet brown.

'Our guess is that they were made within two days either side of Hunter's death,' Fletcher said, following the direction of Alec's gaze.

Alec looked round, then went outside once more. The door stood in a corner of the balcony that ran round three sides of the tower, outside those big windows; and at the head of the narrow brick stairs.

'Have we got Parker's key to it?' he asked.

'This is it. I'd guess there was another one originally. Where it is now . . . We had a good look to see if this key made these marks. Probably not. Can't say for sure.'

Alec grunted, and descended the stairway slowly. The steps slanted down the side of the tower. He arrived at the foot, and a couple of paces took him clear of the corner.

A hundred yards directly in front of him four pegs still stood in the roughly-cleared stubble, unploughed here.

The pegs marked the place where Andrew Hunter's body had been found.

Alec turned to Nelson. 'OK. Go and fetch Parker.' He turned back to Fletcher. 'And there's no sign of a car being parked?'

The older man shook his head. 'None. You don't need me to tell you that that doesn't mean the murderer didn't come by car, only that we can't prove it.' He nodded towards the jumble of derelict huts and the heaps of old concrete and the tangles of bramble. 'Any of those could have hidden a car; or some gateway. If,' he added, 'there was a car and if someone felt they wanted to hide it.'

Alec grinned. 'If "a", then "b". But I'm not sure yet that "a" is true. What I do think is that Hunter was taken by surprise. That means that when he arrived at the airfield it appeared to be deserted. He would have wandered around looking for the man he had arranged to meet—or, assuming the other hypothesis and there was no appointment, then he wandered around looking at whatever he wanted to look at for the purposes of his book—and at some point Person X, who has been watching him the whole time, leaps out from behind a building. But instead of shouting "yoohoo" he comes brandishing a twelve-bore.'

Both men instinctively glanced up at the weather-scarred grey tower and the unseeing windows that gazed blankly out across the Sussex countryside, and the darker circle of glass.

'And Nelson has gone now to bring Person X across to confess?' Fletcher remarked.

'That,' responded Alec, 'is something I can't tell you. Yet.'

Over by the farmyard entrance a quarter of a mile away two midget figures emerged on to the airfield.

'Looks like you'll soon know,' Fletcher commented. 'I'll leave you to it.' He went across to his car and climbed in. The starter rasped, and the car swung round and headed away towards the gate. Alec stood on the bare concrete and watched the two figures grow steadily larger. Then he walked across to his car, took a sacking-covered bundle from the boot, and made his way back to the tower.

'Come on in, Mr Parker. It's your property, after all.'

Parker tightened his lips, and took a few paces into the room. His eyes flickered to the object in the corner, and then fixed themselves again on Alec, uneasy.

'Let me show you one or two interesting things, Mr Parker. Perhaps it's a novelty for you to be caught up in a police investigation. I hope it is. But it should be quite interesting, to a layman. Of course, it wouldn't be merely interesting if one was personally involved. Would it? A murder investigation's a serious thing.'

Parker said nothing, but the muscle at the base of his jaw twitched. Alec looked at him sharply, and continued.

'This room is quite a good example, as a matter of fact, of what can be deduced from seemingly unpromising material. First—' he hefted the padlock in his hand— 'this. Interesting how the padlock is scratched where some clumsy, or nervous, person has been inaccurate with the key. What would you deduce from that, Mr Parker?'

Parker said nothing, though his lips tightened still further and his eyes were those of a dog knowing a thrashing was coming and knowing, too, that he has deserved it.

'No? Well, perhaps it's an unfair question,' Alec conceded. 'I'll tell you what our people deduce from it. They deduce that someone has been in this control tower recently. Within the last three weeks. A nervous someone. What would they be after? Nothing's stored here; nothing *has* been stored here, because not only are the steps too steep and narrow to make it worthwhile, but the dust on the floor tells us its own story.

'So what did this visitor come for? A visitor with a key, you'll note; not a curious schoolkid, or an amateur archæologist. Perhaps,' he suggested remorselessly, 'the . . . visitor came to enjoy the view. It's a good view, isn't it? Do you see the gateway into the lane?—no, stand over here, Mr Parker, why don't you?—and the entrance to your own farmyard? No chance of anyone sneaking up on you unawares, Mr Parker, not while you were up here. But *they* might be unaware of *you*, mightn't they? Well?'

'I suppose so.' They were the first words Parker had uttered. Alec looked at him keenly.

'But I wonder,' he resumed, 'why you—why a visitor—

should bring *a gun* with him, hmm? Step over here and give me your opinion of these marks. What would you say made those, Mr Parker? Do you think it was a gun leaning up against the wall? Like this one?'

'I . . . I suppose it might be. Yes . . . yes, I suppose so.'

'Interesting you should think that. Our own people came to that conclusion too. Now why,' Alec asked with an air of polite thoughtfulness, 'should you—should the person who came here, with a key, for the view—bring a gun. To pot rabbits, perhaps? But it looks to me as if these windows haven't been opened in the last forty years, let alone the last fortnight. So why . . .?'

'I don't know! Look, pack this in, can't you? I don't know what you're trying to prove. I didn't kill him! I didn't kill Hunter. I wasn't on the airfield on Thursday afternoon.'

'Who said anything about the afternoon?'

The two men looked at each other, Parker sullen, Alec speculative, each weighing up the implications of what had been said.

In the end it was Alec who turned away. 'Where were we? Ah yes! Almost done now. Interesting, all this specu- lation, don't you think, Mr Parker. No? Oh well. I wonder if you'd just indulge me a little further. Pick up the gun, will you. The one in the corner.'

Parker looked at him as if he was mad, of course; but mad-dangerous. Nelson was nowhere to be seen. There were just the two of them in the dusty control tower, playing this grim battle of wills. Parker hesitated, then finally moved, went over to the corner, and picked up the shotgun leaning against the wall.

'Take it down the stairs. Carefully! It might be loaded; you don't want an accident.'

Parker looked at him; and then turned and walked out of the room. At the head of the brick staircase he hesitated, but Alec was right behind him, and slowly he began to descend the steps. At the bottom, he stopped. Another couple of paces would take him clear of the tower, on to the open expanse of the airfield.

'Raise the gun,' Alec said quietly at his ear. 'That's right. Now; quickly; step out from the building and if you see anything, anything, fire! Go on! Now!'

Parker had the gun in both hands, half up to his shoulder. For a split second Alec thought he was going to break the spell and stay where he was; then suddenly he stepped clear of the watch tower. Alec ran quickly to one side in time to see Parker clear of the tower, the gun coming up to his shoulder, and Nelson standing twenty-five yards away, on the edge of the concrete. Simultaneously, Nelson saw the gun, and Alec cried, 'Shoot! Shoot!' Nelson panicked, turned and ran into the stubble and Parker, instinctively, to keep the range, ran after him five, ten paces, the gun still half-up.

'Shoot!'

Nelson stopped, and turned, his hands raised in supplication. Parker was still now, and the gun butt was coming into his shoulder and Alec saw his finger begin to tighten on the trigger the instant before Nelson was thrown backwards and fell, lifeless, to the stubble.

'No! Oh no, no, God . . .' Parker was shaking, sobbing. He looked down in disbelief at the gun, and his hands opened and it fell with a clatter on to the concrete. Alec hoped it wasn't damaged; it had given him good service in its time, and his father before him.

'It wasn't like that, it wasn't!' The first shock had gone, but Alec hurried to follow it up while Parker was still rocked off balance.

'What was it like, then, Mr Parker? Did you talk first, was that it? Did you explain what you were going to do to him, make him suffer?'

'I never met the man. I never! Why should I kill him? Why should I want to kill him?'

Alec came up to him and said quietly, 'You and I both know, Mr Parker. What Hunter had found out. What you thought everyone would read in his book.' Behind them, Alec was aware of Nelson scrambling to his feet, and dusting the soil from his trousers. 'Or was it your wife who made you do it? She doesn't much like being married to a farmer, does she? It would be the last straw for her, to have everybody know she was also married to a bastard!'

Parker gulped. 'I didn't kill him.'

'But it's true, isn't it? You're a war baby, Mr Parker. Of the wrong sort.'

'I didn't kill him. I didn't!'

'Where's your gun?'

'I don't know. You've got them.'

'Oh, come on! We're not playing games, Mr Parker. Where is your gun?'

He hesitated. 'I don't know,' he said sullenly. Alec looked at him searchingly. Somehow, he thought it might just be the truth . . .

'I think,' Alec concluded, 'it's time we went back to the farm and I had a chat with your mother.'

CHAPTER 18

Old Mrs Parker sat stiffly in her chair and the force of her hate spanned the few feet between them to where Alec sat at the table. He had prevailed on Parker and his wife to leave them alone; Nelson had both of them penned in the kitchen, making a pot of tea they none of them wanted.

'It came to me through something someone said,' Alec remarked apologetically. 'That your name wasn't Parker by marriage, but by birth. That you were here through the war, working on the farm, while the airfield was built and used on your doorstep. So I found out your Christian name. Joan.'

'What do you want to know?' Her voice was weary, but

unbending. A forty years' secret was to be tossed into the open.

'Who was James's father. For a start. Was it McAllister?' There couldn't be so much shame, even in the mores of another generation, in bearing the child of a good man, who had died before he could marry the girl he loved.

'No,' said Joan Parker, and her voice was infinitely tired, as if the mention of Doug McAllister was unbearable after all these years. 'No, it wasn't Doug. I wish to God it had been. It was Kenny Taylor.'

Alec said simply, 'You'd better tell me.'

It had been the next evening before Joan Parker found out that her lover was dead.

She had heard the four aircraft take off, heard them each head back over the airfield, climbing still, and disappear towards the east. There was no way of knowing which of the aeroplanes was Doug's.

Like many girls in her position, Joan had a pretty good idea of what the Mosquitoes were up to, and how long it would take them to do it, but staying awake to hear them return safely was a luxury she could not afford. There were cows to be milked at seven, and the equipment to be prepared before that; the perpetual grind of farm life which, with the men mostly sucked into the maw of the services, made no allowances for sentiment.

Nor did she expect to hear from Doug until later in the day; when the crews returned from their sweeps over the continent they only wanted to sleep, sometimes till past midday. Joan wasn't perturbed; she would see Doug that evening; he had promised to take her to the Huntsman.

That promise had caused her a good deal of serious thought. Farm life had not given her much opportunity for mixing with boys in a normal social way when she was younger; and when she was sixteen the war had come, and 'normal' became a word with no meaning.

She knew what the pilots meant when they talked of

'taking a girl down to the Huntsman'; she knew of the dark walks into the Forest, and the girls who returned with pine needles clinging to their hair. Doug's was not an invitation of that sort, she knew; but it could be if she wished, and now she debated with herself whether to allow the intimacy of a drink together in the Huntsman Inn, deep in the Forest, to take the course she feared, and hoped, it might. Doug and she had not had many opportunities to 'misbehave', as she termed it to herself; although in wartime, heaven knew, any opportunity was often seized with indecent haste, however brief, and sometimes however public. By and large, Joan and Doug had spent their time together in going to concerts and plays, joining the other crews for an occasional evening in the Dorset Arms; or snatching brief minutes together which, she felt, neither of them would have wanted to use for hurried, guilty passion.

I must be getting loose, she marvelled as she measured out feed for the hens, to be able to think quite coolly about whether I want Doug to . . . to do that with me, tonight. Me, that's always been so prim! But there was a strange, exciting, fearful anticipation that tingled in her belly and suddenly she knew that if it came to it, and it was a fine night and the Forest beckoned, then . . . then yes, she said to herself, surprising herself with her firmness; because it's Doug and because I love him, then I will.

But it wasn't Doug who sauntered into the yard just after six o'clock; it was Kenny Taylor. Joan frowned; whenever they had joined in the evenings at the Dorset Arms she had found Kenny just a little too full of himself. She couldn't see why the other crews allowed him to get away with it as they did, and she shrank from his attentions to her with their insistent heaviness and false jocularity.

No premonition struck her as she dried her hands hastily on the kitchen towel and went down to meet him. And when he spoke his words were flat and neutral, unlike his customary self.

'Doug can't come this evening, Joanie,' he said, watching

her queerly. 'He sent me to say; and to see . . . well, whether I could buy you a drink in compensation. Not the same, of course,' he said with a touch of his usual heavy jokiness, 'as having Doug; but better than nothing, I hope.'

Joan meant to refuse politely. It was disturbing, she realized, to have to acknowledge how much she had been counting on the evening, having once learnt her own mind. She had been going to cross a Rubicon with Doug's help, and now instead she was faced with another dreary evening at home, or a polite drink with a man she didn't much like.

Maybe it was the thought that Kenny might be better company on his own—many boys were, she had long ago learnt that; it was among their peers that they were at their most objectionable—or perhaps the sound of her mother clattering pans indoors; whatever tipped the balance, she changed her mind and smiled briefly at Kenny, who was waiting submissively enough for her reply.

'All right. Just give me a minute to change.'

'Good show. I've got Bertha outside, she's all ready to go.'

'Ber . . .?' Oh, of course, his silly car. Joan disappeared indoors to change and to tell her mother that yes, she was going out yet again and yes she would be back in time to get a good night's sleep because the cows had to be milked in the morning.

God, she told herself as she hastily slipped into a skirt in her room, What wouldn't I give to get away . . . but then, she remembered, perhaps she soon would: about as far away as one could get, if Doug asked her to marry him. There would certainly be no doubt about her answer!

When they came to the junction in Hartfield village and Kenny took the right turning Joan realized that she hadn't asked where they were to go. A few miles further on they turned off into the Forest. That was when she decided it had been a mistake to come.

Kenny glanced at her, his eyes unnaturally bright, as if a demon had hold of him, so that she was suddenly seriously afraid. 'I'm taking you to the Huntsman,' he said, pre-empting her protest. 'I'm afraid I've got something to tell you.'

She knew, then. Premonition and knowledge came merci-lessly, together. While Kenny parked the car, and lifted the bonnet to take the rotor arm, and led her into the inn, and ordered the drinks and set them before them on the table by the fire: during all this, she knew.

He saw it, and when he spoke the demon was gone. 'Doug's dead, Joanie,' he said quietly. 'I didn't want to tell you in front of your parents.'

She couldn't cry. For the sake of saying something—because she couldn't just sit there, numb—she said, 'How?'

'He . . . had some trouble over the other side,' Kenny said. He looked at her, and dropped his eyes again. 'Lost an engine. Came home on one, but he couldn't get over the Forest. It probably wasn't running very well.'

So Doug had died in her own Forest, while she was sleeping. In the pyre of his own aircraft.

'Where?' she asked. Something fell with a little plash on the polished table. I must be crying, she thought curiously.

'Place called King's Standing,' Kenny said awkwardly. 'I suppose you know it?'

'Yes,' she said almost inaudibly. 'I know it.'

'He comforted me,' Joan Parker said bleakly. 'If you call it comfort.' And what she had been going to give to Doug, Kenny took. On a service macintosh, in a clearing in the Forest, looking up at the stars and feeling the weight of a man and nothing mattering, because it was not Doug. 'I went around with him for a couple of weeks. Usual thing. Wartime romance, they call it, but they mean wartime lust. He was only a boy . . . Then he'd proved his point, and he dropped me. Nine months later . . . well, you know the rest.'

He looked at the crippled old woman and understood now the lines of harshness in her face. Understood her un-relenting hostility to the world.

'I suppose it made things difficult at home,' he said inadequately.

There was a spark of sardonic amusement in Joan Parker's eye, and she snorted, 'You could say that.' She added more softly, 'Wartime babies weren't so uncommon; but they were always someone else's. The bad girls had them. And then it suddenly became obvious that their own daughter was a bad girl, too. It killed Dad,' she said baldly. 'It took five years to do it, but it killed him right enough. And then there was the farm to run, and Jimmy just starting school. Mother wasn't good for much.'

Her tone was as bleak as the words themselves; but no harsher than she had been with herself, Alec realized, these last forty years; wearing herself out in bringing up her son and keeping the farm alive until he took it over. To end up crippled and lonely. And, he reminded himself, involved in a murder inquiry.

CHAPTER 19

'How did Andrew Hunter find out about it?' Alec asked Kenneth Taylor roughly. 'No—that's the wrong question. How did you know he'd found out?'

Taylor was uneasy; the skin of his face had turned a curious livid colour that suddenly showed the distinguished grey hair to be dyed. There was no doubt now that he was afraid.

'Did he write to you?' Alec went on relentlessly. 'Telling you—without meaning to—that he knew? Or was he so naïve as to ask straight out for information, believing it was something you had come to terms with after all this time, believing you could face up to it and discuss it rationally now? Well?'

Over in the corner Liz, looking up from her pad, saw the tension between the two men and knew Mr Stainton had

somehow—and just how he did it was a mystery—cut deep
and sure to the rotten source of Taylor's fear.

'Well?'

'How . . . how do you know?'

'I've talked to the Parkers, Mr Taylor. I know it all.'

'The Parkers?' Taylor's eyes sharpened.

Alec saw with sudden misgiving the swift focusing of
Taylor's gaze; but there was nothing for it now but to play
out the game. He had been a fool! It never had been
sufficient motive, he berated himself: what is one wartime
pregnancy more or less? 'I don't suppose it would do much
good to a member of the Assembly to have it made known
that he spent his glorious war years fathering bastards on
innocent English girls.'

Taylor's eyes flickered away. Liz, looking up again, sensed
the change in the room and was puzzled. The tension was
still there; but it had lessened, and changed its quality.

'She wasn't that innocent,' Taylor said eventually.

'You admit it, then?'

'Since you seem to have discovered the whole thing, I
can't very well deny it, can I?'

'You seduced Joan Parker. And you did it the very next
night after her fiancé was shot down.' The memory of Joan
Parker sitting pitilessly in her cheerless room rose unbidden
in his mind, and Alec kept his voice level with an effort.
'Doesn't that seem a pretty despicable thing to have on your
conscience?'

'My conscience is my affair,' Taylor cried harshly, and
Alec, looking at his drawn, pale face, wondered how much
he had tried to push down the memories over the years.

When Kenneth Taylor took Joan Parker to the Huntsman
he intended much more than simply to break the news of
Doug McAllister's death. The lust for vengeance was hot
inside him. The brutality of the programme had something
compellingly attractive about it at first: Doug was dead,
wasn't he? And he, Kenny, was alive, and there could be

no better proof, no sweeter triumph over the dead man, than to take the dead man's sweetheart, on her back in a clearing in the Forest, under the moon.

But somewhere along the line something inside him changed. Maybe it was the suddenness of Joan's insight into Doug's death which did it; maybe the disturbing, nakedly obvious fact that she had loved him. Maybe, even, it was Kenny's unexpected reaction to being alone with a woman who wasn't, as too many others had been, a too-willing accomplice at the wartime game of passion, merely a sad, vulnerable girl made ugly by her misery.

In any event, he found himself unaccountably hurting with her as her tears splashed dully on their table by the fire.

At first Kenny took refuge in anger: even now Doug came between him and peace of mind! Doug the mature, before whom he always knew himself a mere boy! Doug the man of love, not merely of lust; Doug, unforgivably, the uneffusive hero beside whom his own braggart cowardice was so despicable.

Yet the anger couldn't last. Joan's helpless grief was so all-embracing that his own pettiness could not survive beside it. He fought against the urge to sympathy, and then gave in; and as he did so, his own sorrows—for himself, for his dead friends, for the bitter, warring world—choked in his throat and he found himself crying too.

Whichever of them first moved he never knew, but in a moment they were pushing out of the inn, walking, who knew where, under the moon which broke and fragmented among the branches, and then, in a dry clearing, on his mac, or was it hers, holding each other tightly so that the physical hurt merged with the hurt of the soul and both seeped away into the night. He was aware of Joan clutching him in spasms and moaning, pulling him closer, deeper, and of the drained, empty inertia that held him, how long he never knew. He was far too lost in Joan's grief, and his own, to realize the irony of it all, in the clearing, under the moon.

It was a long time before they staggered to their feet and made their way unspeaking to the car and to Hartfield Park.

The two men gazed at each other across the desk in mutual antipathy. 'It wasn't rape,' Taylor murmured absently. 'There were two of us involved.'

'It must have been worrying when you were elected to the Assembly,' pursued Alec thoughtfully. 'To know that there was a time-bomb sitting here in England, waiting to explode. To know that if Joan, or her son—your son—chose they could blow your precious reputation and your more precious seat in the Assembly sky-high.' He looked at Taylor. 'A good enough reason, some might think, to take steps to stop the knowledge spreading any further; to take drastic steps when someone else found out the truth and threatened to put it in his book!'

'He never would have done. You can't publish slander like that.' Taylor was confident now, returning Mr Stainton's shots evenly. Liz, scribbling his answers, knew that after all the interview had all gone wrong.

She could sense it in Mr Stainton, too: he was hunting for his next question, no longer confident of throwing Taylor further and further off balance until he tipped into a confession of having killed Hunter.

Frances Walker was away when Alec rang her the next day, in Manchester for a meeting. He left his name and asked that she should ring him back.

'It doesn't follow,' he commented to Nelson, who had come in at his summons and was waiting while the call was made, 'that because Taylor is telling the truth about one matter, he is not lying about another. The point where he was most worried was when he knew I had linked him to some event which happened at Hartfield Park back in 1944. To that degree, we are on the right track. But when I followed on by suggesting that that event was the seduction of Joan Parker and his fathering of James Parker, I'll swear he relaxed. He knew I was barking up the wrong tree.'

'D'you think James Parker knows this chap Taylor is his father?' Nelson speculated interestedly.

Alec hesitated. 'I don't know. Perhaps Joan simply told him his father had been killed in the war, and he never knew until recently that they hadn't been married.'

'I guess as soon as he went to school the other children would have left him no illusions,' Nelson remarked.

Alec looked up sharply. 'Be careful! For if it was common knowledge that Joan Parker was unmarried and James illegitimate, they neither of them have a motive for killing Andrew Hunter!' They gazed at each other, each considering the adequacy or otherwise of the argument.

Nelson said, to change the subject, 'Taylor didn't deny it?'

'No; though at first he made a half-hearted attempt to suggest that Joan Parker took other lovers. Another reason for believing we were on to the wrong track there. The point is, if it is not that, what is it that Taylor is so guilty about?'

'You want me to find out,' Nelson returned.

'I want you to do some checking, you and Liz. More work on the telephone to South Africa; and more work tracing just where Taylor was at the time Colin Napier's house was broken into.'

'But you said yourself the key to this inquiry is at Hartfield Park.'

'I think it is. But I'm not sure you and I have the equipment yet to ferret it out. I think we must assume that that form letter you found among Hunter's papers was sent to each of the old pilots, even though only Phillips has admitted receiving it. It must have appeared somehow to the murderer that Hunter Knew All. And thus the letter brought about Hunter's death.'

He leant back in his chair and looked at Nelson thoughtfully. 'Nothing on Hunter's bank account yet, I suppose?'

'No, sir. It should be through tomorrow.' He hesitated. 'All this doesn't really answer the question of James Parker and his missing shotgun, though, does it?'

'No,' Alec agreed sadly. 'I'm afraid it doesn't.'

CHAPTER 20

Paul Napier's memoirs were hard going; he was half way through them now, and several times that evening Alec caught himself staring into space, the dog-eared manuscript lying forgotten in his lap, mentally back at Hartfield Park looking down at Andrew Hunter's body lying in the whispering barley. Once, he found himself instead in his mind standing in the little churchyard in the watery sunshine staring down at his father's coffin.

He shook himself and got up, going through into the kitchen to make himself another cup of coffee. When the kettle had boiled he stood there, the mug in his hand, wondering what he had come for.

He suddenly realized that he had reached the point—he was familiar enough with it now to recognize it when he got there, and no doubt this time he was predisposed to depression anyway, after his father's death—at which his confidence was at its nadir. It wasn't that he felt they were on the wrong track particularly; but the whole business seemed so futile. He knew Parker was lying about his shotgun; he knew Taylor was selfish and untrustworthy; he knew that Janssen possibly, and Phillips probably, had been lying about the timing of their visits to Hartfield Park; but none of these facts seemed to matter much, or to have any connection with the black crust of blood on Andrew Hunter's shattered body; or with the bare field at Hartfield where now the dust drifted across the weathered concrete and the endless furrows of the ploughed earth streamed chocolate-coloured towards the distant hedgerow.

Yet experience, which told him that such dejection lay in wait for him at about this stage in any serious inquiry, could add a whisper of encouragement. Because he recognized now—and how many despondent hours might he have escaped on other cases if he had realized it before?—that this was the point where he mentally changed gear. It was not as simple as saying that from now on the graph would trend only upwards; but from now on the mind would be working as it should, and would work at the case as a cat consumes its prey, stripping the carcase, crunching the joints, reaching instinctively for what is meaty and throwing aside what is of no value. It might be a long case; it might even (though this was one thought he did shrink from) be unsolved at the end; but he would have stripped it to the bones and beyond.

He made the coffee and took it back into the living-room. Paul Napier's notes, shabby and disordered, lay on the chair where he had left them. Beside them on the table, Andrew Hunter's blue files: orderly, painstaking, precise. And, now that he had been coached by Dr Walker, not quite so impenetrable as they had been at first.

He picked up the manuscript and weighed it thoughtfully in his hand. It was not that Paul Napier's memoirs were uninteresting; but it was small-scale, day-to-day stuff and poorly strung together. It would have made a dull book, if it had ever been finished.

The trouble was, he told himself suddenly, that he had been setting about them the wrong way. There was no need to subject himself to the whole tedious drag. All he had to do in the first instance was read those parts to which Andrew Hunter's notes gave significance.

He refreshed his memory from the blue files: yes, Hunter's entries, which were chronological, stopped at October 2nd for Janssen and Dixon; for Taylor and Phillips the last entry was that for September 29th. He leafed back to the entries for McAllister and Babe Binney. September 12th, followed by the stark legend DNR: did not return.

Taylor had been uneasy about something; of that much
Alec had been sure. And whatever it had been, he had
clearly felt that Alec had missed it: the relaxation in his
manner could mean nothing else. Therefore it was nothing
to do with his reputed shabby treatment of the daughter,
Joan Parker. Something to do with his life on the airfield,
then; or his flying?

Alec paused, to consider whether his instinctive focusing
on Taylor was reasonable. The fact that he found the
man objectionable was not itself good enough grounds for
regarding him suspiciously. But it was surely reasonable to
presume that a man so obviously self-interested would fight
hard to protect that self-interest; and, moreover, might have
indulged in some very self-interested acts in the past, which
he would now be reluctant to have aired.

He turned back to Paul Napier's manuscript. Leafing
through it, he placed a marker at August 1st 1944, and
another at . . . what should it be? November 1st. Had
Hunter written up his notes after he carried out his research,
or as he went along? Either way, the hypothetical crucial
event must have occurred in the late summer of 1944. Then,
the blue files beside him, he settled down again to read.

The crews came in, not all together for a mass briefing as
they did on the bomber stations, but in their pairs, pilot
and navigator. The flight commander gave them the target;
they came for the intelligence briefing; they went on to the
met office, and ended up in the crew room, where the
navigators marked up their maps and worked out the routine
for the flight.

How many times had he done this, Napier asked himself,
since the squadron came here in May. Fifty? A hundred?
Nearer a hundred, it must be: someone was flying most
nights, and there had not been too many operations lost
due to the weather.

A schoolmaster in civilian life, it sometimes seemed to
Paul Napier that he saw his pupils in these aircrew: pink-

faced, perplexed schoolboys weighed down by their incongruous adult impedimenta of uniforms and flying boots. At thirty-four, Napier knew himself for an old man in this environment, where even the squadron commander was regarded as a hoary veteran at twenty-six.

Because he saw these young men each time they set out and debriefed them when they returned, and because those who returned were so often fewer than those who had set out, he'd toughened himself in his reaction to them, evolving a secret categorization for them: not a joke, or if so a macabre one; more a way of preventing them becoming too much personalized for him.

So he divided them into one of three groups: Bill Janssen, now, who was pushing through the door with his navigator Dixon whom they called Dicky, was a SOD: Should Outlive Disaster. They weren't a brilliant crew, not often in the limelight, but by and large you briefed them, they flew the mission as briefed, they came back and landed without drama. Often with the seals of their gunports unbroken, it was true: two integers of the war, not amounting to much in themselves but adding up, with all the other integers, to a considerable sum. SODs formed the majority of the aircrew on this or any other station.

The ALFIes, on the other hand, tried to fight the war on their own. ALFIes tended not to last long, because ALFI stood for Actively Looking For It. They looked for trouble —and as trouble was usually looking for them, they as often as not found it. They'd shoot down an enemy plane, then get shot up themselves, limp home on one engine and land wheels-up, write off their own aeroplane and—if they were lucky—step out of the wreckage; or if they were not, stay in it as it burned, so evening the score: one German for one British.

ALFIes were rather thin on the ground in the squadron at present. It was just a fortnight since the last pair, intent on shooting up a train near Saarbrücken, had failed to see that it was about to enter a tunnel. Score, one train, one

Mosquito, both burning together in the blackened tunnel mouth.

Napier looked up from the flak map as the door banged open again. Douglas McAllister, almost as old as Napier himself, a BOSS if ever there was one, followed by Babe Binney, like a first-former trailing a prefect.

BOSS stood (ironically) for Backbone of the Squadron: everything that McAllister was, everything that Napier ought to applaud but privately found slightly tedious. Napier greeted him briefly, reservedly. They might have been companionable, he knew, if he could have allowed it; but BOSSes got killed like anyone else—engine failure, or a radar-equipped Ju 88, or flak where no flak should be, could wipe even a careful perfectionist like McAllister from the earth in a moment. It didn't do to invest anything of yourself in aircrew; not if you were to preserve your own sanity, your own ability to do the job, night after night.

After Napier had briefed McAllister and Babe Binney— there was a new concentration of flak reported not far from Flensburg, and a rumour that another nightfighter squadron had been cobbled together to guard Kiel—and they had left, there was a hiatus. There was only one crew to come now of the four that were flying tonight; and Napier wasn't sure at all what category they fell into.

From the line-shooting they indulged in, he'd have classed them firmly as ALFIes. He'd heard Taylor too often sounding off in the mess: berating McAllister for his caution, boasting to Bill Janssen that they never came home without having to clean their guns. Yes, he used to think of them as ALFIes, without question.

Napier opened the drawer in his desk and took out the report which had been forwarded from the radar section and read it again. He almost knew it by heart now; the jumble of bearings and ranges and times. And the conclusion.

It was cursory, merely a suggestion, a possibility. Yes,

that was it. A possibility; not, in other words, an impossibility. But he knew in his heart that it was more than that; and it wasn't the SODs or the BOSSes who, in his experience, were the ones to crack; it was the blustering, devil-may-care, knife-edge types.

The door banged open against the wall and bounced back on its hinges.

'What've you got for us tonight, then, Professor? Flak towers in Brighton or death-rays on the Dogger Bank?'

Napier slipped the drawer silently shut on its runners, consigning the report to the dark once more. 'One of these days you'll be right,' he said easily. 'But not tonight. OK, if you've got your maps I've a new searchlight concentration for you to mark . . .'

The report would wait another twenty-four hours. Perhaps by then they'd know the truth. And then there could be the swift action: the brow-beating of the crew by the angry because embarrassed CO, the shameful admission, and the hasty, surreptitious posting before the other crews were tainted by the proximity of cowards.

Three hours later he watched from the big windows of the darkened control tower as the lights of the first Mosquito swept down the runway. And there the plane itself suddenly was, as it lifted off, a shadowy raptor visible against the western horizon, before it was swallowed up by the dusk.

Ten minutes later a second set of lights wavered along the perimeter track, quivered at the runway's end as the engines were run up, and swept across his view, lifted off and disappeared.

There was a wait then of twenty minutes, until the lights of the last two planes began to move and converged on the runway's end. McAllister took off first; then, a couple of minutes later, Taylor. Napier watched thoughtfully as the navigation lights flicked out and the bat-like silhouette of the Mosquito disappeared westwards and began to climb. He went out to the head of the stairs, and a moment or two later heard, rather than saw, the Mosquito as, having made the height to clear the high ground, it passed back to the north of the field, and the noise of the engines receded over Ashurst towards Germany.

Five minutes later Napier was back in his office. He lifted the telephone and spoke to the officer in charge of the radar unit. Their conversation was brief and cryptic. Napier put the receiver down and sat staring at it thoughtfully.

Like most men who have been in situations of personal danger Alec had a lot of sympathy with fear. He had trembled with terror often enough to hold that against no man; but the trembling hadn't—couldn't have—stopped him going on, doing what he had to do. The soldier, or policeman, who did not admit to being frightened often, and badly, was either insensitive or dishonest, and in either case no good. What mattered was going on nevertheless, because there were men and women who relied on one to do just that; because there was a job to do.

So Alec didn't condemn anyone for feeling fear those long years ago, taking an aeroplane laden with aviation fuel and explosives off into the darkness night after night to go and seek trouble in enemy lands.

But it was one thing to be a coward in theory. It was quite another to be one in practice.

There was no question now of going to bed; only of reading on, digging back through the layers of time to the truth which peeled away from these events like the skin peeling from an apple.

In the small hours of the morning Paul Napier waited for the Mosquitoes to return. At a few minutes after half past two the first aeroplane droned on to the circuit and thumped heavily on to the runway. The airfield lights flicked off again. Twenty minutes later a second machine touched down and ran with a stutter of exhaust towards its dispersal bay. Again the airfield lights were extinguished. Ten minutes later the lights blinked on, a third plane sank gratefully to the ground, and the airfield sank back into darkness.

They went on waiting.

Alec put the manuscript down.

After a while he thought of something else and picked up the topmost of Andrew Hunter's blue files. He opened it and leafed through it until he found McAllister, D. He let his eye glance down the record of training, postings, missions, terminating in the unemotional finality of the entry for September 12th: DNR. Did not return.

Beneath, at the foot of the page, was a set of figures and initials entered in Hunter's precise hand. Mostly they were cryptic: Hunter's own shorthand again, this time applied presumably to the details of McAllister's last flight. A six-figure group caught his eye, and he stared at it thoughtfully, then wandered over to the bookshelf where his Ordnance Survey maps were ranged and took one down.

He traced the eastings and northings along the grid-lines with his finger until they intersected high up on the Ashdown Forest to the west of Crowborough, near the junction of two B-roads. It looked as if McAllister and Babe had nearly made it.

Alec stood with the map in his hand staring sightlessly at the picture on the wall opposite.

CHAPTER 21

It was one of those bright, clear autumn days when the sharp sunlight slants entrancingly through the trees and in the side roads fallen leaves lift and flutter as the cars pass. Near the Ashdown Forest Centre people were walking dogs, and figures on horseback coasted in and out of sight among the trees.

At King's Standing Alec turned the car into the rough

car park. The red Porsche was already there and Frances
Walker emerged as he reached for the map in the glove
compartment and climbed out. Surreptitiously he glanced
at her shoes; she was sensibly shod beneath her dark serge
skirt and waterproof jacket.

'Will I do?'

Alec grinned, and said nothing. The Bristol ticked quietly
as the engine cooled, and he stood, the map spread on the
roof, and looked around.

'Set?'

'All right.'

'This way, then.' And he crossed the road and struck off
into the heather.

A track took them into a small copse. With the memory
of the map in his mind Alec swung a little to his right.

It must be almost the highest spot on the Forest, he
thought, as they stood on the edge of the trees and saw the
heather falling away in rolls and folds all around. Somewhere to the north, just hidden by the fall of the land, two
or three miles away, was Hartfield village and the airfield,
and beyond the fields and woods of Sussex and Surrey
stretched palely away towards the North Downs on the
horizon. A chalk quarry on the far-away scarp winked
dazzlingly like a lighthouse.

A couple of hundred yards down to the right Alec saw
what he had half expected, half feared to find. It was a
fenced-off area which might be taken for a sheepfold; except
that it was too small, almost entirely filled by a little pile of
rocks.

With a last glance in the direction of the hidden Hartfield
Park he led the way down the path, dropping into the
heather, with stunted trees here and there, the bark torn by
deer.

The fold of the land hid the enclosure until they mounted
a rise and there it was not ten yards away. Not a sheepfold;
but a protective post-and-rail fence around a little mortared
cairn of local stone.

Alec walked the last few yards. There was a simple plaque. He read it in silence and a moment later Frances Walker came up and stood beside him and read it too.

They had found the place where Douglas McAllister and Babe Binney had ended their last flight—or perhaps begun it, if you looked at it that way; on the very top of the Forest, almost within sight of home. Perhaps another ten feet, or twenty would have been enough to save them; but they had not had it, and here they had died forty-five years ago in their burning plywood aeroplane.

Frances Walker sipped her drink, then put her glass down, nodding her agreement, unsurprised.

'It's not the first case I've heard of by any means. The pilots who turned back slightly too often because they didn't like the sound of their engine, or the oil pressure was low; something no one could argue about, until it happened a second time, and a third, and a fourth. Then they were posted. Lack of moral fibre. It wasn't so easy for bomber crews. A pilot who lost his nerve would press on nevertheless, because there were six or seven others in there with him, and they were too close to be deceived; and if you were a wireless operator, or a gunner, why, you had to go where the pilot took you, scared or not. They spent their time circling over the North Sea, you say? I don't suppose they were the only ones.'

'I take it they'd both have to be in the plot?' Alec asked.

'In a Mosquito? Yes; there wouldn't be much chance of the pilot fooling the navigator, or vice versa; and then there'd be the log to write up, too. They'd have to cook a complete flight record every time. Oh yes, they'd both be in it. Was that how they were spotted?'

Alec shook his head. 'From what I understand, a radar post picked up an unidentified aircraft, just circling for hours above the sea. Unfortunately someone began inquiring what this German plane was doing circling over the sea every other night, and Napier heard of it from somewhere and started to check the squadron's flight record.'

'And the German was there every time a particular crew was flying, and not there when they weren't?'

'I think so. The night Napier found out for sure was the night McAllister died. September 12th.'

'No indication who it was?'

Alec shook his head. 'Napier was a bit oblique in his memoirs—afraid of libel, maybe. I hoped you might be able to help me find out. It was one of the South African crews, though, he was plain about that.'

'No call-sign, I suppose?'

'No.'

'Humph! What I don't understand is why nothing was done about it at the time. D'you think even Napier might not have known for certain which crew was involved? Normally the authorities would have kicked them out pretty damn quick, before their example became catching.'

'Maybe they did.' He looked up at her thoughtfully. 'Maybe that's something Napier could have told us, if he was still alive. Is it possible to trace what happened to the various crews? I presume it's possible to follow the career of an individual serviceman if you know where to look?'

'Of course. That's what Andrew Hunter was doing. Excuse me a minute.'

Frances left him for a moment and Alec pondered how much to tell her of his suspicions about Taylor. Yet he didn't, to be honest, have any solid grounds for his suspicions: merely an antipathy to a man he disliked and who, he sensed, had lied to him. He glanced up and saw Dr Walker re-emerging, not from the door marked 'Ladies' but the passage where the telephone was.

'Sorry! Where were we?' It was not an apology. Lucy would always come first; must always do so, even if Dr Walker had to pay the price of being thought fussy. 'We were talking about finding out whether any of the crews were posted,' she resumed efficiently.

'Mm. I suppose that's really why I came to you.' He smiled apologetically. 'I thought you might be able to suggest where I should start.'

'Or did you hope I would do the looking for you?' Dr Walker returned shrewdly. 'It would make sense; it's easy enough for me, something I've done dozens of times.'

'Will you?'

'How quickly do you want the information?' she asked cautiously.

'How quickly can I have it?'

She regarded him thoughtfully. 'By mid-week, I should say. Provided nothing comes up at work that I have to sort out.'

Alec weighed it up. It was still only Saturday; but he was acutely aware that time was running out. The South Africans were due, under the terms of their tickets, to leave for home at the end of the week. He'd have to have a pretty good reason for detaining any of them. On the other hand, if he set Nelson or Liz Pink on to the task it would inevitably take them longer. Against that was the fact that he still disliked enlisting outside support.

'There is another possibility,' Dr Walker said, forestalling his answer, 'but it's not a very pleasant one. More in your field than mine.'

'You mean,' Alec said slowly, 'that Napier could have told our man he knew what was going on and agreed to keep quiet—for a price.' It would fit in with the burgling of Napier's house: while Napier was alive, his papers—if the blackmail victim knew of their existence—were no threat; Napier had the information anyway, and publishing it would only cut off his source of funds. Once Napier was dead, the guilty man would have to ensure that nothing incriminating had been left behind. But it posited a blackmail which had endured for forty-five years. And it still didn't tell him who had killed Andrew Hunter.

'What's up?' Frances Walker broke into Alec's thoughts after a while.

He shrugged apologetically. 'Just thinking. The contrast.'

'Between the heroism and the cowardice?'

'You're very perceptive.'

She sighed. 'You don't have to be, really, to see the paradox. One pair of men die fearfully in a burning aeroplane on a hillside, doing their duty. Another pair run away, to spend their patrol circling safely over the sea.'

'The splendour and the folly that is war,' Alec remarked. 'Not a very original thought, but a depressing one all the same.'

'I want to show you something,' she said. 'The reason we came here.' The pub had been her suggestion, her choice, although they had passed three others to get there, and Alec was none too sure just where 'there' was.

She glanced at him as if tolerant of his uninterest and went over to the bar and pinged the bell.

When the barman arrived it was a small roly-poly man with dark eyes, not the youth who had served them. 'I've brought another friend to see your ceiling, Joe,' Frances said.

'Why, it's Dr Walker. Brought another, have you? Yes, you can go through. It's unlocked.'

Frances summoned Alec with a little quizzical tilt of the head and led the way into a back passage through a door marked 'Ladies' and 'Emergency Exit'. Half way along she stopped at the door marked 'Ladies', with a dry glance at Alec. But he had already seen another, unobtrusively plain, door opposite. Frances turned the handle of this second door and pushed it open.

Alec found himself in a little lop-sided room where time seemed, in some senses, to have stood still. There was no juke-box or game machine, and no room for one anyway; only a couple of wooden tables with bentwood chairs and an oak settle and a battered brown armchair with stuffing oozing from the cracked shiny leather and a diminutive bar. The room smelt of disuse, but the furniture was arranged as if custom had only that moment departed.

He looked about him. There was a faded poster on one wall advertising fatstock sales at Tunbridge Wells, and a timetable which appeared to apply to trains from Withyham to Forest Row, Three Bridges and Lewes. A shove-ha'penny board sat silently at one end of the bar. Involuntarily, Alec shivered. There was something other than the still air which struck chill to the senses.

Frances Walker ran a gentle finger along the back of a chair, then turned to him. 'I discovered this place when I was researching my first book.'

'It's eerie. Talk about going back in time!'

She shook her head fractionally. 'Look up.'

He turned his head upward and saw why Dr Walker had led him here on this ordinary Saturday morning.

The whole ceiling of the little room, an area perhaps ten feet by twelve, was covered with scrawled signatures, the white chalk livid against the faded brown paper. Alec recognized suddenly the name of a famous Battle of Britain ace, then another; but mostly the names meant nothing to him; they were the multitudinous marks, in childish rounds or schoolroom copperplate or extrovert swirls and slashes, of a lost generation.

'I hope you're not disappointed?' She came and stood by his side and they both looked up. 'It started as a joke, of course, and became an institution, a good-luck charm. They came here and signed their names on the ceiling and it ensured they'd always come back. Only,' she added, 'sometimes that part of it didn't work so well.'

'Are any of ours here?' he asked at last.

Frances turned away and sat down. 'I don't know. Probably. Do you see why I brought us here?'

And he did see; saw that this silly fragment from the past made sense of the sombre memorial up on the Forest, and made sense of the weakness which led an unknown crew to spend their nights of patrol over the North Sea. Here were the names from a war memorial, the butchers' sons and the squires' sons, the clerks and the farm boys, not chiselled everlastingly in granite but scrawled merrily in their own living hand, the metaphor of their own ephemerality.

'Let's go,' she said.

CHAPTER 22

'The assumption would be,' Nelson suggested dubiously, 'that Taylor, warned in some way that Hunter was on the track of his dirty secret—and I take it to be the cowardice he was worried about, not the seduction of Joan Parker —and presumably frustrated that after Napier had been silenced the threat wasn't over, killed Hunter.'

'Yes. If it is Taylor. And I agree,' Alec answered the unspoken questions, 'that it presumes too much. And the simple fact that we have found a nasty skeleton in Taylor's cupboard is neither here nor there so far as the murder inquiry is concerned unless we can find a firm link with the present.'

'But isn't the burglary at Napier's house that link?' Liz suggested.

'Is it? All we know is that *someone* burgled the house for *some* reason. The rest is speculation; the use of an over-active imagination on my part. And where does James Parker's vanished shotgun fit into all this?'

'I see what you mean,' Nelson agreed reluctantly. 'We can't arrest everyone who happens to have a guilty secret of some sort; and we can't twist all the guilty secrets into one comforting universal theory; they just don't fit.'

'That's right. Don't forget if Taylor's our man, then Stuart Phillips is in it too. So maybe is Colin Napier: perhaps his father passed on his knowledge before his death. Perhaps *he* is blackmailing Taylor. But in that case why didn't Taylor kill him, too, when he had the opportunity?' Something flickered in the back of Alec's mind as he said this, and he tried to focus on it; but it vanished again into the shadows, and he had to concentrate to catch up on what Nelson was saying.

'What it comes down to is that we have two separate crimes: a possible blackmail of Taylor, say by Napier; and the killing of Hunter because he had independently got wind of Taylor's secret.'

'Mm. But it *could* be that *Hunter* was playing the blackmail angle—or that Taylor saw him as a threat in that way. Then killing him would have had a double object. In any event, we'd better do what we can at finding out whether Taylor has been making regular payments in any direction. It's not going to be easy, making inquiries from here to institutions in South Africa.'

Liz looked up expectantly, wondering whether she was to enjoy Christmas in the sun after all.

'We'd better check Phillips at the same time,' Nelson pointed out. 'They were both in it; they've both got as much to lose.'

'Have they?' Alec mused. 'I wonder. I think that's one of the things we'll have to find out.'

Alec sat with a sheet of paper before him, turning over in his mind what they knew.

Unconsciously he began to doodle: a horizontal line. Three circles spaced along it. He shaded in the central circle, drew a low rectangle on top of it, an inverted T. Mosquito, head-on. A reminder, perhaps, that this wasn't a domestic shout-and-bash, tears-and-remorse murder; was a murder, moreover, which must have involved careful planning, correspondence (note: what had happened to the letter Taylor must have written to Andrew Hunter, arranging the meeting?) and cool logistics.

It would also involve—he wrote the headings beneath the doodle—means of transport to the airfield; and acquisition of a shotgun; and the risk of being interrupted, not least by Parker—depending on how far Parker was involved in the murder itself. And Parker was, after all, Taylor's son, he reminded himself.

Of course, if once you posited some sort of collaboration between Taylor and the Parkers, many of the problems evaporated: Parker would provide the shotgun. The farmyard might have hidden the car Taylor used to reach the field. And the risk of interruption would be—if not removed altogether—substantially minimized. If you want to be private, it's much easier in the middle of an airfield than in the middle of a wood, where anyone can sneak up unobserved.

He sat up again, and looked at the notes he had made. Involving the Parkers rather went against his instincts: it was his theory that successful murderers worked alone; but then, successful murderers were the ones who were never discovered. Alec hunted his memory to recall whether Joan Parker had spoken of Taylor in such a way as to imply that she had seen him recently. So far as he could recall, everything she had said pointed rather to the fact that he had passed out of her life totally forty-five years back. Did she even know he was now in the country?

It was curious and unsettling to be dealing simultaneously with the present, and with that distant year of 1944, yet to have the same characters appearing in both settings. Joan Parker now, an old woman, crippled and acerbic; and Joan Parker then, eager and innocent. Kenneth Taylor now, with his tinted hair and undisguised selfishness; and Taylor then, dashing and handsome: no less unprincipled, but venial because of his youth.

They were all different people; just as his friends were different now from the teenagers they had been; but when you lived with them year by year the changes were imperceptible, you were ever young.

Only those who had died, he thought, never aged: McAllister and Babe Binney; and the countless others fixed forever at the moment of their death; caught as in some old

photograph, laughing, youthful, posed beside their aeroplane, a black dog gambolling at their heels.

He tried to put himself in Taylor's place, to imagine
himself haunted for the whole of his adult life by the knowledge of his cowardice, and the fear that it would become
generally known. Even if shame didn't come into it much,
terror of disclosure must have grown stronger as the years
passed and Taylor progressed in business and in the
Assembly.

But still it came down to the same irreducible facts: for
Taylor to be the killer of Andrew Hunter, Taylor had to be
at the airfield that Thursday, and he had to have means of
transport and a shotgun.

Frances Walker rang back on Tuesday morning. It was
quick work, by anybody's standards.

'Excuse me if I keep this brief,' she began; 'I've a call
coming from Boston in ten minutes.'

'Fire away. I've got a pen.'

'All right: four men who flew Mosquitoes from Hartfield
were posted away between September 1944 and the end of
the year. Three of them were pilots. One was Janssen, who
came to the end of his tour in October and was posted as
flying control officer to a squadron in France.'

'Was that normal?'

'At the end of a tour? Yes. No more flying for three
months.' Dr Walker's voice was terse and economical, but
if questions came up, Alec was determined to ask them. Her
call from Boston would hardly, after all, solve a murder.
But already she was continuing. 'Taylor and Baxter went
to a Dakota squadron as replacements for pilots lost at
Arnhem; to be ready for the Rhine crossing. Left Hartfield
before the beginning of November.'

'Baxter?'

'An Englishman. He was killed in February '45. A Rus-
sian Yak fighter shot him down in error over Berlin.'

'Right.' There was no reason why Baxter shouldn't be

the one: cowards were as vulnerable to death as anyone else. Baxter might easily be the one Napier had found. Suddenly he felt a chill strike his stomach. Suppose Napier had done nothing about reporting the coward because the coward had died before he could do so? Then if the crucial date was September 12th, *what if the coward had died that very night?*

He fought to keep the fear out of his voice. 'You said there were four, four men posted away. Who was the fourth man?'

'Dixon: Janssen's navigator. Taylor's navigator stayed at Hartfield to finish his tour. Oh, and I've found out something about Taylor's DFC.' Her voice faded; dimly in the background Alec heard the shrilling of a telephone, and the sound of Dr Walker talking aside to someone else. 'Look,' she came back, 'I've got to go now.'

'Can I ring you if I—'

'I'll ring you,' Dr Walker replied decisively. 'Glad to be of help.'

'No!' he said firmly. 'The DFC—when—'

'July. I'll ring you!'

July! Everything tumbled silently into dust. Alec muttered his thanks automatically; but the phone at the other end had already been put down.

Alec put his own receiver down and stood and stared at it. He had so much wanted Taylor not to be a hero; to be everything that was consistent with cowardice, with being the decades-long victim of blackmail; with callous murder.

He sat down, swivelling his chair until he could gaze out over the trees and grass of East Court, watching a woman dragging her toddler townwards. The point was, Alec told himself irritably, that he had made the old stupid identification between the profession of courage, and the expression of it; and so he had blinded himself to what he didn't want to see. The recollection of the words he had spoken in the interview with Taylor came vividly into his mind. Sometimes this was a dirty, a contemptible job. Because Taylor had been, through fear, mean-spirited and untrustworthy and even malicious Alec had found it easy to believe that he was also incapable of bravery, and had allowed contempt to creep into his dealings with the old man. Did Alec have to learn yet again that bravery consisted in a man going on and doing his job even when terror was playing scornful tricks with his nature?

A DFC proved nothing, of course. Hadn't Taylor himself mocked the award as misguided? But no, he couldn't have it both ways: either Taylor was the boastful empty sham he had taken him for, or he was a modest—and genuine— hero. And if a hero, then not a coward. Not the victim of blackmail. And not the murderer of Andrew Hunter.

Meanwhile another man, who gave the impression of untroubled competence and confidence, had nevertheless been betraying his trust. The confidence even stemmed, perhaps, from the ease with which he had outwitted the rest of the squadron. Risking their lives was for mutts; *he* had more sense.

Paul Napier had known who it was; but he had not acted on his information: that much seemed clear. Someone in that squadron set out each night to cross the North Sea en route for Germany; and never got there: spent the hours of his patrol spiralling endlessly over the grey waves. But Janssen had completed his tour; and Taylor was after all too brave; and nobody else had left the squadron except Baxter, who was dead. And, of course, those others whom death had plucked against their will from Hartfield Park.

So Napier had done nothing. Nothing? Was that really so? In that case, the burglary at Colin Napier's house was no more than a bizarre coincidence.

So why the burglary? Why the television, and the hi-fi, and the microwave untouched? Why the disordered papers? No one, surely, would choose to burgle Napier's house to secure those mediocre memoirs for their own value. It must be—had to be—for the sake of the indictment they contained.

Ergo, Napier had not done nothing. Perhaps he had kept

his knowledge to himself for decades, but in the end he had done something which acted as a catalyst to events. He had asked for money: or, he had shared his knowledge.

If he had merely asked for money, that threat had ceased with his death. The papers might have been sought as a safeguard, of course, to forestall any attempt at blackmail by Napier's son Colin. More likely, Napier had shared his knowledge.

The presumption was that he had shared it with Andrew Hunter, since Hunter was dead. But Colin Napier too, Alec reminded himself, had nearly died. Had that, rather than the papers, been the real object of the burglary: to kill Napier, and provide a plausible motive for doing so?

But still he came back, in an obsessive circle, to the question: if the reason for killing Hunter was a guilty secret, whose was the secret?

CHAPTER 23

'Couldn't we have another word with Parker, sir? Get to the bottom of it? We know he's holding out on us.'

'Do we?'

'About his shotgun. He still hasn't admitted where it is.'

'Probably because he doesn't know.'

Nelson considered this a moment. 'He must know,' he said at length. 'Unless it's simply been stolen. Is that what you think?'

Alec shook his head. 'I said he maybe doesn't know.' He leant forward, his hands flat on the desk, studying the backs, then looked up at Nelson. 'But I think he guesses. Or rather, I think he's afraid to guess in case he's right.'

'That would mean,' Nelson said slowly, 'that he thinks he knows who killed Hunter. If that's so, we can persuade him to let us in on the secret.'

'Maybe. They're a tough breed, those Parkers. If he takes after his mother we'd find him a hard nut to crack.'

'But if we can't break him, and we can't break his mother, who can we get at?'

Alec raised his eyes and met Nelson's, and watched the idea growing in the sergeant's mind.

'You think she's the most vulnerable of them?'

'I think she might well be; if once you can get beneath the varnish. Not only that,' Alec added, 'but I've an idea she could tell us a good deal, if she wanted. I think there are things the others only guess but she *knows*. I think it's time you had a little chat with Mrs Diana Parker. We're getting there, Nelson!'

'Are we, sir?' Nelson looked dubious. 'If you say so.'

Alec looked at Kenneth Taylor seriously. Taylor too looked serious; as if they both knew they had come to a point at which only the truth would be good enough, and where the truth might be, not only stranger than the fiction, but less accommodating, and more painful.

In the end, Alec said simply, 'Did you enjoy your war, Mr Taylor?'

Taylor sighed. He looked his age now, RAF moustache or no. Alec was momentarily reminded of an old man he had glimpsed one year at Henley, shuffling hastily towards the lavatory tent, his pink Leander cap perched on a head freckled with age.

Taylor's voice, too, was that of an old man when he finally replied. 'All these years I've maintained the fiction that I did.' An edge of bitterness crept in and out again. 'No.' He raised his eyes to Alec's, as if searching for merciful judgement. 'No. I hated every minute. I was terrified. Every minute of every day terrified, *trembling*.

'I lived from minute to minute dreading that I would be rostered to fly that night. And then in the cockpit I'd want to retch with sheer . . . sheer funk.'

His eyes pleaded for some understanding. Alec said quietly, 'I've been terrified too.'

'Have you?' For a moment Taylor's eyes held his, as if wanting to believe him. Then they dropped again. 'Well, anyway. There you are. I tried to cover it; keep it from the others; mask it with high spirits. Because I was ashamed. I've been ashamed ever since; afraid to drop the sham. I hid it from my wife . . .'

'I didn't know you had one.'

Taylor laughed briefly. 'I haven't. It didn't last long. Only as long as it took her to see through the act.'

Alec said, choosing his words with the care of one who breaks the news of an incurable disease, 'Some men, men who felt terror too, they . . . coped with it by a more material deception.' He looked up. 'They fell ill; or got . . . lost.' He met Taylor's eye, and asked directly, 'Did you?'

'I didn't even have the guts for that.'

'Did you never turn for home with an engine that *might* have been ailing? Did you never set the wrong course on the compass so as to end up in the wrong place—where there were no guns, no fighters waiting?'

Taylor smiled wryly. 'You don't realize. If I had turned back *once*—and there were times when I legitimately could, when no one would have blamed me—I should never have been able to fly again. It was as simple as that. I had to go on. There was Stu, as well . . . I couldn't show him . . .' He shook his head.

Alec looked at him, seeing the old man convinced of his failure, and seeing too the young one who won the DFC in the face of his jibbering terror, jeopardizing his life for fear of being seen as a coward, and shook his head slowly.

'In fact,' he said, 'there was one: a crew in your squadron at Hartfield Park. A crew who went out every night and never crossed the enemy coast; who flew as far as the North Sea and patrolled it in safety for the duration of their sortie.'

Taylor shook his head wanly. 'It couldn't be done. There'd be the log . . . and the lies. And the radar would pick them up sooner or later. Somebody would spot them.'

'Somebody did,' Alec said quietly.

Taylor looked at him thoughtfully, then shook his head again. 'I'd know,' he said simply. 'We'd all know.'

'If the person who found out kept quiet? If the coward died shortly afterwards anyway, or was quietly posted, or came to the end of their tour?'

'I was posted,' Taylor said, looking at him.

'Yes.' The word hung between them, pregnant. Then Alec said briskly, 'But I don't think it was you. I did, once.' He paused. and said deliberately, 'What about Douglas McAllister?'

'Doug McAllister,' Taylor echoed, and a far-away look stole into his eyes. 'Doug McAllister.'

Alec said, 'He died in September 1944, almost within sight of Hartfield Park. Up on the Ashdown Forest, by a place called King's Standing. The same night,' Alec said seriously, 'that the Intelligence Officer, Paul Napier, found out for sure that there was a coward at Hartfield Park.'

When he landed back at Hartfield Park Kenny Taylor had to fight to keep his hands steady on the controls. They taxied round the perimeter strip to dispersal and swung on to the apron. The ground crew were at the cockpit hatch almost before the big propellers had jerked to a halt.

'What did you get? What did you get?' The tell-tale signs at the gun ports which showed the plane had been in action were always the first thing the ground crews looked for.

Stu looked across at him. Kenny could see the beads of perspiration on his forehead glinting in the shadow, the red marks of the mask bright against the whiteness of his features. For a moment the two of them looked at each other, knowing that they held a secret together which they would hold to their deaths.

Kenny broke the spell, stabbing at the buckle of his harness and stretching theatrically. 'We got some trade,' he told the ground crew. 'Twin-engine job. Over Rendsburg. Piece of cake.'

Stu caught his eye again and held it a brief moment; then he turned away and began to manœuvre awkwardly to negotiate the hatch.

In the warm fug of the hut Bill and Dicky were in a huddle with the IO. Bill turned as he heard their boots scrape on the threshold, and the IO looked up and stared at Kenny over Bill's shoulder.

Kenny made his report; Stu backed it up with the times and positions from his notes. They hadn't carried a camera gun tonight, so there was no film to corroborate the kill.

The phone rang. Bill picked it up, and listened, his eyes vacantly on Kenny. When he put it down his face was expressionless.

'Doug's overdue,' he said, and his voice was strained. 'Group got a position fix from him at the end of his patrol. Nothing since. They think he must have been bounced on his way out.' He hesitated, and swallowed. 'I'm going over to the tower.'

When a plane was overdue those who had returned often found themselves drawn as by some magnetism to the watch tower; to wait, and to will the missing crew home. Only for a new crew did they sometimes not bother: new crews came and went. But if it had been Bill and Dicky, or Stu and Kenny, there would have been a little knot of aircrew still in their Mae Wests waiting there in the dark. So there would be for Doug.

Alison was outside with the truck, and they drove in silence over to the tower. Bill clumped up the stairs and disappeared through the light-trap doors. The others stood waiting on the cold concrete.

Kenny waited uneasily. It could have been him, out there, out of contact. They could have been waiting for *him*; waiting for him to bring his Mosquito staggering over the boundary to belly-flop on the concrete with that spine-chilling squealing as the propellers and cowlings screeched along and the machine finally tipped up and the first flames slipped out from under the cowlings, and licked hungrily along the wings to the fuel tanks. He knew, and his nostrils dilated in anticipation, the smell which seemed to linger over the airfield for days, and the thought that it might be him burning in the wreckage of his plane brought the sour taste from his stomach into his mouth, and made him clamp his sphincter tight.

Let Doug die out of sight; away from here. Let him plunge unremarked into the wastes of the sea. Let him fall into some distant wood, bury himself in some unseen field. What were they waiting here for? In the hope of seeing him die before their eyes?

Bill clumped down the stairs from the tower. 'They think he was about to get a message out when he was jumped,' he said, and his voice was jerky and uneven. 'They got someone putting their transmitter on "send" and then it was cut off.' He shivered suddenly, uncontrollably, so that Kenny looked at him in surmise; so Bill hated it, too.

There were half a dozen of them there now; the three crews who had flown that night, and two or three others who had got wind of the matter and come over to watch and wait until time should have run out and they would know that, whatever had happened to Doug and Babe, their fuel would have been exhausted and they would never now arrive at Hartfield Park.

It was Dicky who first motioned for the others to listen, and raised a finger, head cocked. Then the others heard it, a weird disembodied rumbling.

'He's the other side of the Forest,' someone said. 'It's the echo.'

'Sounds like one engine.'

They listened tensely as the rumbling grew. It seemed to rise a little in pitch.

'Climbing,' Bill jerked out. 'Trying to get over the Forest.'

Unconsciously they were all straining their eyes to the south-east, into the blackness of the night, into the direction from which the sound was coming, as if they could will the aeroplane into sight, will it over the crest of Ashdown Forest and into the safety of the valley.

'The bastard's going to make it,' someone breathed; and at that moment the quality of the noise changed as it sounded direct, without echo, over the crest of the high ground.

It was still sounding, strained but triumphant, as the sky to the south-east flashed suddenly yellow, and then dully blood-red. A moment later the low crump of the explosion reached them. And then there was only silence.

There was a collective sigh. For a moment nobody moved.

'I thought the poor bastards had made it then,' someone said.

Kenny turned away, trembling violently, and intercepted a look of shared horror between Janssen and Dixon. At least he wasn't the only one who couldn't stomach the obscenity of it! So near to home! Why couldn't they have died decently, out of sight? He suddenly realized how much he hated Doug, who even in death had the power to put him in the wrong. Him and his wisdom; him and his maturity; him and Joan.

'Doug McAllister,' Taylor echoed. 'And you think he could have been the one who . . .'

Alec shrugged. 'Somebody was,' he said reasonably.

Taylor shook his head slowly, as if unable to believe what he was having to hear. Then his gaze sharpened. 'But you're investigating Andrew Hunter's death,' he retorted. 'If . . . even if McAllister was what you say—and you're wrong, I know you are—how can it possibly have anything to do with the killing of Hunter? Doug McAllister couldn't have done that.'

'True,' Alec conceded. 'I think, nevertheless, Andrew Hunter had at last got to the truth of the matter. It's all a long time ago. As you say, McAllister is dead. So Hunter might not have felt too many scruples about making it public.'

'But who would want to stop him?' Taylor protested, leaning forward in his chair. 'Doug couldn't have shot Andrew Hunter. Who would . . .?' He broke off, his eyes dulling with realization, and sank back in his chair.

'Joanie,' he said flatly.

'Yes,' Alec echoed grimly, 'Joanie.'

There was a long silence then. Out in East Court an ambulance swung away from the ambulance station and as it reached the main road its siren began to wail. A jet dropped overhead towards Gatwick.

'Your boy . . .'

Taylor looked up, his face contorted. 'I know. I've thought of him these forty-five years.'

'Was that why you came over here? To see him?'

'I should have done, shouldn't I? Maybe that was what was in my mind, I don't know. In the end I hadn't the courage. I could face him; could see him perhaps without him knowing who I was. But I couldn't face Joanie. Seeing her an old woman. Seeing her reproach me for what I did the night after Doug died.'

'It seems to me,' Alec said straightforwardly, 'that you've nothing very much to be penitent for. You felt fear in war; but it didn't stop you doing your duty. You took comfort from a girl when you needed it, true; but gave it to her when she was most in need.' He took a deep breath. 'I'm no one to advise you, Mr Taylor, but I think in your place . . . I'd go and see her. There might not be another chance.'

'No,' Taylor replied slowly, 'I suppose there won't. You're wrong, you know,' he went on after a moment. 'Doug McAllister could never be the one who . . . who couldn't face flying over Germany. Doug . . . he wasn't like that. If he had been, Joan would never have loved him as she did; and maybe I wouldn't have hated him that way, either. And I'll tell you another thing,' he said, leaning forward as if it had suddenly swum to the surface of his memory, 'If Doug McAllister had been a coward, he'd never have had

the respect of his navigator the way he did. Oh, I know—'
he waved a dismissive hand—'Babe would have had to be
in on it too; but Babe *hero*-worshipped Doug. No; it wasn't
Doug. I doubt if Doug ever knew a single moment's
fear!'

Alec smiled a little smile. 'Do you think so?'

The two men looked at each other, reassessing all that
had been said, and a look that was somehow different flowed
into Taylor's face.

'But if it wasn't Doug,' Alec said, 'and it wasn't you . . .
Do you remember a pilot named Baxter?' Taylor's brow
furrowed. 'He was killed a few months later; but he'd been
posted away from Hartfield by then.'

Taylor's brow cleared. 'I remember.' He thought a moment. 'No. Not him.'

'No?'

'Baxter was shot down by the Russians, wasn't he? Over
Berlin. If he'd been the . . . the one, he'd never have been
there to be shot down.'

'I suppose not.'

Alec stood up, and Taylor followed suit, stretching his
muscles a little so as to stand his full height. Alec held out
his hand. The older man hesitated, and looked at him, then
took it firmly.

'What's got into him?' Liz asked as Alec returned from
seeing Taylor downstairs. 'He went in to your office looking as if he'd had sentence of death and he came out like
a man who's discovered he was going to live to be a thous-
and.'

Alec looked at her thoughtfully, a whimsical smile hover-
ing about his lips. 'He's spent forty-five years of his life
thinking he was a coward and a fraud,' he said. 'He's just
found out he was neither of those things. Just another bloody
hero.'

And he disappeared into his office, leaving Liz staring
after him in wonder.

It wasn't Baxter, then. And it didn't seem likely to have

been McAllister. And it hadn't been Taylor. That only left one man.

Janssen.

CHAPTER 24

The house at Edenbridge had known better days. When the road over the Chart from Limpsfield was narrow and dusty-white, and the railways had been more interested in carrying milk-churns than commuters, the place had stood in pleasant isolation in the fields to the north of the town.

Now the fields were occupied by light industry, and on what had been the gardens a close of houses had been erected. Consequently, the house had an air of being under siege: a stag at bay before the yelping hounds which would certainly bring it down before long.

Liz had little difficulty in recognizing the woman who opened the door to her on Wednesday morning as the sister of Alison Janssen. The same relaxed charm, just on the friendly side of graciousness, had lined her face, and echoed in her voice as she asked Liz in. This was a slightly younger version, though; perhaps by four or five years.

There was, inevitably, the offer of coffee, and biscuits came with it, arranged on a pretty plate on the low table in front of the bay window, which gave out on to a sunny south garden. Carefully trained clematis masked the regular triangular roofs beyond the back fence.

'I believe your sister from South Africa has been staying with you,' Liz began when milk and sugar had been proffered and replaced.

'Yes. Did you want to see her?' Mrs Spencer said apologetically. 'I'm afraid she's gone on, now, with her husband, to our brother's place in Leicestershire. They'll be back here on Friday afternoon; they go home on Saturday, you know.'

'Never mind,' Liz said, in what she hoped was an entirely

innocent manner. 'I've obviously missed her. It's only that
I know she went back to a place called Hartfield Park while
she was staying with you, and I thought she might be able
to tell me a little more about it.'

'Oh yes! Hartfield Park! And that's where there was that
terrible shooting accident, isn't it?' Mrs Spencer shot Liz a
keen glance. 'That was after Alison and Bill had left, of
course. Did you think they might have seen someone acting
suspiciously, or something?'

Liz looked at Mollie Spencer carefully. The papers, of
course, had not said when Hunter had died; only when his
body had been found. But could Mrs Spencer really be so
naïve, or was this the clever disingenuousness of a formi-
dable woman?

'Something like that,' she said. 'You didn't go with them?
Back to Hartfield?'

'No. It's only down the road, of course. I've passed
through the village a hundred times, but I've never been
back to the airfield. What for, after all?'

'But your sister, Alison, wanted to see it again?'

Mollie Spencer chuckled throatily as if her body remembered good times. 'They met there, she and Bill. I used to play
gooseberry to them, sometimes, you know. Alison was in the
WAAF; I was still at school, but Ali smuggled me in for station
dances and so forth. Trying desperately to look grown-up in
my high heels and my one and only pair of stockings that a
Flight-Lieutenant caught with his heel and laddered.' She
laughed again. 'He sent me three pairs of nylons a week later.
And I didn't ask where he got *them*; one didn't.'

Liz imagined Mollie Spencer at sixteen. She had the look,
now, of a woman who has known the physical life. And this
was history as Liz had been taught it in school and knew it
from the television, about rationing and station hops and
girls painting lines up their legs to simulate the seams of the
stockings they hadn't got. Curious that you could talk to
someone even quite young—well, relatively—for whom it
was still a memory!

'Mr Janssen was a pilot at Hartfield during the war,' she interposed.

'Oh yes. Well, towards the end of it, anyway. I suppose that would be the summer we invaded; the summer of D-Day.'

The summer we invaded, Liz mused: curious! So people must have spoken once upon a time of 'the year we beat the French at Waterloo'; or 'the year our lads won at Agincourt'.

'Then he finished his tour,' Mrs Spencer was continuing, 'and went overseas. He used to keep in touch with us, and once he sent Alison a big bottle of perfume from Brussels. One of his friends brought it over in his aeroplane. Of course, you weren't supposed to do such things, but everybody did. I don't suppose you can imagine,' she remarked, watching Liz, 'what it was like, can you, my dear? A terrible time; and yet . . . Anyway,' she continued more briskly, 'you haven't come here for my silly reminiscences! I must be letting you get back to your duties.'

'It's been very interesting.' Liz smiled. 'And thank you for the coffee. I suppose your sister *didn't* see anything suspicious at Hartfield when she went back?'

'Not that she mentioned to me. But it was several days before . . . well, you know.'

'Was it? When . . .' Liz trailed off hopefully.

'Thursday,' Mollie Spencer said, rising simply to the bait. 'It was Thursday afternoon they went. On the way to do some shopping in Tunbridge Wells. Such a pleasant place to shop, Tunbridge Wells. Do you go there much?'

'No,' Liz replied. 'No, I don't live quite so close.' She got up, smoothing her skirt. 'I'm sorry to have wasted your time. Perhaps I could ask you to give me your brother's address in Leicestershire? Just in case we want to check on anything with your sister before they return to South Africa. Though as you say, it doesn't look as if she can have stumbled on anything to help us.'

'They'll be back here on Friday.'

'I know; but it would be a shame to spoil their last evening with you.'

'I haven't been much help, I'm sorry.'

But Liz, reviewing the conversation on the pavement of the busy road after she had gained the gate, was not so sure. She stood a moment, tapping her lips with the slip of paper which held the Leicester address, then set off determinedly towards the side road where she had parked her car.

There was a knock on the door of the borrowed room, and Liz opened it and stood aside for Alison Janssen to enter. Discreetly, Liz followed, taking up her customary place on the corner chair, notebook to hand.

Alec had risen at Alison Janssen's entrance, and now watched her expressionlessly as she took a seat. He had surprised himself so far in this case by the ease with which he could misread character: was it possible that he was about to demonstrate that capacity again?

'Sorry to ask you to look in here,' he began. 'I hope it'll be brief: just one or two matters I wanted to check. Not worth asking you to make the journey down to East Grinstead for, but I wanted to clear them up without delay, so we thought it best to come and see you up here.'

'That's all right.' Mrs Janssen had regained, he thought, something of the English accent the years in South Africa had weakened. Liz, watching her, thought the sun and space of the other continent had given her an experienced air which contrasted with the provincialism of her sister Mollie, who had stayed in Edenbridge. She was not, she pondered, certain which was preferable.

'Would you be good enough to give me a list of the things you bought in Tunbridge Wells three weeks ago? I believe it was the Thursday.'

Mrs Janssen's mouth opened in surprise; then she shut it, and lifted her eyebrows instead, more elegantly. 'A list of . . .?'

Alec merely nodded, meeting her eyes.

'Well . . .' She saw he was serious, and continued. 'A skirt. For next winter. A handbag.' She frowned: did he wish her to continue? Alec waited. She raised a hand and began to tick items off against her fingers. 'Two shirts for Bill. Ear-rings for June, that's our daughter. China for the Ebdens, they're our neighbours: Royal Doulton. Um, chocolates for Mollie, port for Jim—he's crazy on the stuff, and his tastes run to the better sorts. I think that's about it.' She looked up. 'I hope that helps you?' she said with perceptible emphasis.

'Thank you. You know your husband's collar size, of course, and what sort of shirts he likes; did you have any difficulty with the port?'

There was a pause. 'Are you trying to suggest,' Alison Janssen said sweetly, 'that my husband wasn't with me? Because I can assure you he was.'

Alec said calmly, 'I'd like some corroboration of that.'

'Oh!' It seemed to be an exclamation of outrage as much as anything. For a moment they looked at each other assessingly. Alec watched the implications of his words sort themselves out in Alison Janssen's mind.

'Do you keep in touch with many of your husband's wartime friends?' he changed the subject. 'Oh—I was forgetting; they're your wartime friends too, aren't they? You were there, at Hartfield Park.'

'Yes, I was,' she said peculiarly. 'Do we . . .? No, we don't.'

'No Christmas cards? No going to stay occasionally? After all, war binds men and women together; you must have stayed close to some of your friends: it's the same impulse that brings you here for the reunion, isn't it?'

'Is it?' She laughed shortly. 'I wonder just why we did come, to tell the truth. It wasn't my idea, I can tell you, not the reunion bit, anyway. Yes, to answer your question, we see a little of wartime friends. Mainly because Bill was one of a small group of South Africans who were together in the same squadron. And I've a girlfriend I was in the WAAF with not so far away; we have lunch together twice a year. But maybe you don't appreciate how large a country South Africa is, Chief Inspector!'

Alec, who had spent some time poring over his atlas and making notes of where each of the South Africans lived, knew she had a good point. Apart from Dixon in Pietermaritzburg, the Janssens, who lived in Durban, could hardly be described as close neighbours of any of their wartime friends. 'So where was your husband while you were in Tunbridge Wells?'

Alison Janssen drew in her breath sharply. 'Really, Chief Inspector, you're not very subtle, are you?'

'Why did he want to stay at Hartfield Park while you went on?'

'Are you allowed to ask questions like that?'

'What time did you arrange to pick him up again?' He looked at her firmly. 'All right. You think those questions are impertinent. So tell me what *did* happen.'

It was not Bill Janssen's idea at all that they should revisit Hartfield Park, Alison said, but hers. Indeed, he was positively reluctant to go; and that rather puzzled her. She could only suppose that he associated it with the deaths of his friends, and the unremitting strain of night intruder operations. But for her part she could not help feeling the nostalgia a woman feels for anywhere where, for her, love flourished; and besides, to be truthful, she had enjoyed her war, what with the glamour of serving on an operational station, and always being in demand at dances and for evening trips to Tunbridge Wells or East Grinstead or London.

Besides, being so close at Mollie and Jim's, it seemed silly not to go by and see if anything was left of the Hartfield Park they knew. She would, for sure, never have another opportunity. The plan was that they would leave Edenbridge about eleven, call at Hartfield Park and wander round, and reach Tunbridge Wells in time for a late lunch.

It had been ironic, perhaps, that they should actually get
lost trying to find the place; the lanes looked different, and
new houses had come, and old woods gone. Bill drove
around for twenty minutes, then suggested they give up. It
was Alison who recognized a turning and persuaded him
to try just one more lane; then they spotted the drive to the
farm and knew they were near. Bill had drawn on to the
verge by the gateway on to the perimeter track and switched
off.

'Aren't you coming?'

'Nothing to see,' he retorted. 'What you want to drag us
here for I don't know. We'll get to Tunbridge Wells and
find we're too late to eat!'

'Don't be silly, Bill. We've plenty of time. I just wanted
to see this place on the way.'

In the end he shrugged and climbed out of the car. It was
drizzly and close, and the concrete through the gateway was
greasy with mud. They walked through until the airfield
proper lay before them. Alison hunched her shoulders into
her jacket and looked about her gloomily.

The old control tower was there, grey and stained, and
with a sheeted combine harvester squatting forlornly beside
it. A hundred yards away the perimeter track met the end
of the main runway. A muck heap steamed gently where
once the Mosquitoes had queued for take-off, straining
against their brakes. Everything else had gone except for
one or two low brick huts now semi-derelict. Could that one
be the crew room where she had nightly dropped the young
men off and picked them up?

'Seen all you want to?'

She looked round at her husband. 'Perhaps you're right,'
she admitted.

He looked round sourly at the endless barley, the drab
tower, the roughened concrete disappearing into the mist.
'Come on. Let's go.'

The mood of dejection lasted to Tunbridge Wells, and
though their route took them past the Dorset Arms Alison

merely looked at it, and looked at her husband, and said nothing.

Alec sat back and regarded her thoughtfully. Of course, the fact that if it were true all this meant Bill Janssen could not be the murderer was neither here nor there: naturally, Alison would lie to protect her husband. *If* she knew he needed protecting. That was the nub.

'Could you put a time on your arrival in Tunbridge Wells?' he asked finally.

'Half past one, two o'clock, I guess.' Janssen had said it had been morning; but then, he had thought—or pretended to—that it was on the Wednesday they had visited Hartfield Park. Alison's recounting seemed to have left her listless. She looked up passively for anything else he might want to ask her. Was there a momentary gleam of triumph in her eye when he thanked her for her time and said that would be all? But the room was brightly lit, and the light was between them, and Alec decided he could not tell.

CHAPTER 25

'So Alison Janssen goes to the airfield with her husband, and leaves him there. She goes on into Tunbridge Wells as per plan. He stays somewhere out of sight . . .'

'The old control tower.'

'How did he get a key?'

'Don't know. Go on.'

'. . . until Hunter happens on the scene. What if Hunter had waited by the gate? Then Janssen would have been stuck; he'd never have got within shotgun range without Hunter turning tail.'

'Assume the appointment specified a meeting by the tower. Hunter would simply think he had arrived first.'

Nelson looked sceptical. 'All right . . . Hunter goes up to

the tower. Janssen waits until he has turned the corner past the stairs, comes silently down, and jumps out. Hunter turns tail and runs; Janssen runs after him; Hunter turns to plead for his life, and Janssen shoots him with . . . with what, sir?'

'What do you think?'

Nelson shrugged. 'Parker's missing shotgun, I guess. Where did he get it from?'

'Same place he got the key.'

'Then Mrs Janssen returns from Tunbridge Wells, picks up her husband, and off they go for tea in Edenbridge, having had a pleasant run out, with Mrs Janssen blissfully unaware that in the interim her darling husband has blown Hunter away.'

'Don't use that damned expression,' Alec snapped. 'Hunter was killed! Murdered! Shot dead! There's nothing comfortable or negligible about it, so kindly remember that and don't trivialize the fact.'

Nelson rocked on his heels, so unexpected was it to hear Mr Stainton lose his temper. 'Sorry, sir.'

'Yes, well,' Alec said grumpily, angry with himself now. 'Anyway, that's theory number one. Theory number two is centred on Joan Parker. Because she has her own guilty secret.'

Liz screwed up her mouth sceptically. 'Would it count for much? I know it's different for her generation . . .' She let the sentence tail away as she saw Mr Stainton's face begin to darken again, and realized she had made the sort of assumption he so often and so pedantically warned them all against. 'Anyway,' she said bravely, 'Joan Parker couldn't have done it. Her arthritis wouldn't let her.'

'We don't know that,' Nelson countered cautiously. And thank you, Liz thought viciously, for *your* moral support. 'And we don't know, for example, the truth about her relationship with her daughter-in-law. If they were close enough to set about the murder together . . .'

Alec grunted. 'We haven't spent much time on Mrs Diana Parker, and she's a woman with some strong feelings. The

prospect of dirty Parker linen being washed in public might
be enough to push her over the top into action. And once
she decided to act, I don't imagine Diana Parker would
have too many scruples about just how far she went.' And
if that wasn't a baseless judgement of character, Liz thought
mutinously, nothing was!

'Want me to get her in, sir?'

'I thought that had already been decided!'

Nelson nodded hastily. 'I'll fix it up for tomorrow first
thing.'

'Good.'

'We're almost there, aren't we?' Nelson suggested, remembering Mr Stainton's own words earlier.

'I wish I could share your optimism,' Alec retorted briefly,
and left. Nelson and Liz Pink glanced at each other as the
door closed and Nelson let out a silent whistle. 'That's what
promotion does for you!' he exclaimed.

'Maybe,' said Liz enigmatically, and turned to leave in
search of coffee.

'Sorry I had to be so brief on the telephone,' Dr Walker
apologized. 'I trust the information was of some use. How
is the investigation going, if I'm allowed to ask that sort of
question?'

'It's drawing gradually to a close, I think,' Alec replied.
'Not least thanks to your help.'

'I've been speaking to Mrs Hunter.' There was a just
perceptible excitement in her voice, and Alec realized this
was really why she had rung. 'She's agreed to the idea of
my finishing off her husband's work and bringing the book
out. In my name, but with full acknowledgement to him.'

'That's excellent news! It sounds as if everybody benefits.'

'Doesn't it? She's going to write to you to authorize you
to pass Andrew's files on to me when you've done with
them. I don't suppose you know yet when that'll be?'

Alec thought quickly. 'I'd have said we'd got everything
from them that's relevant to our purposes. If I let you have

them to photocopy, would you make sure they come back to us in one piece? We'll want to consult them again, not least when we come to trial.'

'You sound confident! Sure. I won't be splitting them up. Simply start new files where Andrew left off. Besides, I do most of my work on the computer. I was hoping you might be able to say something like that.'

'Anyone would think you were sitting at home with nothing to do.'

'I can't wait to get started. It'll be different when the hard work starts.'

'I'll say something else,' Alec replied. 'Why don't you come over and pick them up in person one evening; let me repay you with a meal for your help. And Lucy, too, of course.'

A dry chuckle carried over the telephone line. 'I could probably suspend the obsessed mother act for an evening. Then you could leave jelly and ice-cream off the menu.'

They made the arrangements briefly, and rang off. In a way, Alec thought, it was a disappointment: he had rather taken to Lucy.

'Here you are, then. Mrs Hunter's authorization was in this morning's post.' Alec pushed the familiar blue files along the table, and took his seat opposite Dr Walker.

She was certainly not playing the obsessed mother this evening; in startling (and expensive) red silk Frances Walker was every inch the rich, sophisticated and decidedly attractive woman, from her fashionably styled hair to the elegant strappy shoes beneath her equally elegant, desirably crossed legs. The idea that the impersonal blue files with their dead, dry notes in Andrew Hunter's cryptic jottings could be exciting to this intriguing woman took him momentarily aback.

'I take it you've arrived at the point where you don't need these any more?'

'I think so.' Alec paused, gathering his thoughts together,

seeing the whole jigsaw, with just a few missing pieces that
in their turn would be picked up any time now and snapped
into place. 'I'm pretty sure now it all goes back to that one
night in 1944. The night Douglas McAllister died; the night
Paul Napier's suspicions were confirmed and it became
certain that someone in the squadron was a coward.'

'And you've deduced that that person was Bill Janssen,'
she said slyly.

Alec looked at her in surprise, then grinned. 'I might
have guessed that an expert would get there before a poor
plodding policeman. Though,' he added, 'I'd be interested
to know what led you to rule out Taylor.'

Dr Walker made a little dismissive gesture, and took up
her coffee cup. 'I'll admit to an educated guess there.' She
sipped thoughtfully. 'I've come across other cases, men
doing similar things . . . And then, the obvious cowards
very often went on, gritting their teeth, doing their duty.
And Taylor *did* win the DFC. Rather a good one, as people
used to say. I take it Janssen was at Hartfield Park the day
Hunter died, had the means and opportunity, all that sort
of thing.'

'We're pretty sure, yes. And the motive's a reasonable
one, in his case. He's got a fair bit to lose back home if he
were to be involved in any scandal; though actually I think
it may have been the idea of his wife knowing which finally
drove him to it.'

'Yes,' Dr Walker agreed pensively, 'I can believe that,
perhaps.' She glanced down at her ring finger and answered
the question Alec had not wanted to ask. 'My husband's
dead. An aneurism; one of those senseless things. While I
was pregnant with Lucy.'

'I see.'

She grimaced. 'He left me rather badly off; I didn't work
in those days. Starting Delta was a way of making ends
meet, and a way of dealing with the loss of Edward. I missed
him a lot,' she said simply.

'And now Delta is big business.'

'It's very small business, actually,' she reproved him. 'It just happens that I'm the head of it. Big fish, small pond. Besides,' she added with an amused smile, 'you don't seem to have done so very badly yourself. They say it's a sign of age when the policemen start to look young; but when it's the chief inspectors . . . It's curious to speculate where we would be if certain things had never happened as they did, isn't it?'

'Yes.' Alec thought briefly of his own life, and the circumstances which had nudged him into the army; nudged him out of it, and into the police force. Nudged him in and out of love, once or twice.

'Andrew Hunter's killing is a case in point,' Dr Walker went on, eschewing any more personal trend to the conversation. 'If those various people hadn't been stationed at Hartfield Park together; if they hadn't wanted to hold their reunion in England; if Andrew hadn't been just at the point he was with his researches . . .'

'That's not the end of the coincidences by any means,' Alec replied, and told her about Joan Parker and Kenny Taylor, and the strange trio at the farm. 'One of the things we can't rule out is that the Parkers were a party to the killing for their own purposes. After all, if Janssen was the murderer, he had to get hold of a shotgun and dispose of it afterwards, and leaving his car in their farmyard would have reduced the risk of it being spotted by any passer-by.'

'What about the episode with Colin Napier?'

Alec shook his head. 'That must have been a solo effort. Theoretically we can get Janssen to Hereford to do the deed, as we can any of them—a sightseeing programme can be pretty flexible. Apparently the Janssens were in Cheltenham that night: it's a pretty quick run from there to Hereford. On the other hand, how did he explain his absence to Alison? If the root of the problem is his fear of her finding out his past, it follows that she was ignorant of his part in the killing, and in the attack on Napier. That doesn't mean she hasn't guessed something, and is covering up for him.'

For a moment they both sat, thinking about the ways the crime might have been committed. In the end, Dr Walker asked, 'Do you think now the killer believes the threat is at an end?'

'That,' Alec replied heavily, 'is what worries me.' His eyes rested on the blue files with sudden doubt; when he raised them he realized that she, too, had been thinking the same thoughts. She smiled briefly, and put a hand lightly on his arm.

'You have enough to worry about. Don't worry about me as well. I'll look after myself, don't you fear.'

CHAPTER 26

Diana Parker did not come to East Court at ten o'clock as she had been requested to do; she came at twenty to eleven. And that, Nelson thought sourly, as he watched her settle disdainfully into one of the rather plain chairs, would no doubt be the way she meant to go on.

To tell the truth, he wasn't absolutely one hundred per cent sure where Mr Stainton thought Diana Parker fitted in. Except that someone in the Parker household must be guilty of something. For himself, he would have been inclined to put his money on old Mrs Parker. There'd have been a way she could achieve her ends if she'd wanted to, arthritis or no; and she certainly had an interest in stopping Hunter stirring up the mud of her past.

He wondered whether she would now tell James Parker who his father was; and what it would mean to a man of forty-five to have such knowledge thrust upon him; to find that he had been begotten by an arrogant, affected youth in a handlebar moustache, and that that father was now a doddering, pompous old man.

Diana Parker was waiting for him to begin, and he was reluctant to do so. Her own weapon, he saw, as she arranged her expression into a mask of cold resentment, was to be aloof scorn. Plus a rather chilly sexuality, he added to himself, as she let her coat fall carefully open and crossed her legs with a dry rustle of nylon. Well, the scorn he could swallow, though it left the taint of bile in his throat; and she was mistaken, he thought with sudden grim amusement, if she fancied her style of expensive sexual hide-and-seek would distract or wrongfoot him.

Just as he had opened his mouth to begin the tentative questioning the door behind him opened and Chief Inspector Stainton slipped into the room. He gestured to Nelson to carry on, and took a seat to one side, just out of Diana Parker's direct vision.

'I've asked you here in the hope that you'll feel more like telling us the truth this time,' Nelson began, more confidently than he felt.

'About what, Sergeant?' Diana Parker was very cool, and the 'Sergeant' carried a gentle, goading emphasis.

'About the shotgun.' He watched her eyes. It was his one card, and he took a risk playing it at the outset. But she did seem worried. She reached an automatic hand inside her coat pocket and drew out a packet of cigarettes. She fished one out and put it between her lips, and with a slight hesitation which suggested that she was used to looking for someone else to light it, and didn't like the realization that no one was going to do so, reached for a lighter and flicked it into life.

Nelson deliberately pushed the cheap tin ashtray towards her across the table. It would do no harm to remind her of just where she was.

'Why should you think I know anything about the shotgun?' she asked briefly. 'It's my husband's. It's nothing to do with me.'

Nelson leant carefully back in his chair, and said nothing. Diana Parker's blue eyes shifted from side to side, met his, glanced away. She drew heavily on the cigarette and breathed out slowly through her nose. He wondered whether she had had the insight to see, when she was planning her part in Hunter's death, that she would one day be here, in this chair, answering these questions. She didn't, he told himself, seem noticeably well prepared.

'I understand,' she said, 'that my husband's shotgun has been mislaid. I presume you think he might have mislaid it after using it to shoot that man—what was his name?— Hunter, on the airfield.' Her confidence was stronger now, the voice firmer, the equine face set, unrelenting. 'I would say you are on the wrong track. I would have thought your inquiries would have shown that James could not have been at the airfield when Hunter died.' She raised her head and stared steadily at Nelson.

'Perhaps; perhaps not.' He met her gaze, as stern, as unrelenting. 'But *you* could have been. Or,' he went on as she opened her mouth to protest, 'more to the point, you could at any time have taken your husband's shotgun and passed it to the real killer. That's known,' he said carefully, 'as being an accessory before the fact. That is a serious matter. A person can go to prison for that, Mrs Parker. For a long time. A very long time.'

She looked at him levelly. 'You can't scare me, Sergeant, with your empty threats.'

Bother! The wrong track again. Try another. 'Where were you that Thursday?' He was brisk, pressing.

'I've already told you.'

'Tell me again.'

'I . . . I did some shopping. In the morning. Came back and had some lunch. James was out; he made his own when he got back. Then I went out riding. I often do. It was a fine . . .'

'Where did you go?'

'Round and about. I don't remember exactly.'

'I doubt that, Mrs Parker. Very much indeed. Where?'

She stubbed out her cigarette; reached for another, and checked the movement. There was no doubt she was off balance again. He was, as children said in their games, getting warmer. He stood up. 'Wait there; I'll get a map. Then you can show me, Mrs Parker, can't you?'

He left the room, with an anxious glance at Mr Stainton in the corner; but Mr Stainton seemed unflustered, calmly watching Diana Parker as she took that second cigarette and lit it from the lighter which she snatched from her bag and steadied with both hands.

When Nelson returned minutes later with the large-scale map Mr Stainton was as still and self-effacing as before; Diana Parker sucking at the cigarette and tilting her head to blow the smoke jerkily up at the ceiling, for all the world like the guilty dame in a Hollywood gangster movie. Nelson spread the map out on the table, then swivelled it so that it was right way up for Diana Parker, and came round to her side.

'Right, then. Let's start from the farm, Mrs Parker. Here.'

'I . . . I went down into the village.'

'Into Hartfield; here. What time was this?'

'I don't know. About two, maybe. Yes; something like that. It meant road work, and the traffic's not too pleasant, though Copper's fairly good that way; but it's the only way to get anywhere.'

'All right. And from Hartfield . . .?'

'Along here.'

'Up on to the Forest?'

'No, I didn't have time for that. I turned off when I got to Cotchford Lane.' She placed a forefinger on the map to show the place. The nail was bitten close, and had been varnished, but the varnish was old and chipped. 'That took me to here, past the garage.'

'Into Parrock Lane. Right. Then?'

She was studying the map now, hesitating before speaking; looking, there was no doubt about it, for another way of getting back from Parrock Lane to the farm; but all the possibilities were merely footpaths.

'Let me,' Nelson said softly, 'suggest where you went next; and you can tell me if I'm wrong, can't you? Along

here to the bridle path. Down to the railway. Along the old
railway track. Right so far?' He looked at her keenly.

'I . . . I don't remember. It may have been.'

'. . . Along the old railway, then, to this bridleway here,
Mrs Parker. And if you turned up here it would bring you
back to the farm in a mile or so, wouldn't it?'

'I don't think I went that way that day. I may have gone
up on the Forest after all.'

There was a stirring in the corner of the room. Alec stood
up, and gestured to the corridor outside. When the door
was shut behind them, he said, 'We'll have to get some
sighting of her en route if we want to nail her. As it is, she's
about to wriggle out of it, say she wasn't really there at all,
and you're not going to be able to stop her.'

'I don't see how she can wriggle out of it. From the
railway there is really only one way she could go to get back
to the farm.'

'Yes; across the airfield. And I'd take a good bet,' Alec
remarked grimly, 'that her horse was in a pretty bad way
when she got it back to its stable. I'm wondering whether
those other girls might have seen her. That's where we met
them: coming from the old railway into Hartfield by the
station. It was also the way they went that Thursday.'

'I thought you asked them and all they'd seen was
Hunter.'

'No; I asked them if they'd seen anyone on foot. We never
asked them about other riders. But if what I'm thinking
is right, the question is, how long were they out? Could
they have seen Diana Parker *and also have seen Andrew Hunter
alive*?'

It was three-quarters of an hour before they were able to go
back into the interview room with the information they
needed and confront Diana Parker. It was Alec, now, who
faced her across the plain table and the lone teacup; and
Nelson's turn to sit unremarked in the corner of the room,
which he did, piecing together the jigsaw of the case in his

mind, following Mr Stainton's footsteps and trying to see where they led.

Diana was both nervous and subdued, but the effect, rather than making her look older, was to wipe away the years and restore something of the vulnerability and delicate beauty which her selfish adulthood had all but destroyed. For the first time, Alec found it in him to pity her.

'You must be a good horsewoman,' Alec suggested quietly.

Diana Parker bowed her head and said nothing; as if resigned to being told what had happened.

'When you took the bridlepath up from the railway— we've checked, so don't cheapen yourself with any more lies, now—and it brought you out opposite the end of the main runway; when you cantered, or galloped, down the side of the tarmac . . . by the way, your husband can't be terribly keen on that?'

'I keep right up to the edge.' She added in a low mutter, as if to herself, 'He can't get that last row anyway.'

'Of course,' Alec remarked, 'we'd have seen the hoofprints if your husband hadn't harvested that strip first. By the time the combine and the tractor had both been up there . . . Were you thrown?' His voice was suddenly harsh and insistent.

'I don't know what you mean.'

'Curious, isn't it,' he said in the same hard voice, 'how horses pick up the scent of blood. Did you realize then what it was that had upset him like that? I should think he must have gone berserk. Like I said, Mrs Parker, you must be a good horsewoman, I'll give you that.'

Her head came up at his taunting tone, and her eyes glittered like ice splintering. The stained deal table, the cracked cup, the bare walls, Nelson, were none of them there for her in that instant.

'I *am* a good horsewoman,' she snapped.

'Good enough to stay in the saddle of a horse that's scented blood?' he asked cynically.

'Yes!' she cried. 'Good enough even for that!' Slowly the fire drained from her, as if she was glad that now the lies were done with, proud to speak the truth. She took a deep breath. 'I heard a shot as I came up through the wood, and thought nothing of it. I came out on to the airfield. I guessed there was something in the barley he didn't like . . . you could tell, from the way he shied; and when I tried to lead him back he wasn't having any of it.'

'So you tied him up instead, and went and had a look for yourself.'

'Yes. There's a sort of rail to the stairs on the old tower. I tied the reins to that. Then I went across to see what it was that had driven him berserk.'

'And found Andrew Hunter.'

Diana Parker stared at the table and Alec watched her with pity, and said nothing. 'Yes,' she said at last. 'Yes, I found the body.'

'And . . .?' he prompted.

'I . . . I didn't know what to think. I knew he'd been shot. Oh God, there wasn't any doubt about that! The blood was wet and shiny still. I had enough wit to realize that if I couldn't see a gun, it couldn't be suicide. I didn't know who he was, of course.'

'And you began to think who could have killed him; who *did* have a gun.'

'Yes.'

'James.'

The reply, when at last it came, fell leadenly in the silent room. 'Yes. I should have reported it; gone straight back and rung the police. But I wanted to protect James. I had to!'

'You mean,' Alec corrected quietly, 'you didn't want the fuss.'

She sighed. 'I don't know. No, it was more than that. I couldn't bear to think of James . . . I walked back to Copper and untied him. He was half demented, poor thing. I didn't remount until I was well clear and he'd calmed down; then I just went home. James was out; I could see that; the Land-Rover would have been in the yard. I rubbed Copper down and thought what had to be done.'

'Weren't you a little quick to suspect your husband? It doesn't say much for your respect for him, does it?'

She gave a little shrug, her eyes directed still at the table. 'I wasn't thinking straight. Would you be? I just thought: James has a shotgun.'

'So you decided what you had to do.'

'Yes. I expected the gun to have gone. I thought he'd have got rid of it. But there it was, in the cupboard, with the four-ten and the old twelve-bore that had been his grandad's.'

'But you only took one of the guns,' Alec said pregnantly.

She looked up. 'Do you think I could have a drink of water?'

Alec nodded to Nelson, who slipped out. Giving herself time to think, he told himself cynically. Time to work out which story we'll swallow.

Nelson returned with the glass and set it before her; but she didn't take it up.

'The guns,' Alec prompted. 'You only hid the one.'

'I know. I remembered James had said we were out of cartridges for the four-ten; there were none in the gun-cupboard. And when I . . . I sniffed the barrel, I didn't think it had been fired.'

'Whereas the twelve-bore . . .?'

'Did smell,' she said briefly. 'Besides . . .'

'Yes?'

'The four-ten is my gun. Oh, I don't mean James never uses it; he does, sometimes, for vermin. But he'd use his own gun, he'd use the twelve-bore, if . . . if . . .'

'If,' Alec supplied, 'he had some serious shooting to do. Just so. One last question. When you were on the airfield, did you see or hear anything at all to tell you there was someone else there too? You say Hunter's blood was still wet. You know what that implies.'

She looked up. 'Yes, I know. No. Nothing—nothing at all.'

CHAPTER 27

'D'you believe her, sir?'

Alec glanced at him. 'Do you?'

'I'll tell you that when we recover the gun. If we recover it. It's a hell of a household, though, isn't it?'

'Each suspecting the other,' Alec agreed. 'Each lying, because they didn't know, but feared, that one of the others had shot Andrew Hunter. I think a lot of people have imagined they knew who killed Hunter. Most of them, fortunately, are wrong. She must have had a hell of a time, though, waiting for the body to be found.'

'It looks black for Parker. The gun having been used, and all that.'

'I wonder if it had been, or whether she merely imagined it, because she was so convinced of his guilt. As you say, the first thing to do is recover it. I only hope she isn't stringing us a tale about which pond she threw it into.'

In the flat that night as he ate his pork chop Alec remembered his own remark and thought it worth further consideration. Because if the *dramatis personæ* in this strange entertainment had each suspected, feared, that they knew who killed Andrew Hunter, would they have said, done, all that they claimed they had?

Diana Parker had secreted her husband's gun because she feared he had used it to kill Hunter; for the same reason, because he guessed Diana to be guilty, Parker had lied about its loss. Had Joan, too, lied, fearing for her son and his wife, when she swore she had seen nothing, knew nothing?

Suppose the other veterans suspected Kenny Taylor of
the murder—and Alec himself had held him as first suspect,
after all—would they have lied to save him? Unpopular
as he was, would group loyalty have been stronger than
individual antipathy? And if so, were any of them to be
believed in any respect? Well, that was a familiar problem:
believe nothing until corroborated. But where you couldn't
corroborate, you had, surely, to give weight to your own
judgement.

There was nobody, really, connected with the case who
might not have felt that heart-stopping stab of surmise, that
a husband, lover, friend, sister, might not, after all, have
been capable of pulling the trigger and obliterating a man.

He finished his chop and carried the plate through into
the kitchen, returning with a bowl of yoghurt. Had Parker
remembered, when he found the body of Andrew Hunter
beneath the blades of the combine, those hoofprints in the
soft soil alongside the old runway?

In its way it was remarkable: a barren marriage, you
would have said; a household harsh with antipathy; yet
something, some tie of love or kin, made each quite ready
to perjure themselves rather than let the others be hauled
off to judgement. Whereas Andrew Hunter and Paul Napier,
the innocent—if one could use that word—non-speaking
parts in the drama, had been quite ready to publish any
private grief or personal cowardice in the name of history,
truth and scholarship.

But that was speculation only, he told himself; nothing
had appeared in print; and did he assume, for example, that
Frances Walker would sensationalize her work with such
personal scandals, even if the laws of libel permitted it?

They had ruled Diana Parker out, as he had known they
would; and James Parker, too, whatever Nelson said; and
Joan: the old woman was too reconciled to the hand fate
had dealt her to be eager to take another life in revenge.

No, the noose was tightening around another neck
altogether: the neck of Bill Janssen; Janssen who by his

wife's admission had been at Hartfield Park that Thursday afternoon.

He hadn't, they knew now, used James Parker's gun; that, Alec was moderately confident, would be found, safe and sound, in the pool in the Forest where Diana had thrown it. Therefore Janssen had obtained a gun from some other source.

It was this matter of the weapon which should have worried him, he thought, as he waited for the kettle to boil and stirred the coffee into his mug. After all, didn't they have the motive sorted out?

Did they? Really? Surely a man would kill to prevent his cowardice becoming known, after all this time. Especially if that man were now well-off, influential, in a position of trust and respect. That was reasonable enough, surely? He clenched his fists and sank his head between them. There was something else. It was not in Hunter's notes; and it was not in Napier's memoirs. But there was something there. Must be! Something that gave a logic to the whole business. That meant Janssen not merely could, but *had* to kill Hunter.

His coffee was cooling rapidly; he drank it anyway, conscious of the dangers of flogging the mind beyond its normal endurance. If he left it, perhaps it would come to him in the morning. Perhaps he would see the sufficiency of what they already knew. No need to delve into intricate psychology; they just wanted to show that Janssen and no one else had been at Hartfield Park on the Thursday afternoon with a shotgun and had killed Andrew Hunter. Just that.

But an hour later Alec was still pacing his flat, angry with himself but unable to leave it. There was an answer—had to be. What was more, he held all the clues in his hand!

Stopping at the window, where the curtains were still undrawn though the dark had long invaded the garden below, he told the points off on his fingers.

Janssen had been a coward. Therefore Dixon had been one too. Janssen had been open to blackmail by Dixon, and vice versa. On the other hand, they had conspired to hide their secret in 1944 and could be equally pledged to guard it now. Even to the extent of murder?

Janssen and Dixon had both been vulnerable to blackmail by anyone who had known of their secret. Or who had come to know of it. In the first category was Paul Napier; but he had never made use of his knowledge. Why not? In the second category could have come Colin Napier—attacked, but not killed—and Andrew Hunter—murdered at Hartfield Park. Furthermore, both the Napiers and Hunter presented a further risk: that the facts might get into print in a way which would ultimately lead them to be identified with Dixon and Janssen.

But why had no attempt been made to destroy Hunter's notes? Because the murderer knew that Hunter had not yet recorded the truth?

Forwards and backwards Alec tried the facts; but they still wouldn't add up to anything definite. Suddenly on an impulse he looked at his watch, snatched a glance out of the window at the fineness of the September night, and turned purposefully for the door.

There was still plenty of traffic, enough to delay him several minutes crossing the A22 at Wych Cross. Once over, he flicked the headlights on to high beam and pressed on more eagerly over the Forest. He wound the window down, letting the cool autumn air sharpen his senses and wash away the fog of conjecture and bewilderment.

The lane outside the Huntsman Inn was still lined with cars; light spilled out from the forecourt, then he was past it and diving down to the little stream in the bottom of the valley, before beginning to climb again up the long slope of Kids Hill.

At the junction at the top he hesitated, conscious of the irrationality of what he was doing; but having come so far . . . So he turned right, and a minute or two later pulled the Bristol off the road beneath a clump of firs which etched sharp moon-shadows on the surface of the car park.

The little wooden enclosure sat silently amid the heather. From time to time the lights of cars crested the Forest and they swept by with a swish of tyres; but such brief intrusions did no more than skim the surface of the silence. Even the lights of the plane overhead winking redly among the pale stars could not hold him in the present.

It was chilly here. Alec leant on the wooden fence, and gazed past the little cairn of stones over the darkened Forest and further to the speckled lights of the valleys beyond. It was clear, exceptionally so, and the moon was bright, so that a definite horizon was visible away towards the North Downs. Villages winked their call-signs; distant headlights blinked and crawled and vanished. Behind him the sound of the Bristol as it ticked metallically carried clearly in the cool night air.

He couldn't shake off the idea—and it was what had brought him here, in the face of all logic and rationality on this moonlit night—that everything had its centre in that one single night; that night when Paul Napier had stood and watched the Mosquitoes lift spectrally from the Hartfield Park runway en route for Schleswig and Rügen, and had known that his suspicions were true. The night Bill Janssen and Cedric Dixon had circled tediously for two hours over the sea recording their meticulous lies. The night which led Kenneth Taylor and Joan Parker to take desperate, agonized comfort from each other in some clearing in this same Forest.

The night Doug McAllister and Babe Binney had met a night fighter off the Friesian Islands and these few acres of heather and scrub had crackled with the heat of a high-octane fire and two men had died, horribly, on this spot where he stood which bore not so much as a scar.

For maybe half an hour he stood there, getting colder, and his gaze slowly fell, from the distant horizon to the nearer villages; from the villages to the shadowy folds of the Forest before him; from the heather to the rough cairn, glinting palely in the moonlight. Slowly, his brow cleared.

*

There was a telephone-box in Hartfield, and he fingered his change anxiously as he dialled. There should be enough. If only the woman was in.

While he waited for the number to ring he made a desperate effort to put everything into logical order: what he himself had said about coincidences in time and place. The way Baxter had died. McAllister's desperate efforts to reach Hartfield Park with one engine shot away, and his attempt to get out a last message before radio contact was lost. Taylor angry with fear as they waited for McAllister's plane to clear the hills, and Janssen shaking with nervousness. The hired car; the wet blood, and the deserted airfield.

'Hello?' It was the voice Alec had first heard: cautious, cool. And no wonder, he thought, at this time of night!— and quelled an unbidden vision of the self-possessed Dr Walker nightdressed and soft from sleep.

'Frances? Alec Stainton. Look, I'm sorry to ring you at this time but this is important. Have you got those blue files handy?' Tersely he explained what she had to do. Yes, straightaway. 'Can you ring me back? I'm low on change. Got a pen?'

It was a full five minutes before the bell rang, loudly in the cramped phone-box. Dr Walker was calm and lucid. 'Yes,' she confirmed. 'About two miles. In that moon, no difficulty. No; but I don't know if anybody looked.'

He thanked her quickly and sincerely, and put the phone down. For a moment he stood there breathing heavily as at the end of a race; and it had been, in a way. Then he shook himself, ran his hand over his hair, checked the time—it was no more than eleven-thirty, though so much had passed through his mind, it seemed like the small hours—picked up the receiver once more and dialled Nelson's number. When he answered Alec spoke economically for four minutes and got Nelson to repeat the important bits back to him. Then at last he could put the warm handset down and walk back slowly to the car. He felt suddenly, totally, weary.

The lights were still on downstairs in the house in Eden-bridge. Mollie Spencer opened the door to him at last, with the not quite neutral, faintly accusing expression of someone unused to calls late at night. Alec had time to feel briefly sorry for her. It would be bad enough, before the night was out. In the pretty sitting-room Bill Janssen sat in a comfortable chair in front of the television. The weatherman spoke encouragingly of a fine day tomorrow. Alison Janssen was on the sofa, her feet tucked under her, a mug of something at her elbow. They looked up as Alec entered.

Alec watched the life drain from Janssen's cheeks as realization came that there were no more corners left to hide in.

'I know now, Mr Janssen,' Alec said simply. There was no point in trying to spare Alison, or Mollie. 'I know why you had to kill Andrew Hunter. I know what he'd have found out about that night in September 1944. When McAllister and Binney set out from Hartfield Park for Rügen, but you spent the time you should have been on patrol circling over the North Sea.' He paused, not looking at Alison or Mollie, only at Janssen; his mouth was dry. 'The night,' he said quietly, 'they ran into you on their way back and you shot them down.'

There were no tears. No denials. Janssen's face crumpled a little as a tissue does when it's thrown on to ashes, and Alison only let a single low cry escape her as she watched her husband age before her. Then she was crossing to him, kneeling awkwardly so that she could take his head in her arms and press it to her breast. Only Mollie Spencer looked at Alec with a curious beseeching in her eyes as if he could be merciful if he chose and alter the past.

In their hearts, Alec realized, they had all of them known.

The door opened quietly. Liz slipped through and pulled it softly to behind her.

'She's quiet now. Her sister's coping very well; she'll look after her. We've got on to the husband; he's driving back.'

'Yes.' He would have his own questions to answer. The gun; the silence. Accessory after the fact.

'I suppose he was just trying to protect the Janssens.'

'We'd save a lot of time,' Alec remarked bitterly, 'if people didn't have this irrational urge to protect people they don't really love.'

'Perhaps they don't know whether they love them or not,' Liz replied sadly, 'until something like this happens. Would you have it any other way, sir?'

'No, Liz.' He was suddenly tired, leaden with fatigue. 'No, I don't suppose I would. Time we went, Liz.' Janssen had left, in company with Nelson, in the police car from East Grinstead.

'I'll look in again tomorrow. And have a word with the local minister, perhaps, ask him to keep an eye on them.' She paused. 'It was tomorrow they were to fly back home.'

Alec grunted. Then he looked up, and round, at the pale sky and the moon lurking in the branches of the hedgerow trees, and stretched.

'Come on, Liz. Time to go.'

She came with him in the Bristol, the long twenty minutes in the deserted lanes until they reached East Court and found Nelson with Janssen in the waiting area.

The sergeant on the desk nodded towards the stairs. 'He's in room two, sir.'

Because nobody had said not to, Liz followed Mr Stainton up the stairs. In front of the door of the interview room he turned and saw the incomprehension written across her face.

She said, stupidly, 'But Janssen . . . Aren't you going to charge him?'

He looked at her with a queer, half-teasing smile. 'And keep the murderer waiting?' Then he pushed open the door of the interview room.

Facing them, watched impassively by a young constable, and with a cold hatred on his face as if a thick mask had been finally ripped away, sat Cedric Dixon.

CHAPTER 28

'The shotgun came from Janssen's brother-in-law in Eden-bridge. Who never realized he'd lost it until after the news was out about the killing at Hartfield Park. Whereupon he jumped to the immediate conclusion that Janssen was the killer and he could only save them by keeping quiet.'

'And the key?' the ACC asked. 'To the tower. That must have come from one of the Parkers, surely?'

Alec shook his head. 'No key.'

'No?'

'No. I always thought those scratches were too deep, but I never put two and two together. No, Dixon may have had no intention originally of using the tower at all; but it only had a cheap padlock on it. A man who owns a hardware shop gets a good deal of practice at opening locks, I fancy.

'In fact, the tower was a piece of luck for Dixon: not only did it enable him to surprise Hunter, but it provided a refuge when he spotted Diana Parker coming out on to the far end of the airfield. It must have been a nasty shock when she found the body; but he wouldn't lose his nerve. He'd know that she'd have to leave the airfield to get help, and when she did he took the chance to make his exit. Even then, the tower shielded him from the farmyard. Where his luck failed him was in being seen by the two riders walking back to his car. But that he almost got away with: because the man they saw was carrying Hunter's briefcase, of course, so we assumed it *was* Hunter.'

'And you say Dixon has been living off Janssen for years.'

'According to Janssen. From our point of view the diffi-culty lay in guessing which way the link worked: was Dixon manipulating Janssen, or vice versa? Or were they both in it equally?'

'So how did you decide?'

'Elimination. Whichever of them was the dominant one would have got the other to do the donkey work: making the appointment with Hunter, obtaining the gun. But the actual killing, that couldn't be done by the weak one. So if Janssen did the donkey work, Dixon was the killer. Had to be.'

'Curious. I'd have said that Janssen had more at stake.'

Alec shook his head. 'Dixon had been keeping him thinking so for forty-five years, all the time he had been squeezing him for blackmail. No, it was Dixon who had always stood to lose more if their guilty secret came into the public domain.'

'He's an old man now.'

'Precisely,' Alec agreed. He smiled faintly. 'I don't suppose the hardware business has provided him with much to retire on. He couldn't afford to lose the money he got from Janssen.'

'And this way, he could even find a way of extorting some more.'

'Just so.'

The ACC picked his pipe out of the ashtray, scrutinizing it, and began to fish in his pockets.

'Janssen's singing like a bird, anyway, now it's all out in the open,' Alec continued. 'Busy shovelling the responsibility for Hunter's murder on to Dixon as fast as he can. Some clever lawyer will show he was under duress, of course. We should get him for the attack on Colin Napier though.

'Dixon's really quite a psychologist,' he added thoughtfully. 'Always the right lever for the right person. The killing was to protect his source of income; but I wonder if that was all of it, or whether it was also to give him the ultimate lever with which to work via Janssen on people like Carl Stocker. And of course, he made sure Janssen was an accessory to the murder. Dixon called the shots every time. You know, I'm sure it was somehow Dixon who planted the initial idea in Janssen's mind all those years ago.'

'That they could preserve their precious skins by flying

round and round over the North Sea? Or that the only way to preserve their secret was to shoot down McAllister's plane?'

'Both. I'd love to know just what happened in that cockpit that night.'

The ACC finished cleaning out the bowl of his pipe and tapped it carefully on the big glass ashtray. 'Incidentally, there's to be no case against Janssen for shooting down McAllister. Not after all this time. And what proof have we? Better to let it lie. I've spoken to the press officer.

'Ah well!' The ACC stretched, yawning. 'Glad to have got through your first case as a Chief Inspector?'

'I suppose so.'

The older man looked at him keenly. 'It was a good bit of detective work. Step by step. A textbook case, logical all the way.'

Alec smiled sadly. 'No. But it's nice of you to say so, sir.'

The ACC regarded him thoughtfully but said nothing, and a moment later Alec took his leave.

'What will he get?' Alison Janssen asked.

'I don't know,' Liz said truthfully. The two men had worked hand in hand every time. It had been Dixon who murdered Hunter, but Janssen had found him the gun, lured the prey to him. Forty-five years ago the thumb on the firing button had been Janssen's own.

'He's suffered enough.'

Liz looked at her speculatively. It was almost as if, now that her husband was stripped naked, Alison Janssen had grown in stature, rediscovered her youth. She had discovered him to be a broken reed, and her own strength was the greater in consequence.

After she had gone, Liz went through into the other room. Nelson and Mr Stainton were listening to the tape of Bill Janssen's questioning. Silently, Liz brought a chair forward to join them.

'Him or us,' Janssen's voice said, metallic and whiney. 'We had to get him before he saw us. Then we lost them in cloud. They were burning. They'd tried to get a fix out on W/T but that went dead. Dicky said they were goners for sure. It all happened so quick.'

Nelson's voice, brusque and contemptuous, asking about Andrew Hunter's letter.

'Dicky rang me. Said this guy was going to blow the whistle. I swear I never thought of killing him. That was Dicky's idea.'

Nelson again: he had promised to find a gun, hadn't he? Promised to write to Hunter and lure him down to Hartfield Park?

Janssen's voice droned on, justifying, pleading, confirming; they listened in vain for any hint of sorrow or penitence. Weary of it all, Alec leant forward and stabbed at the off switch.

Later, at the end of a very full day, Alec sat in Frances Walker's living-room in front of the first fire of the autumn, paying her the debt of explanation he owed her.

'It was Janssen's initial mistake which was fatal,' he commented when he had finished. 'After that, he was committed; unable to see a way to break out of the stranglehold Dixon kept on him.'

'The first time they stayed out over the North Sea instead of flying on to their target.'

'That's right. When that had been done only once, and whosesoever the initial idea— Dixon's no doubt, but you never know—then Dixon had a lever. First it was disgrace within the squadron. Then the threat that Alison would find out. That could be averted by a nice, steady financial arrangement that wouldn't cripple Janssen, but would ensure Dixon never had to worry where his next meal was coming from.

'With each year that went by, of course, Janssen fell more and more into Dixon's power. Especially as he was by now becoming something of an establishment figure, with consequently more to fear from disclosure.'

'But even if he hadn't the courage to end the financial blackmail,' Frances remarked, 'he was taking a giant step deeper into trouble by agreeing to become an accessory to murder.'

'Mm; but you can see that he felt there was no alternative. He was absolutely trapped. Of course, from Dixon's point of view it was an ideal situation. Hunter's letter must have put the wind up him something rotten: all of a sudden, after forty-five years, Janssen's guilty secret, which only Dixon knows, is about to become public knowledge. End of meal-ticket.'

'Or,' remarked Frances, 'start of a new and better one.'

'Just so. His hold over Janssen was in danger of being broken, but he had the opportunity to give himself an even better one, which he could use not only to secure his future financially but to add his considerable weight to Stocker's fight against liberalization. Now he could implicate Janssen not merely in a forty-year-old act of cowardice, devalued currency, but a new, fresh-minted crime; the worst crime in the book. He, Dixon, would help his friend out by doing the actual killing; but Janssen must supply the gun and arrange an alibi—which he did, with the Tunbridge Wells trip. No wonder he was so reluctant to visit Hartfield Park that Thursday! But he daren't risk making Alison suspicious by an absolute refusal. In a way, Dixon was recreating the situation he had manœuvred Janssen into in 1944, when he first tightened his hands round Janssen's throat: securing his own ends, while all the time giving Janssen the conviction that *he* was the one in *Dixon's* debt.'

'People, again.'

He nodded. 'Not just an academic exercise; neither your work, nor mine.'

Dr Walker acknowledged the perception with a brief, absent smile. 'When I first started this sort of . . . of history, it was real, important, because I knew people who had been involved. My father; his friends. Then when I left that field and started on the book about the Italian campaign, I lost touch with the fact that real people were involved. It was all second-hand. Not a matter any more of men dying, people being wounded or heroic or confused: merely history.'

'Will your book—Andrew Hunter's book—be better, for remembering again that they were real men; that that generation has not yet passed away? That the wounds are still open?'

'Maybe.' She appealed to him, half angry, half petulant. 'What do I say now, about Kenny Taylor, and Bill Janssen, and Cedric Dixon? About the cowards who shot down a friend rather than have their cowardice exposed?'

'I don't know.' He thought of the two men who had fought to bring their crippled aeroplane back; of the chill air whistling through the damaged fuselage; of the stink of burning, and of burnt flesh; of the doggedness and skill which had not been enough. 'I should have thought there were heroes enough to even the account.'

'Yes.'

They sat staring into the fire, which talked to itself in clicks and rustles of what it too had seen. Alec felt, all of a sudden, a faint draught against his cheek, and turned, at the same time as Frances Walker sensed her daughter's presence.

Lucy stood sleepily at the door, her hand just slipping from the handle, on a level with her cheek. Alec saw fear and love and irritation chase each other across her mother's face.

'Couldn't sleep,' Lucy muttered accusingly, and took a hesitant step into the room, fingers to mouth.

'Were we disturbing you with our talking, darling?'

'Mm.' The girl accepted the excuse gratefully, and ran across to climb on to her mother's lap. When I was her age, Alec thought, we had a Prime Minister who had fought at Omdurman. Young men boasted as they sold cars in Great Portland Street of the men they had killed not ten years before. Once, with my father, I met a man who had played football in No Man's Land in the Christmas truce of 1914, had shared diffident bars of chocolate with men he would kill tomorrow.

By the time Lucy is her mother's age, by the time, even, she is a woman, she will marvel to meet the pensioners still able to mutter about Dieppe and Normandy, and tanks in the desert and thousand-bomber raids. And it will all pale beside her own Northern Ireland, her own Gulf War or Afghanistan or Falklands, or whatever, until those too vanish backwards into history as my own wars have.

He looked up, realizing he had been dozing off, hoping nothing of what had drifted through his mind had been uttered from his lips; but he needn't have worried. Nobody was awake to hear.

There was a car in the yard, but it was not Taylor's hired Sierra, but a Rover with a local registration and the sticker of Central Garage, Hartfield in the back window.

It was Taylor, nevertheless, who answered his knock. Alec raised an interrogative eyebrow, and the South African smiled weakly and stood aside for him to enter. There was something subtly different about him, which Alec could not put his finger on. Had his hair cut, maybe; that might be it.

Joan Parker was in the sitting-room where he had first seen her, but this time the television was off, and pushed back against the wall. She looked at him sharply as he entered, and nodded him to a seat. Alec found himself looking at her with curious interest, as if the events of so long ago had mapped themselves in her face; and perhaps they had.

'I've come to tell you what's going to happen,' he said. Behind him, Taylor slipped into the room, and crossed to sit beside Mrs Parker—as Alec still thought of her. Suddenly, he realized what was different: Taylor's moustache

was gone. A pale patch on the upper lip showed where it
had been.

'We're not proceeding against Diana,' Alec said simply.
'Obstructing the coroner; wasting police time; either would
be possible, but it's not worth it. Vengeance isn't our style.'

Joan Parker acknowledged the news with a barely perceptible nod. 'She'd have found prison little to her taste,' she
commented with grim humour. 'Not the right class of people
at all.'

'How's your son taking it?'

Joan Parker was silent, as if the answer to that was beyond
her. Taylor glanced at her and, surprisingly, answered
on her behalf. 'It's a busy time of year on the farm,' he
volunteered. 'I think he's using his work to keep his mind
off it.'

Alec thought of James Parker pent in the cab of his tractor
for the endless hours of ploughing and rolling and drilling,
and wondered whether he was pondering the curious fact
that the chilly, harsh-spoken woman he was married to had,
in the end, loved him enough to lie for him. There were
worse things to discover about one's marriage. 'Maybe,' he
agreed non-committally.

There was a pause, and Alec made up his mind to go.
'You decided to miss your plane, then,' he said to Taylor.

'I'm staying on,' Taylor replied. 'For a while, anyway.'

Alec tried to look surprised. 'Oh. That's your car in the
yard, then?'

'Yes; something to get about in. I thought of looking for
a cottage to rent, not too far away.'

He'd be lucky, Alec thought privately. He looked at the
assumed nonchalance in Taylor's face, and thence to Joan
Parker's customary hardness. Did he discern a hint of
softening, after all these years? They were, after all, both
lonely people; and they had not been strangers, once, long
ago, in a clearing in the Forest.

'Well.' He stood. 'I'll be on my way. I'll see myself out.'

But he turned the Bristol not towards the lane but past

the old outbuildings on to the mud-stained concrete of the perimeter track. He speeded up a little, and the tyres thrummed on the scabbed surface past the aprons and hard-standings where once Typhoons and Mosquitoes, their engines and cockpits shrouded in canvas, had hunched patiently waiting for the next summons to battle.

At the runway's end Alec turned and, a moment later, drew off by the control tower and switched off the engine. The tower squatted where it had done for almost fifty years, looking out with sightless eyes across the valley towards the skeletal trees on the distant boundary. There was no birdsong, here in the centre of the airfield, just the drone of a jet fading towards Gatwick, and the distant stutter of a tractor in the meadows down by the Medway.

Up here the ploughing was over. Even where Andrew Hunter's body had been found the soil had now been ploughed, rolled and seeded like the rest.

Soon the first green tips of next year's harvest would feel their way through the surface of the soil towards the watery October sun.

THE END